7 Figure Publications presents . . .

I0679355

Murder Breeds Mayhem

by

Pierce J. Anfield

7 Figure Publications
PO Box 9334
Augusta, GA 30916
http://7figurepublications.com

(Paperback)

ISBN-10: 0-692-15982-7
ISBN-13: 978-0-69215982-8

Library of Congress Cataloging-In-Publication Data:
LCCN 2018953933

Editor, Linda Wilson

Cover design by Lisa Sims of Passionate2Design

Published November 2018

Dedication

Beloved Son and Brother, Cordero Giovanni Anfield

Sunrise: 02-03-1988

Sunset: 12-31-2008

Gone but never ever forgotten . . .

Acknowledgments

I would like to give thanks to my Higher Power for giving me the patience, strength, and the ability to pen my first novel. I give great thanks for being blessed to have a beautiful family, who are indeed my motivation to overcome my struggles.

I'd like to thank my beautiful mother, Tonya Larry for always being there for me, and my step-dad, Tyrone Larry for going hard when it was definitely needed. Thanks to my maternal grandparents, James and Elveria Jackson, may they Rest in Peace. Thanks to my paternal grandparents, Bennie and Gloria Palmer and Henry and Barbara Cannon for sticking by me through the good and the bad times and taking my father's place since he couldn't be here himself. I could never thank you enough. Thank you for all that you have been to me and for all that you still are.

I would like to shout out a few good people doing this bid with me down the road, fighting to get home to their families as I am. Nick, Geoffrey and Larry, y'all fools keep your head up and know that better days are ahead. It won't be long before we are out and making a difference. Sometimes it takes a small time-out for us to see that life is not something that we should take for granted. My dawg, Hard2Guard from New York, even though he jacked the rec in the championship game 2018 open league in Estill. They know we are a force to be reckoned with on the court. Everybody from the spot Augusta in Estill from 2016-2018, y'all know what's going on. I'd like to give a big shout out to everyone doing a bid; it ain't easy. Much love, and I can wait to y'all free. Shout out to all my rounds from Florida, HD, Freddy G, and Free. I'll see y'all on Miami Beach somewhere.

A Poem to My Cordero

Cordero Giovanni Anfield is the name that you were given.
God made a decision on this particular day,
and I drive myself crazy wondering why you couldn't stay.
As I ponder and look back, I ask God why,
no please . . . not this day.
Let the choice be mine, make it my time.
I would have stood tall so you could stay alive to see it all.
I would have said . . .
He has his whole life to live and kindness is his way.
But obviously God doesn't work that way.
For whatever reason, He wanted you that day.
I wanted to look in your eyes and say,
Surely I will see you again someday.
Ten years have gone by and still, it feels like yesterday.
I thank God I had the chance to hear your voice, feel your touch,
and be graced by your face.
And if I live to be a hundred years old,
I'll still ask Him why couldn't you stay.
We love you now as we loved you then
By the Grace of God, we will meet again!

Love,
Mom and Me

CHAPTER 1

Son-of-a-bitch! Fred Sanders thought as he suddenly spotted the caravan coming down his block of 2300 Travis Pines. He stood up from his seat on the porch. Before the vehicle came to a complete stop, men wearing steel-toe boots hit the ground running with guns aimed at the house across the street. In a flash, Fred was crouching behind the bushes surrounding his porch; then he dashed off to the side of his house, ducking behind his black F150. It had been a while since the former all-around athlete had moved that fast. He panted, trying to catch his breath. Having just smoked a blunt filled with loud contributed to the fire set in his lungs. *He must've set me up! Droppin' this shit off at my house!* Fred thought, referring to his connect, who had dropped off five pounds of loud at his house instead of at the trap spot. His connect would be out of town for a while. Fred's heart pounded in his ears. Saving his own ass crossed his mind. But knowing the weed was inside because of his foolishness, kept him where he belonged. He loved Tiffany and Marquise too much to let them get caught up. Fred peeked around his truck. Waiting.

SWAT officers approached the residence across the street like Navy Seals invading Bin Laden's compound. A guy was bent over inside the Dodge Magnum Wagon. "Police! *Search warrant!* Let me see your hands!" one of the officers shouted. The guy wearing earbuds popped out of the Dodge Magnum Hellcat with eyes wide, startled by the commotion. At that exact time, the SWAT team knocked in the front door of the home with a steel battering ram.

"Drop your weapon!" a trigger-happy cop screamed, letting off shots from his AR-15. Like a chain reaction, a barrage of bullets from other officers followed, tearing into the unarmed man.

"What the—Did they just shoot? Hold up . . . What the fuck just happened? I can't believe . . ." Fred spoke to himself. From his viewpoint, even he could tell the young man was holding a cellphone. The man's body absorbed the last .233 round of many, then crumbled to the ground.

With guns still aimed, several officers eased up to the man sprawled out on the sidewalk, bleeding into the cement, gasping for any air he could get. One officer kicked away his cellphone. His comrades filed out of the house, their eyes taking in the scene. Another officer, much heavier than the others, pushed Trigger-Happy in his chest, scolding him. A pushing match ensued.

An officer with more stripes stepped between them, taking Trigger-Happy's gun. He was then led toward the house and sent inside. Minutes later, he exited the residence and looked around suspiciously. About five seconds passed before he bent at the knees and dropped the object he held behind his back right beside the body. Then he walked off hastily. Officers who remained inside wrestled the shirtless man out of the door in handcuffs.

"You bitches killed my brother!" the man ranted, after seeing his brother's bullet-riddled body. "All you bitches are dead! Every last one of you muthafuckas will die for this!" He spat in one of the officer's face, then locked eyes with the trigger-happy cop, who suddenly dropped his head. He head-butted the officer behind him, creating a gash in the center of his forehead. The officer fell back after grabbing the injured spot. "Y'all planted that gun!" He tried to head-butt the officers on his left and right. The officer on the right stepped back, but the man turned and kicked him dead center in the chest. The suspect got one last kick in before Trigger-Happy hit him across the head with a flashlight, knocking him unconscious.

"Aw, that's some bullshit!" Fred complained as he held his position, watching the young man lying motionless. Within a few minutes, an ambulance pulled up to the scene, and an EMT attended to the man.

Eventually, the shirtless man regained consciousness and was now strapped to a gurney in the back of the Gold Cross Ambulance. "Everybody involved dies! Every one of you!" he yelled at the top of his lungs before the doors finally closed.

From a thin crack in his mini blinds in his living room, Fred Sanders watched the ambulance pull off. He remained at full attention while officers brought countless guns and pounds of weed out of the house. News media descended on the area like vultures. The body had been quickly removed from the scene and was probably already at the Georgia Bureau of Investigations (GBI) Crime Lab. He shook his head. *Nobody would've survived the number of holes they put in that dude. That was some bullshit. The young brother didn't stand an ounce of a chance.*

Cameras flashing snapped away his sympathizing and alerted him to the detectives pretending to look for clues while news personnel tried to be the first to report the bust to the world. A tow truck rolled up the street and backed into the yard. The driver hopped out and shut his door with his eyes on the Hellcat, red polish glistening in the night. It was on its way to later be sold at the city auction. Fed up with the entire scene, Fred closed his blinds, glad he'd finally let his cousin talk him into getting a home security system. He just needed to think about what he was going to do with the situation he had just captured.

CHAPTER 2

An hour earlier . . .

After bagging up the last ten of the fifty pounds of weed inside green deep freezer bags, Tyrod King mentally calculated the profits they stood to make, as his twin brother Tyreek finished up his phone call. He'd been dealing with this cat named Fish for almost six months. At first, Fish was cool to Tyrod. But within a month he noticed a change in Fish that his brother Tyreek just couldn't see.

"Reek, this dude went from coppin' two ounces of loud and being short every week, to coppin' a pound. *And* Percocet 30's in small bundles," Tyrod said, staring out the window at Fish coming up the block.

"So what," Tyreek shot back nonchalantly. "Fish is all right."

Tyrod mean-mugged him. "'Reek, when niggas upgrade their status in the game, their appearance changes too. Dude still wearin' them same dirty ass Jordan's. His gear ain't about shit. Ass be showin'. Somethin' ain't right wit' that nigga. I'm tellin' you."

"Okay, Rod." Tyreek shook his head with a smirk.

Tyrod stormed his way into the bathroom and slammed the door. When Fish came around, Tyrod wouldn't do any transactions or make any calls. Tyreek was ending his deal with Fish by the time Tyrod made his exit from the bathroom. Fish glanced around the room, and then met Tyrod's gaze.

"'Sup, Rod?" Fish said. In response, Tyrod gazed around the

trap the same way that Fish had. Again Fish greeted Tyrod and received the same silence as before.

"Rod be trippin'. Don't mind him," Tyreek said and bumped fists with Fish.

"It's all good. Peace, 'Reek," Fish replied, then made his way out the door. Tyreek locked it behind him.

"I *hate* that dude, 'Reek," Tyrod stated as he pulled back the curtains and stared out of the cracked mini blinds. He watched Fish back his '94 Crown Victoria with government tires out of the driveway in a hurry, turning on his lights. Tyrod frowned, wondering if his mind was playing tricks on him. He was damn near positive that Fish flashed his lights while speeding down Travis Pines. "What the . . . 'Reek, I really think this nigga just flashed his lights, bruh!" Tyrod said.

"Bruh, chill," Tyreek replied, stuffing the rubber banded bills inside his pocket. "Fish is all right. I told you he said he met somebody from outta town that he be taxing that couldn't get the work."

"He can tell you anything, but have you met him?" Tyrod asked, glimpsing at the guy sitting on his porch across the street. He closed the blinds.

"Naw," Tyreek stated, texting on his phone. "But would you let a nigga meet your plug?"

"Hell naw!" Tyrod sat at the rickety table, grabbed a Swisher Sweet cigar, and busted it down by removing the tobacco.

"My point." Tyreek placed the new Android phone on the glass table littered with scales, weed stems, and sandwich bags. Tyrod fired up the kush and moonrock-filled blunt. He choked violently after taking one pull, then passed it to Tyreek while on his way to the kitchen. Tyreek hit the high-grade weed like a Newport king. His cellphone buzzed and vibrated against the table. He placed the remaining eight pounds inside his black Prada bag before checking to see who it was, blunt still in his mouth. He stood to leave. Tyrod returned from the kitchen, downing a glass of water. Tyreek passed his brother the blunt, then texted on his phone.

"Bruh, I'm out," Tyreek said. "I'm gon' check in with Keno about opening that spot off Richmond Hill Road." He placed his phone in his pocket and his pistol on the table. Tyreek never took his "trap gun" outside. Instead he kept a Glock 23 with the extended 22-round clip inside a hidden compartment in his Dodge Magnum.

"All right, 'Reek. Be safe. Man, you need to start parking down the street. I tell you that all the time," Tyrod reminded him. It did look odd having that red ass Hellcat sitting outside the trap, with a lot of traffic coming and going on the block. Tyrod followed Tyreek to the door. "I'm serious, 'Reek. Be safe, man, and don't be speeding." All their lives Tyrod felt the need to watch over his stubborn little brother.

"Nah, none of that," Tyreek said. "I'm good."

"That's what's up. And let me know when you get with Keno. We ain't paying no high ass rent. Can't make a profit like that. Plus we still need Columbia County in our pocket 'cause them white boys pay crazy numbers," Tyrod stated. The twins shook hands, then embraced each other.

"No doubt." Tyreek started his car, then pulled out his phone.

Tyrod shook his head. *That boy gonna die fucking with that phone.* Tyrod's cellphone vibrated on the table next to where Tyreek laid his glock. He grabbed his Samsung Edge and read the message:

COPS JUST TURNED DOWN WINDSOR SPRING. HEADED THAT WAY DEEP.

Tyrod heard the rumble of Tyreek's engine outside and

hurried to the door to let his brother know. Tyreek was notorious for doing a million things before he got in his ride and drove off. Just as Tyrod grabbed the doorknob and turned it, the front door flew open with a resounding "BOOM!" A flashbang grenade went off, disorienting Tyrod's senses.

"Search warrant!"

Dazed, Tyrod spun around, and came face to face with a ski-masked SWAT officer brandishing an AR-15. Another officer slammed him to the ground. Someone else kicked him in his ribs as he fought desperately to get to his brother. More officers filed inside the trap house in groups of twos or threes. Gunshots rang out from outside, each shot sending a jolt of energy surging through Tyrod's body. Tyreek was all he could think of as he silently begged, *Please don't let them hurt my brother.*

Seconds later, a cop ran inside and grabbed Tyreek's gun off the table. Tyrod fought harder to get away from the hands trying to restrain him. Although he was yards away, he heard Tyreek cry out as searing hot pain pulsated in several parts of his body.

CHAPTER 3

Cop cars were all over the area, and yellow tape cornered off an area between two apartment buildings. Denise King had stopped on CNN after flipping through the channels on the 75-inch TV. A news anchor occupied the left side of the screen. The right side showed footage from a helicopter. The caption rolled across the bottom:

Cops shoot unarmed black male multiple times.

She turned up the news to hear Kelly Thomas, the news reporter, talking to a colleague on the scene. "Well, Kelly, so far we've found out the victim in this case was unarmed when he was shot by police. Police say they were responding to a disturbance call, and upon arrival they encountered the victim, whose name has not been released, pending notifying the next of kin. Sources tell us that the victim was being fully cooperative with the officers. At that time, the victim, who is believed to be just sixteen years old, ran from the officers.

"After pursuing the victim for several blocks, they lost him somewhere inside Pinnacle Place Apartments. A K-9 unit was called in to track him, which led them to the area just beyond the yellow tape behind me. As officers surrounded the apartment, the victim came running out toward one of the responding officers, who then shot him, I believe, five times in the chest. First responders were called, but he was pronounced dead at the scene."

"Thank you so much, Tom," Kelly said. "As everyone has just

heard, another unarmed black male, possibly just a teenager, was gunned down today. This will be the twenty-first killing by a cop, and it's sad to say, the twenty-first black man.

"Joining us today is former Chief of Police here in Richmond County—"

Deeply sighing out her sympathy, Denise was fed up with black men and women being killed off by the police. The killings were happening all over, in Chicago, Detroit, New York City, Miami Gardens, Jacksonville, Cleveland, and New Orleans. Now they had made it to Augusta, much too close to home. It was bad enough that white cops with hidden agendas were blaming the shootings on blacks. Denise turned off the television and headed to the bathroom, suddenly worried about the safety of her own twin sons. She said a brief prayer.

Following a long hot shower, she went into the kitchen for a cup of tea to calm her nerves. Watching the senseless shootings of black men and women by cops on the news was depressing. Thoughts of her sons stayed with her as she placed her arms on the kitchen island and tried to exhale her stress away. One look at the stainless-steel appliances and custom cabinets, as well as every other room in the contemporary furnished house was unsettling. She was thankful for the comfy lifestyle her sons provided her, but their well-being was most important, and it forced her to look at the circumstances even closer. Her boys were always buying her nice things and spoiling her. Denise remembered a time not so long ago when she could barely make ends meet. Now she was quite apprehensive about all the nice things she had; high-stake risks were involved. No matter how much she wanted things to appear on the up and up on the surface. Denise knew her sons' employment did not match their income.

Her youngest son Tyreek was talented at building websites and had a few clients with big names. Still, there was no way they were paying him that much. Not with the top-of-the-line clothes he bought and the fancy cars he'd recently purchased. Her son Tyrod was into real estate and loved nice things too, but he was far more laid back than his younger brother. Tyrod had always been the more mature one, the take-charge kind, and definitely didn't tolerate a lot of nonsense. Like their father, Tyrod would fight in a heartbeat, and she often wondered if he would kill if he felt he needed to. Even if it was the police. She ended that thought as the worry began to flare up.

Denise took out a tea bag and her 'NUMBER ONE MOM' cup, the first Mother's Day gift the boys bought her when they started their grass cutting business several years ago. They were so proud when she opened the box, and laughed at her when she started crying. Years later, she cried even worse when they drove her up to her new three-bedroom house and handed her the keys. She flipped on the Keurig with her thoughts on the young man murdered and how deeply hurt his family must be. The fear of Tyreek and Tyrod getting shot always took her breath away, so she tried not to entertain the thought. But this evening she couldn't stop her mind from racing. Whenever worry distressed her, she had no problem calling their cellphones until she knew they were both safe.

Denise headed to her master bedroom and set the teacup on her nightstand. She got comfortable on her California King-size bed, then dialed Tyrod's number. It rang several times and finally sent her to voicemail. Slowly she inhaled and exhaled and finally left him a message. She also sent him a text asking him to return her call. *Maybe Tyreek will answer*, she thought as she dialed his cellphone. It too rang many times and sent her to voicemail. She left a message and texted the same request to his phone as she'd done with Tyrod. *Where are they?* she thought, as she watched her phone. *Shoot! I better busy myself with my schoolwork until they call me back.* Although her sons didn't want her to do anything except shop and enjoy life, Denise was taking online classes for medical billing and coding. She knew she had to make her own money and soon; the money her sons always gave her produced this guilty feeling in her gut when she thought of its origins.

She recalled having to sometimes work shitty jobs, or date some sorry ass dude just to keep a roof over their head. Back then she'd mastered the art of skimming money from one bill to pay the next and stretched their meals by going without eating so her sons wouldn't go hungry. Whenever funds would get really hectic, she'd have to rely on a man to give her something, or get it the best way possible. Their school clothes were mostly hand-me-downs from the local Goodwill, and there were times when a married man that she dealt with would pass his kids' clothes down to them. Whenever they were really lucky, they'd buy clothes from Walmart and shoes from Shoe Show in South Gate Plaza. In many ways, Denise did want to lay back and just chill out, but Tyrod and Tyreek's blessings were still the fruits of drug dealing. She needed her certificate and a steady income from a legitimate job pronto. Glancing at the phone once again and willing it to ring, she cursed when it didn't.

"Where the hell are y'all?" she asked out loud. "I gotta keep myself busy. These boys will have me up all night worrying." Denise opened up her class assignment and started reading it on her MacBook.

KNOCK. KNOCK. KNOCK.

Startled, Denise jumped as her fingers stilled on the keyboard. *Who in the hell is that?* she wondered. No one ever just stopped by at random, other than Tyrod and Tyreek, who always called first. And she had slowed all the way down on dealing with men, not only because her sons felt it never got her anywhere, but she was also tired of feeling used. Again she glanced at her phone. No missed calls or texts.

Setting her MacBook down, she slowly pulled back the drapes and stared at the brick driveway. A dark Dodge Charger with tinted windows was parked carelessly in front of her double garage. The antenna sticking high off the trunk quickly alerted her that it was the cops. Her heartbeat tripled, thumping harder the closer she walked to the front door. "Please, let whatever they want have nothing to do with my sons," she repeated every step of the way to the door as she tied her robe closed.

Taking a deep breath, she opened the door. A white, middle-age unshaven male stood in the doorway. He had that "I hate doing this job" look.

"Yes, how may I help you?" she asked, glancing at the second cop. He appeared to be a veteran who was used to knocking on people's doors. He was the first to speak. Both men wore Nike warm-up suits with Nike running shoes.

"Ma'am, I'm Detective Scott," the veteran stated, brushing past his companion. "And this is my partner, Detective Noah. We're from Richmond County Sheriff's office. Do you mind if we come in to talk to you, please?"

"What is this all about?" she asked. *I'm not going to just invite them into my home. He barely flashed his badge.*

"It's about your sons, Tyrod and Tyreek King," he stated, looking down at his yellow notepad.

That warning signal struck her as her heartbeat stalled then sped up. Denise stepped aside with her hand over her heart, fighting to maintain her composure as Detective Noah closed the door behind them and followed her into the family room. "What's the matter?" she asked, spinning around to face both detectives. "What about my boys? Are they all right?" Denise was barely able to breathe.

The men exchanged glances. Fear set in deeper, knowing all too well something terrible had occurred. Her eyes teared up. *Please let them be alive,* she prayed.

"Ms. King, tonight our SWAT team and federal agents executed a search warrant on the 2300 block of Travis Pines, where your sons ran a drug house. Upon arrival, they approached the house, and your son Tyreek was reaching inside his car. Our officers identified themselves, and at that time, he produced a semi-automatic handgun. They instructed him to drop his weapon. When he refused to comply, shots were fired, killing him at the scene. I'm so sorry, Ms. King," he said, looking her in the eyes.

"No-o-o!" she shouted. "No-o-o-o! It . . . it-it can't be! No . . . oh Jesus! Please!" She held her hand tightly to her chest, crying hysterically.

"Ma'am, your son Tyrod King was arrested for drugs and gun charges in this case as well. He was treated for minor injuries at University Hospital, then turned over to our deputies," he said, looking down at his notepad.

"No . . . Nooooo!" Denise screamed louder. The color drained from her face as she fell too fast for either detective to prevent her from hitting her head on the marble end table.

CHAPTER 4

Twenty-five-year-old news reporter, Alexus Robinson started on her article about the police shooting in Pinnacle Place Apartments as soon as she reached her desk. Her crew covered the story as it was unfolding, but details were still sketchy, except the identity of the victim, who was sixteen. She finished her report of the shooting, then moved on to Augusta State University and Fort Gordon bringing cyber security to the area. It was a fast-growing field, which was guaranteed to bring jobs to the city, increase property value, and bring another 20,000 people there. It was also going to be the number one facility for Cyber Defense in the USA, possibly the entire world.

Angela Brooks, manager of Crime Development stories, poked her head inside of Alexus' office. For over ten years, Angela worked hard to scramble her way up to the top. She earned her position and peeped the same drive and dedication in Alexus. She was quick to dash hope from other eager interns' ambitious eyes by telling them that she was grooming Alexus to take over her job once she retired.

Where other reporters would cut corners just to get the story out, Alexus would show up around the clock, so she could interview whomever the story featured, in depth. Willing to go beyond the call of duty, Alexus would seek out the interviewee in the most undesirable locations. Often she would have exclusive reports that no one else had, and eventually she'd garner a dynamic resume once she decided to move on to something bigger. She had been working with the local news station for over two years and now did her reporting live from the field.

"Lex, how's it going?" Angela asked, taking a seat beside her with her clipboard in her hand.

Alexus continued writing without a glance at Angela. "Just finishing up my last-minute touches before the eleven o'clock news."

"Well, you may want to pass it down to Steve."

"But, this is my story, Angela. I've been working on this shooting of a black teen all evening." Finally, Alexus looked up, dropping her pen on the desk.

"Trust me on this. This is bigger." Angela passed Alexus her clipboard. Alexus's mouth dropped. "God! Two shootings in one day?"

Angela nodded. "I know, right." The elderly white woman shook her head. "When will all this killing stop?" Alexus greatly admired Angela's drive and compassion for people, which were the two reasons the women had grown so close. "But, hey! It's a sad truth. No crime, no job," Angela said, rising from her seat. She headed toward the exit. "So take Jake with you, and don't forget to pass your other stories over to Steve." Angela then dashed out the door.

When dealing with Angela, no wasn't an option. But she was right. This story was big! Alexus could use this to move up the ladder. She packed up everything after briefing Steve, then she buzzed Jake, who answered on the first ring.

"Meet me in the parking lot pronto," she said, then ended the call. Alexus knew they were not supposed to drive their personal vehicles, but she needed to be the first reporter on the scene. Jake had taken the "12 On Your Side" magnetic logo off of their field vehicle and slapped it onto Alexus's SUV.

Racing to her vehicle, Alexus hopped in the driver's seat while Jake tossed his camera and equipment into the backseat. "Seat belt," she said, tossing Jake the brief report she'd gotten from Angela once he sat in the passenger's seat. He read over it as she zoomed across the Thirteenth Street Bridge headed to Travis Pines in her super-charged Audi Q7.

They arrived minutes later to a hectic scene. Police cars had the area blocked off, and rows of blue and red flashing lights could be seen as soon as they turned down the street. After she checked herself in the mirror, making sure her lip gloss was still fresh and shining for the cameras, Alexus exited her car several houses down from the action. "We're late! Fox 54 and Channel 6 are here already." She pouted.

Jake set his camera stand outside the car and grabbed his black bag containing his most valued Nikon camera. He pulled the camera out of the bag, checking the lights, even though the investigators had plenty of lights set up to finish combing the scene. "All set," he said, walking to her side of the car with his camera on his shoulder and the stand in his hand.

"Let's do it," she stated, strolling toward her next big story.

As Jake set up his camera on the stand, a tow truck was slowly pulling off with a red Dodge Magnum sporting Forgiato rims with pin stripes going down the side. The other news station crews were being backed away from the area they were shooting from, as the officers widened their search area. Alexus stopped and tried to get information from a few officers and detectives, to no avail.

"Hey. Could you tell me why they backed y'all away?" she asked a reporter from Fox 54.

"Because those assholes said they were going to search the yard next to and across from the house to make sure they had no drugs hidden in their yards," he responded.

Her breath seemed to stop as she got a closer look at the car being towed. Her grip tightened on the microphone. The license plate on the car read "3 KINGS."

"Tyreek!" she whispered to no one in particular. "Oh my God! I have to go!" Alexus tried to catch her breath and calm her palpitating heart. No names were released to the news station, but one thing was for sure: one man was dead and one man was in jail.

"What's the matter?" Jake asked, running after Alexus. "You know we can't leave. We'll get fined. Maybe even fired!"

She didn't wish anything bad on Tyreek, but Alexus repeatedly prayed that Tyrod was okay. Tears filled her brown eyes. Jake stared at her in utter confusion.

"That's my brother-in-law's car!" She passed him her car keys. "Just explain that I have a family emergency and had to leave. Hell, if I lose my job, so be it," she said, calling for an uber. While waiting, Alexus pulled her cellphone out of her purse and dialed Tyrod and Tyreek's numbers. She got no response from either phone. She was calling Ms. King just as her uber driver arrived.

"Hello?" a male voice finally answered.

"Ms. King?" *Who the hell is this?* The call dropped suddenly. "Hello?" Alexus said to the dial tone.

* * * * * *

Alexus stood at the emergency room front desk waiting on the nurse to look up Tyrod and Tyreek's name in their system. The heavyset blonde sat behind the computer typing away at the keyboard. She scrolled up and down the screen.

"I'm sorry, ma'am, but these computers are not showing either name," she said, looking up at Alexus, who had transformed from a beautiful reporter to a stressed-the-hell-out fiancée. Now her shoulder-length hair was frizzy from running her hands through it. Her eyes were stop-sign red and puffy.

"They must be here. I work for News 12, and the report I received says either one or both were brought here," Alexus insisted, having forgotten they were probably not in the system because they were brought in by the police. "It's King. Look again, please," she said as she glanced down at Angela and Jake blowing up her iPhone. She couldn't answer until she knew the fate of her family.

"Sorry, ma'am. The only King we have is a Ms. Denise King," the woman stated.

"Not Denise King. I don't . . ." Alexus stopped mid-sentence. "Wait a minute. Is that Denise M. King?" she asked, then gave her Denise's address.

The nurse had to release hot air dealing with Alexus, but eventually admitted, "Yes."

"What room?" Alexus asked as her mind kicked into overdrive.

"I'm sorry, ma'am, but it's hospital policy. We can't let reporters know that type of—"

"Lady! That's my mother-in-law!" Alexus shouted, on the verge of losing her professionalism. "What fucking room is she in? I need to know now!" She banged her hand on the counter, startling the nurse.

"I'm sorry, but you really need to calm your little self on down. Alexus Robinson, I'm only telling you this because I do watch you on the news. You know good and well you can get me in trouble with what you're asking me. It's room 329. Elevator C." She pointed Alexus in the direction she needed to go.

Alexus hurried off the elevator and rushed straight up to the ICU desk. "I'm looking for Ms. Denise M. King," she stated, trying to control her heavy breathing.

The nurse, dressed in green scrubs and a face mask and a hair net punched in the name. Alexus tried not to fear the worse, even if this was the floor where people's lives hung in the balance and could slip from bad to worse in a split second.

"I'm sorry," the nurse said, staring in Alexus's eyes. "But Ms. King received a substantial amount of brain damage from the fall she took, then suffered a massive heart attack."

CHAPTER 5

Dirty ass cops murdered my brother in cold blood, then tried to plant a gun on his body to cover their tracks. They all gon' pay. One way or another. They gon' pay. Tyrod was in a trance thinking about Tyreek as he was being escorted through the rear of Phinizy Road Jail into the boxing area where he was searched, then placed inside the x-ray machine to make sure nothing was concealed on or inside of his body. Finding nothing, Tyrod was ushered to booking, where he was fingerprinted, photographed, and sent to see a nurse.

Once she confirmed that he was stable enough to be placed inside general population, he was led inside a cold, stale holding cell littered with piss and toilet paper, along with sandwich wrappers, cookie paper, and clear juice packets. From there, everything was a haze. He was functioning. But not functioning. He didn't want to believe that his brother was gone. *I still can't believe this. Seems like just yesterday when we first got put on.* Tyrod sighed and flashed back to the day that had changed their lives majorly. Now he didn't know if that day was a blessing or a curse.

Headed home, exhausted from playing full-court at Diamond Lakes Recreational Center, the young teenage brothers netted their biggest gain when they simply walked on the grass to avoid being hit by a speeding car. A navy book bag lying beside the thick roots of a tree caught Tyrod's gaze. He picked it up, and they continued on their way.

"Finders keepers," Tyrod said, throwing it on his back. During the entire walk back home, Tyreek kept trying to peek inside the bag, but Tyrod denied him and told him they'd have to wait until they got home.

Once home, they showered and quickly ate dinner. Then they rushed to their room for the night. "All right, Rod. So what do you think is in the bag?" Tyreek asked.

"Let's find out," Tyrod answered, tossing it on his bottom bunk where they both sat. They checked its contents. Their eyes bulged the moment they both pulled out a freezer bag bulging with high-grade marijuana. Another bag, similar in size and weight was inside with individual baggies of weed. Tyrod also removed a digital scale, cocaine, a semi-automatic Patriot .45 caliber with a chrome slide and a black rubber grip. And a whopping $4,865.

"Four thousand, eight hundred and sixty-five dollars, Rod!" Tyreek said after he finished counting the money for the second time.

"Yeah, I know," Tyrod said with a smile.

"What we gon' do with all this stuff?" Tyreek excitedly asked, eyeing his brother handling the product like he'd done this a million times. Tyrod had never touched any drugs, but he knew hustlers who did, and when money was in place to be made, he had a vengeance to get paid.

"We ask around for prices on what we got, but we gotta be careful 'cause we don't know who it belongs to. Once we find out prices, we build up our clientele and sell small amounts for the most money." Tyrod stacked the contents back inside the book bag.

"What about that?" Tyreek asked, pointing to a few money stacks and the gun that he didn't stash away.

"We save both and don't spend no money," Tyrod said, preparing for the next day. "We on now . . . we on, lil bro."

"Let's go!" a guard shouted the order, bringing Tyrod back to the present.

After showering and changing into regular jail attire, an orange jumpsuit, he was led back inside the holding cell, where the concrete walls were covered with drawings and writing. It didn't take long to hear Fish's name mentioned by a couple of dealers from the Hill Top area, who were also raided that same day, and a few guys were roughed up as well. "I know it was that fiendin' ass nigga Fish!" one of them said. "It had to have been that bitch!"

Tyrod kept his head against the wall, and Tyreek in his mental. His heart shattered to pieces just thinking of how he'd seen his better half riddled with bullets. Thoughts of he and his brother hanging out together flashed rapidly through Tyrod's mind, from the sandbox to the moment he last saw Tyreek. His heart just didn't want to believe that his brother was gone.

"Where you from, folk?" a dread-headed youngster asked Tyrod. He didn't respond. "I know this nigga heard me," the dude stated to no one in general. He stood and then paced in front of Tyrod, hitting his fist inside his hand, ranting about being tried and disrespected.

Staring straight ahead without blinking, Tyrod listened to every word the dread-head spoke. Dread Head didn't know of the anger, revenge, and murder that was taking root inside of Tyrod, who was envisioning cracking his skull.

"King!" the booking officer called.

"Yeah," Tyrod said, dryly.

"You want to make your call before you go back?" The potbellied man with a played out Afro pointed at the phones on the wall beside the holding cell. "Use the code on your band to dial out. You got five minutes."

Unable to reach his mother, Tyrod called Alexus. After several attempts that went to her voicemail, she answered.

"Lex? Baby?" Tyrod said.

"Oh my God! Rod! Oh baby. Thank God you're okay," Alexus said.

Hearing her voice almost made him cry. "Them bitch-ass cops killed 'Reek, baby. He's gone," Tyrod said, with his hand clenched around the phone. His eyes shot daggers inside the holding cell. Dread Head was still talking shit.

"Jesus, no!" Alexus stated. "Noooo, baby. Noooo!"

"Listen, I need you to call Hank Cushman's law firm and have him to come down ASAP! Those bitches planted a gun on 'Reek a few minutes after they shot him." Tyrod watched more people being brought in, almost hoping one of them would be Fish. "Man!" he said, shaking his head. "Damn, baby. Who's gonna tell this shit to Mama? It's gonna kill her."

"Baby, I got you." She sniffled. "But I have to tell you something, and I don't want you to overreact."

"Overreact about what? I'm fuckin' locked up and I—" Tyrod sighed, not wanting to take his dilemma out on Alexus, his only link to the outside world. "What is it, Lex?"

"Denise passed out when she got word of what happened to Tyreek," Alexus said. Tyrod closed his eyes briefly and bit his lip. "She fell and hit her head, baby. It's really bad . . . I'm so sorry, Rod. I—"

"Is she alive, Lex? Tell me the fucking truth!" He punched the window to the cell. The officers headed in his direction.

"She had two heart attacks on her way to the hospital. The doctors are not sure of the extent of her injuries, so please, let God handle this."

"Handle what? Lex, what are you talking about?" Tyrod grew

agitated in his state of amazement with the news about his mother.

"Denise is in a coma, bae. They won't let me see her. But, bae, listen—I'm gon' get on the lawyer shit now and see if you have a bond. But please, don't do nothing to get in any more trouble, Rod. Please, baby, don't do anything to make things worse. Please. I need you home."

"Make sure you stay by Mama's side," Tyrod ordered. "And get me the fuck up outta here!" He knew she was fighting back tears; he hated to see or hear her cry.

"I will," Alexus said, meaning every word.

The officer signaled that Tyrod's time was up. He killed the conversation and headed back to the cell. Mind in a daze, he bumped into the talkative guy.

"Man, watch where—" Dread Head began.

Tyrod hit him with the force of an air bag being deployed. Dread Head stumbled backward and swung wildly as Tyrod clocked him with a two-piece, knocking him to the floor. Then he sat on his chest and beat him with every grain of strength he possessed.

Officers rushed in, one hitting Tyrod with a taser gun as the electricity raged through Tyrod's body. Once his body stopped convulsing, the officer grabbed his hands, placing them on his head. The officer carried him to be locked down, away from the other inmates. There he could grieve the loss of his little brother and prepare for the worst with his mother. Wiping the solitary tear that dared to fall, Tyrod said aloud, "I owe every one of those cops a bullet right between the eyes. Revenge is a must."

CHAPTER 6

Hank Cushman sat inside of his spacious office, planning the opening statements for his next trial. He wiped sweat from his wrinkled forehead, not having a solid defense for his client that was caught dead in the wrong. He did what he could to assure his client that he would receive the best defense possible at trial. His client was hard-headed and stuck in his ways, which Hank was totally against, and he refused to plea out to the five years that was on the table.

Cushman's law firm was established in the year 2000 and made a good name for itself in downtown Augusta. Hank had won unbeatable cases that surprised others, some even shocking himself. Furious when cross-examining witnesses and attacking the state's evidence and their method of obtaining it, Hank was a client's dream and the prosecution's worst enemy.

His lifestyle was extremely good for him. He hired office staff to assist with calls, appointments, and briefings, in addition to the four paralegals and two field agents that usually aided him with digging up information in the streets for clients. In certain instances, he even hired private investigators or a detective to follow people sometimes.

In the past year, Cushman's demons had caught up with him. He did a lot of online gambling and investing in stocks. His fever grew after a hot hand, which encouraged him to go harder in his investments and in Vegas. But one morning, he woke up and it was all crumbling around him. The stock market crashed and several bad gambling picks had him robbing Peter to pay Paul. Once his wife Christy discovered that he'd wiped out their kids' college funds and their family savings accounts via a notification text from their bank, it was too late.

"I can't believe you did this to us," she cried her final words out to him. Then Christy packed her and their three kids' bags.

Hank could only hang his head as she stormed out the door without ever looking back. His ringing phone snapped him back to the present, but also to the aching hole Christy left in his greedy heart and his now miserable life. Her leaving was only the beginning of his end. More checks were bouncing, and business was so bad that he staged a car accident with a former client for a settlement, which he had already blown. And each of his four paralegals had quit, along with his two field agents. He performed his own investigations as scarce funds wouldn't allow him to hire a private investigator.

Dismissing the disappointment that constantly attacked him from every angle, he picked up the phone, flicking a crumb from the sandwich he ate earlier off his desk. "Hank speaking. How may I help you?" he asked, after his secretary put the call through.

"Mr. Cushman, my name is Alexus Robinson, and my fiancé, Tyrod King was arrested tonight in that drug raid on the 2300 block of Travis Pines." Hank immediately began to see point spreads and paying his car note. He took a fresh legal pad out of his desk drawer and grabbed a pen from the holder. "I'm not sure of all the charges against him, but he said to contact you," she said, speaking low.

"Sure thing, Ms. Robinson. I can find all of that out for you in a little while with a few phone calls. But I need to get some info from you right now, so I can move forward. After I figure out the charges, I will be able to give you my prices, and there will be a retainer fee. Depending on the nature of the case, it varies, just so you know," he replied.

"Okay, that won't be a problem."

Twenty minutes later, Hank had the list of charges against his new client. He was hoping for a bigger case for a bigger retainer fee, but this one would do for now. From what he was told, forty-eight pounds of marijuana was seized, along with four handguns, two extended clips holding thirty rounds, and two assault rifles that had been modified with bump triggers, allowing the guns to shoot faster and deliver a brutal force. Also, $165,000 and a bag full of Percocet 30's. Something he could definitely use.

He finished his briefing, then set out to meet Tyrod King at the jail with big plans on the Boston and Blazers' game. Hank was going all in on the 25-point spread in Boston's favor.

A single thought stopped Cushman in his tracks. Why had Mr. King called his firm out of all the other firms in Augusta?

CHAPTER 7

Lieutenant Dan Eddy walked into his office inside the FBI headquarters on Walton Way, across from the old county jail, also known as 401. He leafed through files of information on the drug bust from the day before on the King Brothers, and was amazed but not shocked by what was discovered. Not only was there plenty of drugs and cash, but there were handguns and assault rifles. The guns no longer held the .223 caliber rounds the AR-15 Bushmasters were designed to hold. They now carried one hundred 7.62x39 millimeter rounds. There was no doubt in his now racing mind that this had already attracted the attention of federal agents.

After having found both brothers at the house in possession of so many drugs and guns, he got the judge to sign off on warrants to search their residences. Team One arrived at Tyrod King's home first. When they didn't get an answer, they kicked in the door. No one was home as they searched each room, clearing the premises for the safety of the search team. Fanning out, each officer took a room inside the spacious 3,500-square-foot home while admiring the exquisite chandeliers hanging from the fourteen-foot ceilings. As well as the floor-to-ceiling windows, a swimming pool, hot tub, full basketball court. ATVs, dirt bikes, and motorcycles also littered the grounds.

An hour into the search, the only things uncovered was even more money and firearms. The deed found in the unlocked wall safe confirmed the residence belonged to Tyrod King, and until he could provide sufficient evidence to prove he paid for it all legitimately, it was being seized along with everything inside and outside of the estate.

Confirmation came from Team Two that their search was complete and yielded the same results: firearms, cash, and expensive cars and other accessories. Altogether, eleven cars and $765,000 in cash were taken, not including money spent on the houses and gems inside, clearly pushing it over the $1.5 million price tag.

* * * * * *

Alexus stood over Denise, uncertain of how to feel anymore. Tyrod's mother was hooked up to every monitor the hospital had to offer, and her hair was shaved in a horrendous Mohawk so the doctors could close the seven-inch gash on her head. Her skin was ashy, and her face had instantly aged by ten years. Alexus wondered if Denise was fighting to survive her injuries, despite receiving the devastating news that she had lost a son. For sure she'd be worried about Tyrod, who suffered as much of a loss as she had, especially with Tyreek being his twin. Even after this, Alexus knew this would be one hell of a tough road for them to get through. Denise would probably need physical and mental therapy after she woke up. *If* she woke up.

Someone from the business office stopped by to explain the expenses associated with Denise's hospital stay, and the case manager expressed her uncertainty of Denise waking from her coma. Alexus covered her mouth and closed her eyes as tears fell down her cheeks. Unemployed, with no medical or life insurance, Denise's reliance on her sons hadn't turned out to be the wisest decision. It was only day one, and Alexus estimated Denise's medical bills at five figures and rising. She had given this situation her full contemplation, and knew that street life came with a lot of risks. In most cases, the end results were never favorable.

Eventually Alexus sat in the chair beside her future mother-in-law. Denise King lay as stiff as a board, and according to the monitor that seemed to lag with its beats, her heart rate was weak. Anguished, Alexus rubbed her forehead. The doctor had already let her know that Denise's brain was severely damaged, and the injury was causing major swelling. And if they couldn't control the cerebral edema, her life would be in jeopardy. Brain surgery was their only option to relieve the pressure.

Earlier that morning while the doctors changed Denise's bandages, Alexus used that time to secure the attorney for Tyrod and finally contacted the television station. She was given a leave of absence, and Hank Cushman was going to meet with the district attorney and Tyrod later that day. *Why didn't Tyrod call so I can update him? Damn I hope this man didn't get in any trouble.* She knew his temper, and given his situations, this could not be good.

Without a doubt, Alexus was in love with Tyrod, but the lifestyle he led was placing a huge strain on their relationship. They saw less of each other because of his all day and night hustle. Her career as a reporter kept her just as busy; she had dreams to fulfill. Never once had she considered how Tyrod would not fit into her future plans. She assumed he'd eventually want out of the game especially once he became a husband and a father. Originally, Tyrod didn't even want her to go to college or work, but Alexus was already wise to the bullshit. She'd seen and heard of too many women ending up with absolutely nothing once their man got caught up. She knew that would never be her in a trillion years. Therefore, she raced to the University's registration building the moment she received her high school diploma. As it stood now, Tyrod's line of work was not promising. It held no long-term retirement plans, and at any given time the white man could take it all away with a signed piece of paper. That's why she refused to have any knowledge of his trap houses or his connects. She believed in "don't ask don't tell."

"I gotta get outta here. I can't do this right now . . . too much thinking for just a few hours!" Alexus said as she made her exit from the hospital.

Torn between anger, sadness, and frustration, she sat alone at Texas Roadhouse, once again on an emotional rollercoaster, courtesy of Tyrod. As much as she wanted to spend the rest of her life with him, at some point she expected a change, but it seemed as if that time had come and gone. Yes, they were high school sweethearts, and she understood back then that selling drugs was a means to an end. But Tyrod was smart, and he spoke of building a future and a life with her that didn't include connects, workers and soldiers, trap houses and fiends. She wanted a legitimate life, one in which they'd go out on dates, and enjoy spending quality time at home. They were now twenty-five. Alexus wanted a partner she could trust without worrying about him getting robbed or killed or fucking the next bad bitch she came across.

She sipped her margarita at the bar while waiting on her order. Normally she wasn't a drinker, but when pressure mounted, she would use a drink to knock off the edge. The waiter placed her order in front of her with a fresh basket of rolls.

"Is there anything else I can get for you, ma'am?" he asked with a smile.

"Yes, let me have your steak dinner with steamed rice and string beans," said the gentleman standing next to her. He grabbed one of her rolls as he removed his Gucci shades.

"Umm . . . excuse me." Alexus, the shapely, five-foot five-inch chocolate beauty gave him a once over with her slanted brown eyes.

"I'm sorry. But I *had* to get your attention." He stood a little over six feet tall, medium build with a mocha complexion.

Alexus gave him a closer look from his head to his feet; she was able to assess that he cared about labels. From the button down he wore to the belt, slacks, and shoes. Everything held an expensive brand name. She didn't know why the thought entered, but his swag made him sexy as hell.

"I'll buy you dinner if you want me to."

She had been approached many times, but not by someone who demanded her attention in such a way. She didn't know what it was, but she found herself saying, "Yes, thank you."

The guy made himself comfortable in the seat beside her. "You don't mind, do you?" he asked innocently. His dark hair was wavy, and his face held the prettiest dimple she'd ever seen.

"I don't mind at all," she responded. He ordered a drink for himself and one for her.

"So what's your name? You look familiar. And why're you eating alone? And the most important questions is: why are you so damn beautiful! You pretty much forced me to come over here and talk to you."

"My name is Alexus," she said as she suppressed a big grin, "and who said I was by myself? For all you know, my husband could be meeting me here, and you just invaded our dinner."

The waiter handed him his drink and set Alexus' drink in front of her. Her uninvited guest gave a light chuckle, then said, "That could be true, but it's not the case. If you were meeting someone, you'd probably be sitting in a booth or at a table waiting. You wouldn't be sitting here." He sipped his drink, then placed it on the bar. "You can't be married, for my sake," he added.

"Maybe you're right, but for your sake, I am married. It's just that my husband will not be joining me. We got into an argument, so I came here to clear my mind and have a drink," she lied, picking at her food. *Shit! Why'd I just make that up? My business with Tyrod isn't for everyone to know. Note to self: no more revealing any personal info.*

Some drinks later and with her belly full, two hours had gone by filled with laughter and conversation like she hadn't had in a long time. After they'd parted ways, she was still smiling, glancing at her phone as it lay against her steering wheel. He was now listed in her contacts under "Doctor's Office." Although it was briefly, his conversation and attention was what she sorely needed. Alexus caught her smile in the rearview mirror and quickly erased the big grin. Her man was locked up, and his mother was in intensive care. *Shit! What am I doing?* She pulled off aggressively, headed back to the hospital, wondering how a complete stranger had made her feel that giddy in just 120 minutes.

Denise's condition hadn't changed since Alexus had returned, and she hadn't really expected it to. She knew Denise was in pretty bad shape, so she said a quick prayer and decided to head home for the evening.

As Alexus turned onto her street, she was filled with relief. She was desperate for a hot bath and a quick nap. Cat naps on the pullout bed in the hospital room were nothing like being in her own comfortable bed wrapped in her down comforter. Plus, she needed to get out of the clothes she'd had on for two days. A patrol car sat in front of the house she and Tyrod shared. *Hmm, that's strange . . . maybe the cop is just finishing up some paperwork.* When she turned in the driveway, he exited his vehicle and approached the driver's side of her car as she stepped out.

"Good evening, ma'am. Did you used to live here?" he asked, after speaking in his walkie-talkie.

"Yes, *I do* live here," Alexus replied.

"This house was seized today by the federal government." Her mouth dropped open. "Until it can be proven that this house was legally bought." He walked to the back of her car, reading the plate number as he spoke into his walkie-talkie.

"What? That's crazy! Of course it was bought legally. I do have a—"

"Yeah, I see women like you all the time. Y'all always trying to use your low-paying job to cover the cost that dope dealing boyfriends spend on a house that costs a fortune. I'm sorry, but I'll have to ask you to leave the proper—"

"The car is registered to Alexus Robinson," someone responded from the other end of the walkie-talkie. The officer headed back to his car.

Dumbfounded, Alexus stared at what used to be her home. She walked to her empty mailbox, refusing to break down and cry.

"Can I get a few things that I'm gonna need?" she asked.

"No you cannot." He slammed his car door. She headed to her car and pulled out of her used-to-be driveway in a hurry with not a single thought of where she'd stay for the night.

* * * * * *

Georgia Bureau of Investigations officers and Richmond County Sheriff Department (RCSD) officers knocked on the doors of several neighbors on Travis Pines, trying to get witness statements from anyone who saw the shooting. Even though it was an open and shut case, they still had to follow protocol with a lot of man hours spent doing follow ups and paperwork, all in the name of the law for Lieutenant Butler James, and GBI Investigator Charles Reid. Elbowing his partner, Reid nodded at the house catty corner from the drug house where Tyreek King's blood had once stained the sidewalk.

At three in the morning, he'd spotted the hawk camera

monitors that were positioned on the outside, two facing the house where the shooting took place. In the department, a video was more reliable than 100 witnesses. Witnesses told the story from their point of view, so it could be 100 different accounts for one incident. A slick grin spread across Reid's greasy face. Lieutenant James' face paled. He led the search team on the day of the shooting and gave the order to the detective to get the gun.

Although he wore a mask during the bust, his supervisor and fellow officers knew he was the lead officer because he wore light gray camouflage, while everyone else wore green. Reid rapped on the door, then took a step to the side to peep in a window in search of movement inside. Music filled his ears. An F-150 pulled into the driveway. The driver got out, locking the doors to his truck using his remote.

"Any reason for the unwanted and unexpected visit?" Fred Sanders asked with a straight face.

"Yes, I'm Investigator Charles Reid with the Georgia Bureau of Investigations and this is Lieutenant Butler James with the Richmond County Sheriff's Department. We're doing an investigation into the shooting death that occurred across the street. And noticed you have surveillance cameras pointing toward the scene. Do you mind if we look at the footage?" Reid asked, pointing to the cameras.

"Sorry, sir, but they don't record—only feedback to a TV monitor," Fred said, stretching his arms across his chest.

"We see the ADT sign out front, sir, which means it does record. We could get a warrant, and there's no telling what we might find. So make it easy on yourself," said Reid, spitting tobacco onto the pavement. Fred eyed the wet spot with disgust, disrespect swelling in his chest. Where he came from, that was a fight.

"Suit yourself," Fred replied, stepping over the plants in front of his house and retrieving his water hose. He turned on the spigot and sprayed the pavement, removing the tobacco and wetting the officers in the process.

"Okay, you did this to yourself," said Reid, motioning for James to follow him. "I'll get a warrant," he mumbled to his partner. "He's gonna give us whatever he's got."

Lieutenant James looked down at his feet, then at the house as they headed back across the street. The red light on the camera indicated that there was indeed a video of the incident. He pointed it out to Reid. Without words being spoken, both men knew there was a reason Fred did not want to release the tapes. They had to get the video one way or another.

With newfound fear, Lieutenant James's face changed color. He separated from Reid once they returned across the street to check on the progress of their officers. "I've been on this force for nearly twenty years," he ranted as he stood alone, "and I refuse to let the death of a worthless street punk end my career. I'll kill his black ass first." His angry eyes settled on Fred Sanders, who continued watering his yard while meeting Lieutenant James' gaze with a challenging one of his own.

CHAPTER 8

Tyrod entered the courtroom on Walton Way after being driven from the jail, along with eleven others in the county van that smelled like ass and unwashed feet. All of the men were placed inside a holding cell outside the courtroom until their names were called. Tyrod was first.

"Case number 2:36cr043, State vs. Tyrod King," read the courtroom clerk.

Tyrod stepped forward with his lawyer and stood at the lectern with his hands at his side. His insides pulsed with nervous energy; he'd never had his freedom placed in a white man's hands before. Even though this was a bond hearing, the judge could still deny it and send him back to jail until he went to court for sentencing.

"Your Honor, on June 4, at 8:30 p.m., officers served a search warrant on the property of Mr. Tyrod King. Four handguns with extended clips were found, two modified assault rifles, forty-eight pounds of weed packaged for re-sale. Also, a bag containing fifteen hundred prescription Percocet 30's and $165,000 cash. We ask that no bond be set in his case," said the prosecutor, looking like the devil in heels, with her red hair and evil frown.

"Your Honor, I would like it to be known that my client was not the only one involved in the drug bust," Hank Cushman said in rebuttal. "Another person, his brother, was killed there. And that's whom these items belonged to. My client has been living in Augusta, Georgia his entire life and has no ties outside of this area, which does not label him as a flight risk. He's married, and the charges on my client, we expect to be dropped in the future. We ask

41

that bond be set at a reasonable price, so he can tend to his mother, who is in a coma as we speak." Hank adjusted his silk tie.

The Judge looked at the papers in front of him for several moments, then at Tyrod, who was still numb and unsure of what he'd do if he had to spend another night in that hole. "I'll set bond at $75,000, requiring the defendant to report back here every thirty days for calendar call until this issue is resolved," said the Judge, banging his gavel and moving papers aside. The set bond gave Tyrod a sense of relief.

Hank extended his hand to shake Tyrod's hand. "I'll meet you at the jail."

"Thanks, Cushman." Tyrod shook his hand. "I need you to contact my wife and let her know bond has been set. She'll know what to do from there." Tyrod was then escorted back to the holding cell to be transferred back to Phinizy Road. Although he should've been excited about getting out, he felt nothing. The only thing that could possibly make him happy was a cemetery full of SWAT and DEA agents who'd shot and killed his brother.

* * * * * *

That afternoon Fred Sanders backed out of his driveway, headed for a meeting with one of his young runners. Even though the bust from the previous day had nothing to do with him, he still took precautions. The cops snooping around his house asking for copies of the video, which he quickly denied having, left a bad taste in his mouth. And gut instinct also told him that he had not seen the last of the two officers. He made it to the Checkers on Windsor Spring Road.

"Aww damn! I forgot my burner," Fred complained. He never did business on his contract phone, so in order to call his runner, he headed back home to get his flip phone.

Once he completed his turn on Travis Pines, Fred phoned his

wife, intent on asking her to bring his phone outside. Surprised that she didn't answer, his gut twisted. He called again. Same result—no answer. Something was wrong. He pressed down on the accelerator.

* * * * * *

Desperate, Lieutenant James dressed like a street bum in a dirty gray hoodie, navy khaki pants, and black socks with dingy white gym shoes. All this, in hopes of not being recognized. From Oketo Drive, the street over from Travis Pines, he watched Fred Sanders leave his house. Robert Holmes, one of the officers placed on administrative leave, pending the outcome of the shooting, accompanied Lieutenant James on the stake-out. They covered their faces with ski masks as they jumped the fence behind the house, entering the backyard.

"Check the windows," James ordered in a whisper, keeping a watch for neighbors.

Holmes did as his superior directed. Not finding one, Lieutenant James kicked the back door in, and Holmes quickly followed with an estimated thirty seconds before the security system sounded off.

Within seconds, a terrified woman appeared before them, and instinct forced Officer Robert Holmes to squeeze the trigger.

Boom!

The shot rang out, hitting the female above her left eye. Her head recoiled from the impact, and she dropped instantly. Wide-eyed with shock, her mouth was set in a perfect O.

"What the fuck! Are you insane?" yelled Lieutenant James, checking her pulse. "Find the fucking DVD and any desktop or laptop computers. Then let's get out of here. Now!" Holmes took three steps forward to begin his search.

Boom! Boom!

Two shots rang out from the weapon of a startled Lieutenant James. The bullets entered the little boy's body as he rounded the corner in search of his mother.

"Oh *fuck!*" James said, not missing a beat in finishing his search. Racing over to the DVD player in the living room, he swiped all the DVDs lying on the TV stand into a black JanSport backpack. Then he ejected the disk out of the DVD player. Holmes handed him two laptops that James also stuffed into the bag.

"I found these. No desktops pcs are in here," Holmes said.

Lieutenant James exited the house the way he came in, followed by Holmes. Both had just committed cold-blooded murder during a home invasion. Sure grounds for a death sentence.

* * * * * *

The door was open and the molding around the door was ripped, some parts in shreds. From experience, Fred knew it had been kicked in. With only eight shots in his compact and .40 caliber, he prayed he found his mark and that he was not too late. Fred positioned himself in a shooting stance as he peeped around the side of his house to the backyard.

Two men were half-way across his lawn when Fred's first shot went off, catching a guy in the back. The other guy spun around as Fred crouched down low and released a slow, precise stream of bullets in his direction. The first guy fell to the ground after being hit two more times. The other shot flew wildly over his shoulder as the second guy ran away.

Keeping his gun out in front of him, Fred approached the man lying in his yard. Fred placed his hand on his jugular. He had no pulse. Instantly, Fred raced back into his house. The wind was quickly knocked out of his body. Tiffany had a quarter-size bullet hole in her forehead.

"Oh shit, Tiff!" Fred said, kneeling beside her to see if she was still breathing. *Where's Marquise?* he immediately thought, looking around. Four feet away, his son lay in a puddle of blood, clinging to life. He coughed up blood and shook, as Fred rushed over to him and cradled him in his arms. He pulled out his cell and called 911.

"Don't do this to me! God, no . . . no . . . please no . . . noooo!" Fred cried, holding his son as he choked on his own blood. Marquise took his last breath and died in his father's arms.

CHAPTER 9

Tyrod expected to see Alexus as soon as he walked out, but it was cool that she wasn't there. Or at least he hoped so. His first thought was of his mother. *Damn, I hope ain't nothin' else wrong with mama.* Tyrod approached his lawyer, and they shook hands.

"Mr. King, your wife informed me that she could not provide me with the funds to bond you out. She had about $3,500 in her bank, which she is getting now. The rest will be taxed on your bill," he said, walking around to the driver's seat of his Mercedes Benz S550.

"Hell no! Can they do that?" Tyrod asked, knowing the answer. *These crackers do what they want to do. That's why I'm gon' do what I wanna do.*

"Afraid so, Mr. King. They more than likely got a warrant after your arrest," Cushman said, guiding them onto Peach Orchard Road. "And it is the law. The police can seize your house and any property you have until you can prove you paid for them legally."

Tyrod stared out the window, shaking his head. "Can you take me to Travis Road? I need to get my car and your money." All he had left was the money inside his glove compartment, which wasn't much. Provided the police hadn't found it.

"No problem," Cushman replied. "You know, I was wondering something."

"Oh yeah? What's that?" Tyrod asked.

"Why did you choose me out of all the other lawyers?"

"It's not rocket science. You're good at what you do when you do it. But I just need a lil quiet for a minute, Cushman. Okay? I

47

mean, I just lost my lil brother and my mom's in a coma. So I need to think for a moment."

"Sure thing." Cushman focused on the road ahead and kept to the speed limit.

Turning off Mack Lane by the animal shelter, Cushman pulled in to park. Tyrod got out of the Benz and headed straight to his Dodge Challenger SRT Hellcat. Reaching underneath, he removed the magnetic box holding the key in place. After taking out his last fifteen grand, he paid his attorney the remaining $8,000.

"Thank you," Cushman replied, placing the money inside the center console. "And I will be looking into the seizure of your property. Anything illegal inside?"

"Money, but every gun was bought legally," Tyrod said, pulling out a Newport 100.

"I'll be in touch then," he said, before pulling off.

Tyrod passed him, burning rubber, only to find Travis Pines blocked off with cop cars.

* * * * * *

Alexus withdrew the money needed to pay Tyrod's lawyer from her Wells Fargo Bank account, leaving her with a little over $2,000. With everything seized, she could only hope he had funds put away to get them somewhere to live. Her job alone could not accommodate the lifestyle they'd become accustomed to, and at this point, an Applebee's meal would be a luxury.

Turning on Windsor Spring Road, she headed toward Hank Cushman's law office, anxious to know what happened with Tyrod's bond. She grabbed her iPhone out of her Louis Vuitton tote. Scrolling down her contact list, she was interrupted by an incoming call. UNKNOWN was displayed on the screen. She ignored it, not being the type to answer private calls. Just as fast as she could reject the call, it hit her back. Again, she let it go to voicemail. Twice more it rang and she ignored the calls. It rang for a fifth time and she could not resist.

"Hello!" Alexus snapped, suddenly changing lanes and barely missing a 750 Li in front of her.

"Is that how you answer the phone for your man?" Tyrod asked.

"Tyrod! Baby, where are you?" she asked, beyond excited to hear from him.

"I'm at the Kuntry Store about to head home. How long before you can meet me there?" he asked.

"Baby, stay there! I'll be at the store in like five minutes," she squealed with delight, now speeding and weaving through traffic.

As estimated, Alexus pulled her Audi into the parking lot within her five-minute time frame. She exited her car, and Tyrod got out to meet her.

"Hey, baby! I missed you so much," she said, jumping onto him and wrapping her legs around his waist while kissing him. She held his face tight, not wanting to let go.

"Wow! I need to be gone a little more often, if *this* is the welcome I'm gonna get. Let's head home so I can shower, and then go visit Mom. How's she doing?" he asked as he placed her back down on the ground. People entering and exiting the store were watching them with mild curiosity.

"The same, baby. Nothing has changed. She may have to undergo surgery to reduce the swelling in her brain. But we cannot go home!" she said in the voice she used to deliver bad news.

"Why not? We're right around the corner. It'll only take ten minutes," Tyrod said, not seeing the harm in taking a shower to get the jail house stench off his body. He'd also just smoked a blunt and didn't want the odor following him through the hospital's hallway.

"Because we *have* no home. The house has been seized because it's in your name, and you cannot show how you received the income to buy it. It belongs to the Feds now," Alexus said. She went on to tell him how the cars and even items inside the house could not be accessed.

Tyrod stood in front of the store in a trance. Everything he had worked so hard for had been taken, including his brother and mother.

"Okay. Well, until we get everything situated, we'll stay at my mom's house. When she gets out of the hospital, we'll get us some place to stay," he said, relieved that he hadn't put his mom's house in his name as well. He could deal with not having anywhere to go, but not his mom. Images of his dead brother being shot multiple times and his mother lying in a coma flashed in his head. He clenched his fist and bit down on the inside of his jaw.

"Rod," Alexis said, getting no response. "Tyrod!"

"What!" he shouted, licking away the blood from the side of his mouth. Alexis jumped when he raised his voice.

"Nothing. That's all right. Let's go on to your mom's house. Okay, baby?"

"Yeah, yeah . . ." He nodded. "They think it's all good out here . . . think they gon' stay on the police force and keep killin' black folks until retirement. I bet they really be believing that shit, Lex!" Tyrod looked at Alexus with mild amusement. He smiled and laughed so hard until he was doubled over, clutching his stomach.

Alexis grew uncomfortable and headed to her car without another word.

CHAPTER 10

Fred sat inside of homicide detective Reid's car along with Lieutenant Forrest, the officer in charge of the local GBI field office. Fred's body shook with rage, and pain gripped at his heart as he looked at the officers moving about his yard that was now taped off and filled with law enforcement officials.

"Mr. Sanders, we are indeed sorry about the losses you suffered here today, but we need to ask you some questions." A brief paused followed. "Can you tell us what time you left your house prior to the shooting?" Detective Reid asked.

"Around two," Fred answered, sniffling.

"And what caused you to turn around so quickly and return home?" he asked, writing notes on his yellow legal pad.

"I left my phone, came back to get it, saw my door had been kicked in, and the rest is history. Why you questioning me like I am a suspect or something?" Fred asked, looking at the detective, who finally took his eyes off the scene in front of him.

"Not at all. I am just covering all of our bases. Sorry about that. Do you by chance know either of the people involved in this crime? Any reason you know of that someone would be kicking in your door? For money, valuables, or do you sell a little drugs?" he asked, staring a hole through Fred.

Pitifully shaking his head, Fred glanced from Lieutenant Forrest, then back to Detective Reid. "Always assuming the black man selling drugs to survive. I don't know why the hell they did what they did. I only regret not killing both of them crackers!" he shouted, hitting the back of the driver's seat as tears streaked his face. Fred balled his hands into fists, and then placed them on his lap. He lay his head on top of them. Both law enforcement officers glanced at him.

"I know this is very hard for you, Mr. Sanders. As soon as you are up to it, I would like to have another sit down with you, if that's okay?" The detective fished out a card from his wallet and held it in front of Fred's face as he sat up wiping tears away.

"Nah, I'm good. Keep your card for someone who's going to use it. But for future reference, you better hope you catch the other guy before I do," Fred said, opening the car door.

"What is that supposed to mean, Mr. Sanders?" Lieutenant Forrest asked, speaking for the first time. The lieutenant wore his forty years of age very well, looking ten years younger with a low faded haircut. But the black slacks, white shirt, and beige jacket screamed veteran.

"What the fuck it sound like? His life is on a countdown!" Fred replied.

"Shit!" both officers exclaimed as their witness slammed the car door, knowing they didn't get merely as much info as they should have.

* * * * * *

Grief-stricken and head held low, Fred rocked back and forth in his F-150, cradling a family picture taken weeks prior. Puddles from his tears formed inside the frame. His son's life was snatched away before he had a chance to live it. Marquise would never grow up and venture out and start a family of his own. His wife Tiffany also had a list of nevers that Fred truly regretted. She'd never have more children or complete the college degree she'd wanted. Tiffany was only thirty years old and had stressed over not finishing college. She was finally able to enroll and had completed one semester. School meant everything to her, but her family meant more.

Two days later, Fred had finally contained himself enough to return home and relive the moment all over again. His tears had been real as the cops delivered the devastating news that his son and his wife were gone forever. When the questions arose about his security system and the video, Fred insisted his cameras were functioning but did not record. After the cops' first attempt to retrieve footage of the shooting of the man across the street, Fred had his recordings sent to his lockbox. The disc the intruders did take out of the DVD player was from a kid's movie he'd burned off the internet.

Now Fred sat watching the video of the cops jumping the gate and running up to the rear of his home. He froze their images on the screen and zoomed in as close as possible, focusing on the culprit's eyes. "The next time I look into that devil's eyes, that son-of-a-bitch is gon' suffer!" He knocked Tiffany's favorite vase off the table.

CHAPTER 11

Is this shit really real? Tyrod wondered and waited for somebody to shake him awake. He kept a straight face once he walked into his mother's hospital room and saw her lying there peacefully. Her chest rose and fell in an easy rhythm. Her eyes seemed a bit busy as they moved from left to right behind their lids. "Damn," he whispered, after kissing his mother's cheek. "Ma, I need you to wake up so I can take you home. You gotta get up outta here, Ma."

"He's right, Ms. King. Who else is going to help me plan a wedding?" Alexus added, grabbing Tyrod's hand and squeezing it. He eased his hand out of her grip and grabbed the railing on his mother's bed.

"Lex, why you mention a damn wedding during a time like this?" he asked, clearly irritated.

"Oh, baby. I didn't mean anything by it. I just wanted to talk to her as if she's still aware. What if she can hear but not talk?" Alexus said. Tyrod sucked his teeth and cut his eyes.

"Lex, this ain't a good time, that's all."

"Rod . . . an administrator stopped by earlier to discuss your mom's hospital bill."

"Lex, what the fuck I just say. Damn!"

Tyrod stormed out of University Hospital, unable to hold back the floodgates any longer. Tears streamed freely after seeing his mom and realizing his brother would never again be by his side. He felt all alone with his back against the wall. He hopped in the

55

car and peeled out, nothing feasible was coming to mind. "Think, think, think, Rod," he said as he drove along.

At first he thought about sneaking into his home, hoping the cops overlooked anything he could use to make some cash, but he remembered a patrol car was there keeping watch. Everything was probably gone anyway. He knew Tyreek's residence had also suffered the same consequences, so there was no sense in even going on his street. Besides, it would have been too painful walking through his house. Having no other choice, Tyrod headed to his mother's house, passing by their old apartment building where they had grown. A memory from the past struck him just then.

"Tyrod! Tyreek! Get in here!" Denise had yelled.

Tyrod paused the video game and went into the living room followed by Tyreek. They went to see what had their mother interrupting them while Tyrod was kicking his little brother's butt once again in Call of Duty.

"Ma, what's wron—" Tyrod said, but was soon speechless.

A cop stood beside Denise in their dimly lit living room. The cop stood beside the one black chair with peeling bonded leather. Chipped paint decorated the dingy, beige walls that glistened from the hot, muggy Georgia temperature.

"Did you two steal anything from the school?" she finally asked as roaches crawled along the long wooden table positioned in front of the chair. Both boys immediately shook their heads.

"No, ma'am," Tyrod replied, speaking for both of them.

"As much as I want to believe you two, I'm wondering where you both got the money you been giving me." Denise's dark brown eyes narrowed. "I highly doubt the ten dollars I gave you to start a lil candy hustle at school brought in that much money."

Denise's beautiful brown-skin, pretty face, and shapely body didn't escape the average-looking cop's gaze. Nor did the mice running across the floor and into a small hole in the corner of the room, creating embarrassment for the single mother and her two sons. The cop handed her a piece of paper. She cut her eyes from it to her sons, reading the printout of the teacher's cellphone that was stolen. The iCloud showed the exact location of the phone before it died. The security feature also snapped a picture of Tyreek inside of his bedroom.

"Tyreek, where is this phone at?" she asked, disappointed that they were indeed stealing.

"In the room," he replied, with his head held down. Tyrod had warned him not to turn it on in the house and was mean mugging him.

"Can I go check?" the well-built officer asked.

"Yeah," Denise stated.

Tyrod and Tyreek's heart sank, unable to stop him from discovering everything they'd stolen, hidden at the bottom of their closet inside a bag. The officer emerged from their room holding their treasures, along with a few other items they'd stolen, but decided to keep for themselves.

"Jesus Christ! I can't believe y'all stole all this shit!" Denise exclaimed, placing her hands on top of her cheap weave.

"We were just trying to help out around here," Tyrod explained.

"So we don't have to go hungry, and our bills can be paid," Tyreek added.

"Well, I don't need y'all help!" she replied.

"Damn, Mama. I sure do wish that was true today," Tyrod said aloud. Frustrated, he sat on the stairs thinking. Seventy-five thousand dollars was needed for the hospital and fast! Not only did he not have a plan, but he also needed to plan his brother's funeral. He paced the floor, played music, took a power nap and still woke up with no immediate answers. Tyrod decided to head back to the hospital.

Alexus was in the parking lot getting her sweater out of her car when he returned. She hurried over to him with both joy and worry in her big, brown eyes.

"Let's just figure this out together," she said, giving him a reassuring hug. "We can come up with some money; we just have to think."

He chuckled as he lightly broke their embrace with a gentle shove. "Whatchu know about gettin' money, money? I have to make funeral arrangements for Reek and pay $75,000 to the hospital ASAP. You got plans to get to that type of dough?" Tyrod asked, with his voice raised.

Alexus wiped away his tears as they continued to fall from his eyes. "I don't know anything about getting big money. Only what I work for. I do know about being there for who I love, no matter the situation," she said, planting a kiss on his lips. Tears of her own threatened to fall as she stepped back.

"Thanks, baby. You my ride or die, but I gotta figure this shit out somehow. Just help me out with Reek's funeral arrangements?" he asked, sorry that he raised his voice at her. The last thing he wanted to do was lose her too. "I don't think I'll be able to function throughout that ordeal."

"Yes, of course, baby. Anything for you," she answered. "I love you, Rod."

"I know. Me too." He needed cash to somehow materialize.

* * * * * *

Keyshawn Hughes was Tyrod's old connect from Atlanta. He operated out of a low-income area near Morehouse College off Lee

Street. This area was always crowded with junkies looking for a fix. The West End Mall and the Marta train station shared the same street and brought in a lot of traffic from many different walks of life. A year ago, Tyrod met Keyshawn after he and Tyreek had come to the Blue Flame Night Club to enjoy themselves during Super Bowl 51. The entire city was out in their Atlanta Falcons gear, including Tyreek. Tyrod, on the other hand, showed up in his New England Tom Brady jersey. He received all kinds of comments and disapproving looks, and most importantly, big bets. Keyshawn and Tyrod had a ten-thousand dollar bet alone, and Tyrod had another ten-thousand amongst three other people.

At the end of a historical game, marking the greatest comeback in Super Bowl history, Tom Brady pulled it off, 31-28. The Falcons fans were enraged. Some knocked over tables, spilling pitchers of beer and liquor on the floor. They ripped off their Julio Jones and Matt Ryan jerseys and ranted about the ref not calling a fair game. When the money started to exchange hands, one guy that Tyrod bet with, decided he didn't want to pay.

Tyrod approached the dude, who was accompanied by four other men, some bigger than him and Tyreek. "Hey, man. Game's over."

"Shawty, I don't know who you talkin' to, or what you talkin' 'bout. Gon' 'head wit' all dat," the guy said, looking beyond Tyrod.

"So you don't know what I'm talking about?" Tyrod asked, placing the money he collected in his pocket, except for the $4,000 the guy was refusing to pay him. Tyrod clenched the Moet bottle tight and stepped closer to the sore loser and his entourage. "A bitch nigga ain't never took shit from me," he expressed.

The dark-skinned guy laughed in Tyrod's face, showing a mouth full of gold. *"Bitch nigga?* You must not be from around here talkin' like that, fuck-boy. I murk shit, Shawty." He stepped closer, inches away from Tyrod's face.

Keyshawn stepped between them and gave Gold Mouth a knowing look that said, 'I know damn well you not trippin' 'bout no petty cash.' "Damn, Wayne! Four thousand dollars ain't worth the fuck shit, shawty. Pay the man." Keyshawn eyed Wayne and his crew.

"The fuck nigga ain't even from 'round here. Let him get it in blood," Wayne stated, holding firm.

"Fuck nigga?" Tyreek said, with his face screwed up. "Let's see who the real killas are." He grabbed his coat. "Meet us in the parking lot." Tyreek was no longer willing to observe and wait on an outcome.

"No need for all that," Keyshawn said, pulling out a wad of bills. He counted out four thousand and placed it in Tyrod's hand. He then turned to Wayne. "Now, you owe me, nigga. Be at my spot no later than twelve p.m. with my shit."

"Let me walk y'all boys outta here," Keyshawn said, turning back to Tyreek and Tyrod.

"A'ight, Keyshawn. Twelve p.m.," he said. Wayne ice-grilled Tyrod and smirked before walking off. ". . . *Bitch!*"

From that day on, Tyrod started dealing with Keyshawn and would come up and shop with him once a week, or he would come to Tyrod. However, Keyshawn was not what he appeared to be. Once Tyrod began buying coke from him, Keyshawn began to hit him with the finesse. Tyrod could drop a whole brick and wind up losing four ounces. Anytime Tyrod even dropped a thirty-six, he'd always come back with forty-eight or better. It didn't make sense that now Tyrod kept taking constant losses. Tyrod approached Keyshawn with the situation.

"Man, you cutting me to death," he complained.

"That's what it is, shawty," Keyshawn replied.

From that point forward, Tyrod cut all ties with him. But now he needed Keyshawn more than ever.

Tyrod pulled his Hellcat into the Taco Bell parking lot on Lee Street. Keyshawn pulled up alone in his Range Rover Sport. He hopped out, iced up, looking like a few bricks, and strolled over to Tyrod's car, getting in the passenger seat.

"Shawty, this muthafucka here . . . Shawty, how much it run you?" Keyshawn asked, dapping Tyrod up, looking over the interior of his car in admiration.

"Seventy-five thousand from the lot. And I got an extra seventy-five thousand into it on the upgrades I had done to the engine. He told Keyshawn about the twin 118mm turbos and intake, along with the upgraded pistons, headers, trans, and suspension.

"True shit. You ever want to get off this, shawty, let me know," Keyshawn said as he silenced his ringing cellphone.

"For the right price . . . it's gone. But listen, I need to grab a few joints from you, though. About ten bricks and fifty pounds of gas," Tyrod said, cutting to the chase. He was shooting big, not having enough money to buy even one brick. But why not go for the gusto?

"Damn, you doing it like that now? Augusta been that good to you?" Keyshawn asked and adjusted his seat.

"A little sum'n-sum'n. Not too big," Tyrod said, not playing into the hype.

"Cool. I can have it in about two hours. Pull up to the Magic. You know the spot?"

"Yeah, across from the bus station," Tyrod said, being familiar with the area. "Everything still the same price?"

"For you, seventeen for a brick, $2,500 for the bags. You good with that?" Keyshawn asked. He used to charge eighteen and $2,800, so a little cushion was good.

"Yeah, that's good. See you in two hours," Tyrod said. He got out of Tyrod's car and jumped back in his. Keyshawn never brought his prices down for anything. No matter how many times Tyrod had dealt with him, or how much he bought. Either he was trying to lock him in, or they both were "capping," as they said in the ATL. Humans were creatures of habit, so Tyrod had to be careful dealing with him.

* * * * * *

Some of the sexiest women in the world could be found inside Magic City. Women of all ethnic backgrounds strutted around the club, preparing to take the stage so that they could get their money up. Tyrod left the club and stood outside in the midst of a crowd, waiting for their bus to arrive. His car sat in the back of the club's parking lot, as he checked out the scene from afar. After standing for twenty minutes, he spotted Keyshawn as he pulled into the parking lot. A CT6 Cadillac filled with the driver and a passenger, pulled in behind him. The CT6 pulled alongside Keyshawn's driver side door. The passenger pointed in the direction of Tyrod's car.

His cellphone rang suddenly. "'Sup, folk?" Tyrod stated as he watched them from across the street. He wasn't sure what they had planned, but he had nothing to lose. His Glock 17 pressed into his pelvis, and his extended magazine rested against his hip bone. No one knew he was in Atlanta, and Keyshawn only knew him as Ty.

"I'm out here. Where you at?" Keyshawn asked, looking around the parking lot.

"I had to use the restroom. I'm inside the club. I'll be out in a minute," Tyrod said, ending the call before he realized there was no music. He walked toward the Korean store that was next to Magic City, and ended up in the back of the store via an alley. He approached the end of the Magic City building, getting a better glance at the CT6.

Two young, dread-headed men sat inside of it, facing the front of the club. One held a cellphone to his ear, no doubt talking to Keyshawn. Tyrod removed his Glock from his waistband and screwed on a silencer, then placed the gun inside the small of his back. He crept up toward the car.

"Say, bro, you know how to get to the Phillips Arena from here? I'm late as hell," Tyrod asked, startling the men inside, who had assault rifles propped between their legs. The passenger ended his phone call.

"That shit that way, shawty," said the driver, pointing to the left. He sat up, trying to block Tyrod's view of his weapon.

"Okay, thank you, bro. Can I bother you for a light?" he asked, patting his pocket. They both mimicked Tyrod's action. Tyrod snatched the Glock from behind his back, and pointed it, alternating between the driver and passenger. "One chance to live! Which one of these cars got the work . . . y'alls or Keyshawn's?" he asked the petrified occupants of the car.

"It's in the back of Keyshawn's truck. Please don't kill us!" the driver pleaded. The passenger's hands moved toward the weapon resting in between his lap. A silenced round to his chest stopped him.

"Oh shit!" the driver screamed, before a round found his frontal lobe. Tyrod leaned him over, then strolled to Keyshawn's car like nothing happened, Glock concealed. He opened the back door and slid inside, placing the gun to the back of his head.

"Damn, shawty, it's like that?" Keyshawn said, looking at Tyrod in the rearview mirror. He placed his trembling hands on the steering wheel and shook his head.

"That's what it is, *shawty,*" Tyrod replied, quoting what Keyshawn told him when he confronted him about the weight of the funny ass coke he'd sold him.

Keyshawn turned to look at Tyrod. "That's what this is about? Shit that happened almost two years ago."

"Nah, it's about my family. They come first. You're just a fallen soldier." Tyrod pressed the gun to his right eye.

"Take it . . . you won't leave here alive." He smirked.

"I like that CT6. I started to buy one, but the Hellcat had more of a sportier sex appeal," Tyrod whispered.

Keyshawn's eyes widened. Tyrod shot him in the eye, sending brain matter flying against the windshield and splattering his face. He ducked out of the Range Rover, grabbing the three duffle bags at his feet, and wiping his face with the sleeve of his shirt. A woman screamed as he dropped the bags inside his car. A crowd had already gathered around when he drove slowly past Magic City. "Bankroll Fresh" played softly on his Bose speakers as he headed to Interstate 20 East. Back to Augusta.

A little over two hours later, Tyrod sat on the bed at the Holiday Inn in Columbia County and pulled out the contents of the bags he took from Keyshawn. What was supposed to be cocaine, turned out to be all cut, except one brick. The rest were dummy bricks. The fifty pounds of gas were good. In total, the package would net Tyrod close to $175,000, giving him enough to send Tyreek off in style and pay up his mom's medical bills.

He phoned a few of his folks, getting plays lined up for the next day. All but fifteen pounds were set to go for $3,500 apiece. The brick went for $23,000. He phoned Alexus and told her to meet him at the room and to bring him something to eat. She wanted to stay with him, but eventually agreed that staying with her best friend was better so he could do what he had to do without any distractions.

The following day, he cleared the remainder of the work off to his folks. Then he took the $75,000 to his mom's house and decided he'd have Alexus write a few checks, and they would get money orders to pay off his mom's hospital debt until it was paid in full. His relieved moment of taking care of his mom quickly disappeared when he went to pick out a casket for his brother. He fought harder than he ever had to, to keep his emotions contained and almost lost it when he and Alexus arranged for his mother's old church to be decorated with floral arrangements in Tyreek's favorite color, red—just like his Dodge Magnum Wagon. Even more difficult was picking out a suit for his deceased twin. Time swooped Tyrod up and took him back in time to the day when he had to force Tyreek to speed up his routine while he was getting dressed.

"Man, could you hurry your ass up?" Tyrod had scolded Tyreek, who'd been in the bathroom for over an hour after shaving then showering. While Tyrod was laid back and casual, his little brother was finesse.

"Bruh, you can't rush a player, especially when he's gettin' all dapper in Gucci." Tyreek stayed looking fly in a designer T-shirt, hoody, bomber jacket, gym shoes, all Gucci.

"Baby, I need you to go online to the Gucci website," Tyrod said as soon as Alexus answered her phone. He knew Tyreek wouldn't want to be buried in a suit, so he had her order a shirt, slacks, socks, frames, and a watch fitting for him. Just thinking about his brother made him swallow the lump in his throat. He coughed to push back the tears. Tyreek would be buried in what he loved! Tyrod prayed he wouldn't have to plan a funeral for his mother also.

CHAPTER 12

The hearse made its way from Fred's house to Windsor Spring, headed for Broadway Baptist Church on Barton Chapel Road. Fred opted to drive his own car instead of riding with Tiffany's family, especially after feeling the negative vibes from her mother and father. At the church, the caskets were pulled out of the back, then rolled to the front of the church where Tiffany and Marquise's pictures had been placed earlier in the day.

After the opening prayer, the singing, eulogy, reading of the obituary and final words, the funeral came to an end. Many words of comfort were spoken to Fred, who gently nodded his thanks, but he was completely numb on the inside. His only thoughts were on finding that other cop who broke into his home and killed his family. As he walked to his car, oblivious to his surroundings, he heard a voice behind him screaming. He stopped walking and Tiffany's mother, Mrs. Sims met him face to face.

"This is all your fault. Dealing drugs and bringing that mess to your home. My baby was trying to make something of herself. But you . . ." Tiffany's mother stabbed him in the chest with her finger.

"C'mon, Martha. We've gotta go bury our daughter and our grandson. C'mon now, sweetheart. Please," Mr. Sims begged, pulling her away. She fell into his arms.

"Our baby is gone. She's gone. My grandson is gone. Marquise . . . oh, little ol' Marquise . . . my lil ol' grandbaby," Mrs. Sims groaned. "Please God help me! Please help me, Lord!" she screamed, causing a scene. Tiffany's family rushed over to Martha as well, glaring at Fred and also blaming his drug dealing for Tiffany and Marquise's murders.

"But this had nothing to do with me," Fred tried to explain. "I swear it didn't. But I know y'all want to believe what y'all want, so I'ma just leave it at that." Tiffany's mother and father never came around because they disapproved of Fred. But she was deeply in love and carrying Fred's child and no one could stop her.

"Gone on to your truck, son," Tiffany's paternal grandmother said, suddenly grabbing his arm and gently pushing him along. She glared back at her family, ashamed by their behavior. "I'll see you at the cemetery. You're in enough pain as it is." He heeded to her words and headed to his truck as his hurt and anger simmered.

In a flash, Fred was in his truck and slammed the door, grateful to be alone. Tears blurred his vision as his heart felt torn in pieces. He glanced up and saw the two hearses parked beside each other, containing his loved ones. He burst into gut-wrenching sobs, knowing it was only a matter of time before he caught up with the cop who'd gotten away.

* * * * * *

Tyreek's procession pulled into the Good Shepherds Baptist Church on Olive Road. High-end luxury cars led the way, bringing him forward in style. Alexus had the inside of the church decorated with all his favorite sports teams, along with pictures of him through various times in his life.

Tyrod entered the church first. Several people expressed their condolences, but he felt as if none of it would do him any good. "Sorry for my loss?" he complained to Alexus. "What are they sorry for? They ain't the evil muthafuckas that shot my bro down like a dog,"

"Baby, people mean well. They just mean they are sorry that

you lost your brother, that's all. Don't be so hard on people. Most of the time they really don't know what else to say."

"I'll tell them what *not* to say. Do you know how many times I've heard 'I'm here if you need me?' How about just don't say that shit. Where were they at when Mama was scraping pennies just to get by? That's the time they should've been there! Where were they when the cop she was dating was beating her ass? We needed them back then. Not now! So fuck 'em! Fuck every one of 'em!" he shouted. Alexus looked around, embarrassed. She wrapped her arm around him and led him to the first pew on the front row.

Being that they had no real close family, only a few distant cousins and aunts and uncles twice removed showed up. Most of the people in attendance were from the street, or people they grew up with, sporting pictures of Tyreek on T-shirts, pants, and hats. People from all hoods came out to show his brother respect.

After the preacher spoke about a life lost too young, he proclaimed, "The police are killing us blacks, and getting away with it. But there are times when we find ourselves in situations we create for ourselves." He dabbed at his nose with a rag, wiping away the sweat. "We still do not deserve to be shot down in the streets like animals." He wrapped up his speech an hour later with a prayer. Tyreek's casket was wheeled outside into the awaiting hearse. He and Alexus entered the limo. It pulled up behind the hearse, and everyone else fell in line for the lengthy funeral procession to the cemetery. He remained silent during the entire drive there and so did Alexus.

Tyrod had to steady his breathing when they entered the cemetery on Deans Bridge Road and Richmond Hill. Workers had placed chairs around the burial site, along with a green tent overhead. A second site like Tyreek's had been prepared as well, only yards away.

After the pastor's final words were spoken, Tyrod asked Alexus to leave him alone and wait in the limo. He released a dam of tears after everyone cleared out. "Bruh, I'm gon' miss you every day!" he said. "Sorry I couldn't do nothin' to stop this shit from happening. If I could, I would switch places with you in a heartbeat." He breathed hard. "But you gon' forever live through me. And I'm gon' take care of Ma. I miss the times of us growing up and making a way out of no way. I wish we could just smoke one last blunt, have one last conversation, or count money before the re-up." He cast his eyes to the heavens for a brief second. "God got you up there . . . I can feel it. I love you, Reek. Fly high," he said, as his voice began to crack.

"I'ma do all I can to make sure you didn't die without someone answering for it. You hear me, bruh?" As Tyrod stood, a shadow passed across his face. He spun around on his feet. A dude stood behind him, his face stricken with tears. He held a bottle of liquor in his hands.

"You want a drink?" he said, extending his arm out with the bottle in it. The same turmoil apparent on his face as Tyrod's. "Looks like you could use one."

"Thanks, I really could use it, man. Sorry for your loss," Tyrod said, accepting the bottle from him and nodding toward the plots behind him. He laughed inside as he heard himself speak the same words he despised: "Sorry for your loss." *Maybe Alexus was right.*

"Same to you, homie. Same to you," Fred said, extending his hand. "The name's Fred." He wiped away tears that threatened to fall from his eyes.

"Rod," Tyrod said, accepting his hand, then passing him back the bottle after he took a deep gulp.

Fred downed most of what was left. "That was my wife and my

son, man. I came home . . . My door was kicked in. I killed one of them son-of-a-bitches," he spat. "But they had already killed them. They murdered my family in cold blood. My son breathed his last breath in my arms. Looking in my eyes."

With sympathy Tyrod listened; he had never seen a man so broken before. And despite his anguish, he listened to the brother pour out his heart. Fred's head dropped. "And all this shit happened because I wouldn't turn over a tape showing the police killing this dude during a raid."

Tyrod stared at Fred, shaking his head. He frowned. There were only two recent police killings in Augusta, Tyreek's being one of them. "Where did this take place?" he asked.

"Huh? What you mean?" Fred passed the bottle back to Tyrod, who downed the rest before tossing it into the trees nearby.

"I mean, where did the police kill the dude during the raid?"

"Oh. On Travis Pines . . . across the street from my house," Fred said, standing to wipe his eyes dry and stretching his arms. "What happened to your people?" Fred pointed to Tyreek's grave.

Tyrod glanced at his brother's grave and shook his head. There, standing in front of him, was the person who had video footage of his brother being killed by the police. Tyrod was 100% sure that Tyreek had no gun on him. "So, the people who broke into your house were after the video? Were they cops?" he asked, as he pulled a Newport from his pocket, lighting it.

"Yeah, they both were cops. The one who got away, came to my house asking for the DVD. He was a GBI investigator."

"You still got the video?" Tyrod asked.

"Yeah, I do. Why?"

"Because, I'm the dude he was talking to that night. That was my brother!"

"Oh shit! Man, I'm so sorry, bruh. Those bastards killed my

family trying to get their hands on the video. I told them I didn't have a recording, but they came back anyway. My family died because they wrongfully killed your brother," Fred said, his voice alluding to all types of emotions whirling within him.

"I wanna see the tape," Tyrod said, clenching his teeth. "We won't be able to right our wrongs, but these folks will pay for what they did to our families."

"So . . . what you got in mind?" Fred asked, throwing the cigarette to the ground.

"Only God knows what's in store. You game?" he asked, pulling out his keys.

"Oh, fo' sho'!" Fred said, as they began walking toward their vehicles. "Just follow me."

"I gotta get to this repast first and drop my fiancé off. Let's meet up in a couple hours."

"That's what's up," Fred said. They exchanged information, and Tyrod dapped Fred up as they parted ways. Tyrod felt like taking off with Fred right then because the idea of having evidence that showed Tyreek was unjustly shot made his heart soar. He grinned for the first time that day.

"Ay yo, Fred!" Tyrod called out.

Fred turned back. "What up?"

"I'ma skip the repast, just let me tell my fiancée I'ma roll with you, all right?" He couldn't waste another second letting Tyreek's death go unpunished.

* * * * * *

An hour later, Tyrod sat across from Fred in his living room on the contemporary plush gray sofa. The flame burning inside his soul grew larger each time he watched the bullets pierce Tyreek's body. "Them muthafuckas! You see that foul shit, man! Hold up, rewind that!" Tyrod shouted. Fred did as requested.

"Aw damn! Yo' brother was just holdin' his cellphone. It's clear as day, Rod. The officer fired his weapon as soon as your brother turned around. Bitch ass was scared. Them other cops just started blasting off too. Oh my God! They didn't even know what was going on. Just started shooting . . . Damn!" He pressed play, and Tyrod relived his brother's murder all over again.

The lead cop went into the house and came back out and dropped a gun near Tyreek's body. "Ay yo, back up a little, man. Then pause it when you get to his face." Fred had done just that.

"There! Right there! That's that nigga right there!" Tyrod shouted. He got up and pointed at the screen. The person Fred had frozen on the screen was a part of the raid. Even though they wore masks, those green eyes never lied.

As soon as the footage ended, Tyrod contacted his lawyer. Fred burned a few copies of the DVD for him. Tyrod turned one of them over to Attorney Hank Cushman. After watching the video of Tyreek being murdered, Cushman took possession of it and assured Tyrod he would be on top of the issue. Heads were not only going to roll; there would be a huge shake-up within the Richard County Sherriff's Department. A shake up didn't mean shit to Tyrod. He was expecting heads to be chopped off and grinded into little pieces.

* * * * * *

Excited by the new evidence, Tyrod entered his mom's house with a mind full of diabolical ideas. A sweet Dove soap scent and vanilla candles graced his nostrils. Walking to the rear of the house, he heard the water turn off. Alexus was bent over the tub when he entered the guest bathroom like a lion entering its den, manhood at attention, pressing against his Armani slacks. Water trickled down her plump ass and rolled down her sexy, thick thighs. He gripped his erection and licked her back.

"Aahh!" Alexus screamed, jumping around to face him. "You scared me, boy!" Snatching the towel off the towel rack, she ran it through her natural hair and dabbed her face. "How are you feeling?" she asked, pecking his lips. She stood in the mirror drying off her flawless structure.

He eyed her as she toweled down. His dick throbbed so hard, he could feel his pulse shooting through its length. "I'm good, baby. No more tears. I gotta be strong and move forward. That's what 'Reek would want, so I gotta give it to him."

"That's good, baby. You know if you ever need someone to talk to, you got me." Alexus began to lotion up her body, starting from her breasts and passing over her toned abs.

"Let me finish that up for you." Tyrod removed the Victoria's Secret lotion bottle from the marble countertop. She turned, facing him. A smile spread across her face. Tyrod put an adequate amount in the palm of his hand, rubbing them together to lull the chill. He rubbed down her right thigh first, hitting the front and back as he made his way down. Getting past her knee, she propped her leg up on the toilet, bringing him face to face with her waxed tunnel of love. Tyrod lotioned her leg and foot, then rubbed up again, this time stopping by her sex box and placing light kisses on her lips, giving much tongue. Aroused, her clit was now fully exposed from its refuge. Repeating the same motions with her other leg and foot, he stopped back by the love shop; his tongue abusing her center as it flicked fast and furiously across her clit.

"Ooh shit, boy! Eat this pussy, Rod," she cried as she propped her ass against the sink. She arched her back, running her hands over his head. After a few more seconds, Tyrod turned her around, putting lotion in his hand. He smoothed his hands across her ass cheeks. Getting down on his knees, he spread her cheeks apart, exposing her asshole and moist pussy. He ran his tongue across her clit, then her asshole.

"Mmm—yes!" she moaned as she rotated her ass against his face. He ate around the rim of her ass while placing two fingers inside her moist honey hole. "Please! Eat more! Eat!" she said, bouncing her ass in his face like she was twerking to her favorite song. Tyrod stood, kicked off his black gators, and damn near ripped off his slacks. His boxers came down also, giving him quicker access to his length.

Seeing his erection, Alexus dropped down to the floor on the balls of her feet. She grabbed his full erection and passed her tongue around the head, rubbing him across her lips and taking him into her warm mouth. Slurping and moaning as she sucked his soul from his body while bouncing on her toes, massaging her clit in a fast, circular motion. At the height of pure lust, Tyrod grabbed her head, pumping in and out of her mouth while knocking at the door of her throat. He threw his head back in pleasure as she gripped his ass cheeks, forcing him to enter her throat. Threatening to erupt, he pulled back from her captivating head game and helped her to stand. "Head still getting the best of you, huh?" she asked with a sexy, devilish grin, as Tyrod led her to the room.

They climbed onto the California king, ready for the real deal. Alexus lay across the bed, rubbing her pussy and licking her chocolate nipple. Getting in between her legs, Tyrod beat his dick against her clit mildly, then slowly entered her tight, wet sex cave. "Yess! I needed this," she said, as he made his way deeper into her home. She contracted her muscles against his soldier, as he marched in and out of her beautiful battlefield. Pinning both of her legs beside her head, he thrust inside her roughly and received a positive reaction from Alexus. She bit down on her lip as she took the beating he was inflicting on her honey pot. Tyrod pumped hard and fast, releasing any anger and frustration that had accumulated inside of him. He flipped her over, ass sticking up in the air, and forced his member inside of her. Her pussy coated his dick with juices.

"Aaahh, you killing this pussy!" she screamed in pleasure, as he gripped her hair aggressively and pulled her head back toward him. Alexus rose on all fours, matching his pace and licking her lips. Moving forward and out of his grasp, she pushed him down onto the bed as she stared deep into his eyes. Leaning over, she grabbed a burning candle off the nightstand, then mounted his dick slowly, gripping his tool with her muscles and slowly dripping hot wax onto his chest. The feeling was unexplainable. Her bouncing on his manhood with hot wax hitting his body sent his sex into overdrive. His back arched in pleasure, as he could no longer take it. Tyrod took all of his rage out on her walls, pounding away hard and steady as the pressure built up. She set the candle down, biting her bottom lip like she always did before she released.

"Fuck me harder! Yes, fuck me! Fuck me . . . fuck, fuuuuck!" she screamed while matching each thrust, as they both activated their sex sprinklers. He gripped her ass cheeks, pulling her close as he released each drop deep inside of her.

"Wow, I could use more of that," she said, lying her head on his chest while still panting. She gyrated her hips as his dick still rested inside her.

"You can have more if you want it. You know what to do," he said, rubbing his hands across her voluptuous ass.

"Is that right?" Alexus asked, not waiting on his response. She slid his dick out of her pussy and into her mouth. He gripped the back of her head, ready for round two. For a brief moment, his mother and Tyreek flashed across his mind.

"Focus, baby," Alexus said, stopping all action. "Everything is going to be all right."

"You're right, Lexus, baby. It will be. Keep going, baby," he said, smiling seductively. Just thinking about how sweet revenge was going to be, rocked him up like granite. The perfect idea manifested just then.

CHAPTER 13

Two weeks later . . .

"Hey, beautiful. What's up?" Tyrod asked, holding his cellphone to his ear.

"Hey, baby. Nothing much." Alexus exhaled.

"Well, I've got some great news to cheer you right up. You ready?" She didn't respond. "I love how excited you are to hear my good news," he said.

"And I love your sarcasm, baby. What's going on?" Something in Alexus' voice seemed off.

"All of the officers involved with Tyreek's murder got charged with manslaughter, and all charges against me got dropped. What you think of that?"

"Yes, baby! Yes! That's fantastic, Rod! It really is."

"And check this out, Lex. Cushman already filed lawsuits against the Richmond County Sheriff's Department, and he filed motions against each officer individually."

"See, that's what I'm talking about! That is good news, baby. They need to pay for what they did to Tyreek. He didn't deserve that."

"And that's not all."

"Oh my God! I know what you're gonna say! I got wind of the news a little while ago. Those other six officers were arrested at the RCSO station earlier today. They were all doing admin duties because of the investigation."

"It's nice to know they asses got loaded into a paddy wagon, and then transported to Phinizy Road County Jail. Let them see how that shit feels for a change."

"Yeah, but they all just posted bond too."

"Not all of 'em. All except Lieutenant Butler James. He disappeared like a vapor."

"What do you mean?"

"When James' house got raided by state and federal cops, everything was gone! No clothing, furniture, or any signs that someone lived there. They even checked his financial history. No activity on his credit cards. His accounts were wiped out two days after the double murder."

"How'd you find that all out?"

"Cushman has some ears in law enforcement. And this Lieutenant James has a Special Ops military background, so tracking him ain't gon' be easy. A man with his background can only be located if he wants to be found."

"That is crazy!"

"I know. And I saved the best news for last. You ready?"

"Always."

"All the charges against me were dropped, and the court released everything. I'm selling it all, the house and the cars. I'm only keeping two cars and Reek's house."

"Really, baby?"

"Yeah. Something in my heart won't let me sell it. Think I'll use it as a place to just chill and think when I want to be alone."

Alexus' landline rang, and she quickly answered it. She said yes much more than a couple of times, then thanked the caller and hung up.

"Who was that, Lex?"

She was silent, which meant one of two things: she was pissed off about the call, or she was worried. He put out the Newport burning in the ashtray, not knowing what to say or do. "You want to talk about it?" he asked.

"Rod, baby . . ."

"What is it, Lex?

"Well . . . I know the timing is bad, and we said we were going to wait. But baby . . . I'm pregnant." She sniffled.

"What!" He jumped off the sofa and started pacing, thinking about the danger of his plans. He'd have to make sure he came out of it safe and sound now.

"Rod?" Alexus said. His original goal was by any means necessary. But in just a few seconds and with a few words from Lex his entire plan was altered. In less than a year, someone's life would now depend on his survival. He knew Alexus was waiting on his full reaction.

"Wow! No shit, baby?" he finally said. "I'm actually gon' be a father?" Genuine excitement forced his heartbeat to race. *With death comes new life*, he thought.

"Yes. Where are you? I thought—"

"I'm on my way." Tyrod broke every speed limit getting there, anxious to embrace her. He always said if he ever had a kid, he wanted a son. A daughter would be fine, too. But he had dreamed of raising a boy. Either way, becoming a father would be a chance to prove he was more man than the bastard that knocked up his mom, and then ran out on them.

In record time, he made it over to his mom's house. Rushing through the door, he grabbed Alexus up in his arms. "Thank you, baby. Thank you so much for carrying my seed."

"I love you, Tyrod King," Alexus said. "I'm so happy, baby!"

"Me too." He was so thrilled, he could barely contain it.

"Rod, we've gotta start planning for our future and our baby's future," she said with a serious expression.

"I know we do. But one thing I know we'll do for now is continue staying here at Mom's. We need to save some dough."

"That makes so much sense to me, baby. I need to save as many checks as I possibly can. And I'm really hoping Ms. King gets better so she can bond with her grandchild."

"But the reality is that her condition ain't changed at all. I'm hoping that moving her to Grady's Trauma center will help."

"It will. They probably have better doctors in Atlanta that deal with life-threatening issues like your mother's. Everything is gonna be all right, baby. Watch." Tyrod's cellphone rang.

"Yeah, man. What's up?" he asked, kissing down Alexus's neck. "We can meet in an hour."

"Meet with who in an hour? Is Ms. King okay?" Alexus asked.

"Yeah. Baby, this is Hank Cushman," Tyrod whispered, holding the phone from his ear. "We gotta discuss my lawsuits. I'm hoping I can sue the officers and the department until there is no law enforcement agency left in Augusta."

* * * * * *

"Hello, Mr. Sanders." It was Lieutenant Forrest and Detective Reid greeting Fred once again. "We have a few more questions we'd like for you to answer, if you're up to it."

"I'm really not up to it," Fred responded with a shrug. "Not much to say really. You asked me to come down here to the station and now here I am." He looked around the small room. Standard desk and chair. Two-way mirror and two officers. Both standing on opposite sides of the room. Straight-faced. One blonde haired and blue eyed. The other a green-eyed ginger. *Am I supposed to be a witness or a suspect?* Fred thought and immediately refused to be seated.

"Mr. Sanders, three murders occurred on your property—one being your wife and the other, your son, and we're just trying to get to the bottom of this. Surely, you want to help us solve this case. Get you some justice."

Five seconds of silence passed before Fred spoke. "Lieutenant Forrest, right?"

"Right."

"I can't help you do your job. I'm not a cop, didn't go to the academy or nothing. Just a regular citizen who's just lost his wife and kid." Fred shrugged.

"Mr. Sanders, I'm really sorry for your loss, and I know of no words that can help ease your pain, but I'd love to solve their murders to offer you some closure," Lieutenant Forrest replied. Fred stared straight ahead.

Reid, the GBI investigator cleared his throat, breaking the silence. "Well, let me catch you up to date. Detectives thoroughly inspected the crime scene, and we all wondered why an officer of the law was found murdered outside of your home. We suspect robbery as the motive."

"Okay," Fred responded, offering nothing else.

"Three people were found dead that day. Evidence showed that another shooter was at the scene, one that fled, leaving only a few shell casings behind. The casings were the same brand issued by the department. Either someone had rounds like the department, which isn't likely, or another officer was involved in the shooting."

Lieutenant Forrest intervened. "Yeah. This seems to be the more logical explanation, but whom and why? Do you have any idea of who the dead cop was, or have you heard anything around the hood about his accomplice?"

"Neighborhood," Reid corrected Lieutenant Forrest.

Fred met the officers' gaze and folded his arms. Lieutenant Forrest took a seat. Reid sat on the right side of the desk and opened a folder and began reading from a document. Lieutenant Forrest said, "Inside of your house, the only thing that seemed to have been disturbed were the DVDs. The entertainment center had been ransacked, revealing a few prints, some unusable. Someone was obviously looking for something." Lieutenant Forrest's right brow rose. "Is there any information you can offer us regarding the DVD?"

"Nope. Don't know anything about that." Fred shrugged and placed his hands at his sides.

"GBI and local federal investigators were initially called in because an officer was shot and killed," Reid said. "His name was Officer Timothy Holmes. While investigating Officer Holmes' background, the department noticed that he was on a leave of absence, pending the investigation of his involvement in the shooting death that took place across the street almost a week prior. A total of six officers were placed on leave, pending an investigation of the shooting.

"After inspecting the exterior of your house, we began to form a theory. We believe that your security camera—the one facing across the street where the first shooting occurred—that, from that angle your camera footage could provide us with crucial evidence. However, you—the homeowner, Fred Sanders, aren't going to cooperate. That much is obvious. I just don't understand why you won't let us help you."

"Look, I've already said the cameras were working, but they did not record."

"Mr. Sanders, we know otherwise—we're very familiar with the type of security system that you have installed in your home. But since you don't want to help us out, we'll just have to move forward on the case using the evidence collected from both the current crime scene and the previous one located across the street. One thing's for certain, both incidents are indeed connected. Again, I'm truly sorry for your loss," Lieutenant Forrest said.

"Thank you for your time. And I'm sorry for your losses as well," Reid added.

"Yeah well, be more sorry for whoever caused me those losses," Fred murmured. "We're done here, right?"

"Unless you have anything else to offer," Reid said.

Fred tilted his head just slightly, annoyed with the dumb question. "Have a good day, officers." He left the gloomy room, muttering curses during the walk to his car and even until the time he made it home. The quiet of the home filled him with too many memories and insurmountable grief until he made a mad dash out of the door and back into his truck.

Unable to live in the house where Tiffany and Marquise's lives ended, one week later, Fred moved into a small house as far away as possible from his old neighborhood on Travis Pines. Even heading in that direction made his heart throb with longing. He was grateful for Tyrod though. Hearing from him regularly kept him sane and also got him out of the house and far away from the depression that kept trying to crawl all over him. Tyrod and Fred went out for drinks and talked about anything but their problems and women. On the outside, Fred seemed to be dealing with everything just as well as Tyrod. But guilt kept creeping in, making Fred relive his decision to withhold the tape from those cops. Over and over he wondered, *Did I do the right thing? Would Tiff and Marquise still be alive if I had just given them the tape?*

He was glad, however, that Robbie's Bar and Grill provided him with an escape from his troubles. The crowded bar became Tyrod and his favorite meeting place. It had a backroom with a flat screen TV that his regulars used whenever it was too crowded.

Fred sat in that room listening closely to Tyrod because he knew firsthand what the loss of a loved one felt like. Tyrod had Fred's full attention as he met his gaze.

"I know you're hurtin' on the inside real bad, man. I feel that same shit. But I know from experience that, that pain can lie just beneath the surface and you can just go on like nothing ever happened at all. But that mental and emotional shit be eatin' a brotha's insides up. That's how dudes be offing themselves."

"Rod, I ain't thinking about killing myself, man. That's why I smoke."

"I'm just making a point, bruh. That's how men fall off—when guilt or depression be on a man's ass. He start feelin' sorry for himself and wanna start fuckin' with coke or crack to dull those thoughts. If you ever need to talk, I'm here. And I'm gon' do the same wit'chu."

"That's real talk right there, Rod. Thanks man," Fred said, dapping him up.

"It's something about you, Fred, that tells me you a solid dude. You all right with me, dawg. I got a lot of respect for you, bruh."

"That's what's up. 'Preciate that. Just tryna take it one day at a time, man. It's all I can do to keep from falling apart."

"So check this. I gotta bounce this idea off you, just to see how you'll respond. I've been giving this some serious thought, so hear me out."

"All ears, dawg. Go 'head."

"I've been thinking it's too many men like us who don't know what to do once shit like this happens." Tyrod shook his head, staring at the ice in his drink. "I don't know what I would've done without my girl."

"Yeah, man. My wife was a straight up ride or die," Fred said, wiping his hands on a napkin. He didn't want to seem as if he was that much into his feelings. "But I can ride solo and still be cool." He waved for the waitress to bring them another round. They were watching the news of a double homicide, when the tears a young man couldn't stop shedding in front of the camera made Tyrod want to reach out to him.

"Man, see! That's what I'm talking about! We need to do something to help that young brother," Tyrod said, full of compassion.

"You took the words right out of my mouth, Rod," Fred replied.

"Let's make it happen."

"When?"

"Right now," Tyrod said, pulling out his cellphone and making a call. Once the call ended, he and Fred conversed until the bar closed, and then they headed to a club and talked some more about what they could do to help the young man and other men like him who were left to deal with the violent and senseless murder of a relative.

That following day during a late afternoon, he and Fred visited the young man and helped with making funeral arrangements. They also took on most of the expense. Helping the young brother made their pain and his a helluva lot easier. The young man had come home from college and found his mother and her new husband stabbed to death by his father, an ex-cop.

"We need to get a group together," Tyrod suggested a few days later as they sat at the bar at Robbie's.

"Like a support group?" Fred asked.

"Yeah, man. We never talk about our pain—our loss. We try to hustle, smoke, or sex all that shit away. And real talk, bruh. None of that shit ever works."

"Or . . . we just pretend the shit don't exist . . ."

"So let's create a forum for dudes like us—where we can talk some real shit. Speak the truth about what it's like when these dirty cops take away the only person you feel something for. And how, despite the justice you know you're due, it somehow never comes. How can we turn that shit around? Maybe other cats got the answer. Or maybe the answer is: we get justice the way we see fit. Since the scale of truth seems to rock either way in America when it comes to officers of the law."

"That's a damn good idea!" Fred agreed. "Like it or not, we're all united through pain."

The name stuck, and it didn't take long before word got around about a support group that helped men deal with the violent and tragic loss of their loved ones. The first meeting took place at Butler Manor, a home Tyrod and Fred originally rented to entertain females or relax without having to go home. The group grew quickly to ten members. Most attendees were from the hood, tired of being victimized and bullied by the biggest gang in America, law enforcement, which made them all out to be villains and trouble makers. The men were a diverse group and in need of somebody to hear their voices. They all tried to make sure they kept a positive outlook on their lives, even though their pain ran deep, some even deeper than Tyrod and Fred's. They all agreed that someone had to keep track of the injustices the police committed and right them all.

CHAPTER 14

"Yo, would it be cool to post up a sign for the *United Through Pain* support group meetings in here? I wanna try to reach as many men as we possibly can," Tyrod said, hopeful that other men would benefit from the meetings.

"Absolutely. It's definitely needed. Go right ahead, man," Robbie replied. Tyrod had already informed him of the group's purpose, and Robbie also knew about the cops killing Tyrod's brother and Fred's wife and son. "Hey, make sure you tell the young cats that if they're stopped by cops that their number one goal should be to get home safe. So that means be polite even if they don't deserve it and don't say shit, even when the cop is an asshole. Let him talk his shit and just report his ass later. Going home alive and well is always the end result."

"I think we'll make that our first discussion," Tyrod said. "I hate cops."

"Robbie, I don't know about that be polite shit, especially if the officer is being disrespectful and abusing his authority." Fred shook his head from left to right.

"The goal is to make it home alive, Fred. I already said that. Listen, man. You ain't gotta get on his level, especially if it's real low."

"Real low like racist, hateful, and just plain evil."

"Right. If you go off, all you'll be doing is helping to provoke him so he can justify shooting the top of your head off. Y'all dig what I'm saying?"

Fred looked down, thinking, and then he met Robbie's eyes. "Yeah, that's true."

"So keep your hands where he can see them and do what he asks. And by all means, don't run if you don't wanna get shot in the fucking back. These racist ass cops couldn't care less about taking the life of a black man, woman, or child."

"Thanks for always keeping it one hundred," Fred said, dapping Robbie up. "We appreciate you, and we'll most certainly make sure we tell all the members about your spot."

Fred and Tyrod were seated inside Robbie's bar in their usual spot, enjoying their perfectly cooked steaks, as they talked about life. They both checked their watches. Their support group meeting was set to begin in an hour. They drank their beers and wolfed down their T-bones and baked potatoes and then headed to Butler Manor.

Word of mouth brought nineteen-year-old Shawn "Scooter" Daniels to his very first meeting. Average height, baby faced with a nappy fro. He was dressed in khakis, a button up, and Jordans. He was quiet, yet listened attentively to each of the attendees as they spoke. Once everyone finished, he stood to finally tell his story.

"Two years ago . . ." he nearly shouted. The whole room was held captive by the long pause that followed. Scooter looked around the room. "I lost my father during a traffic stop." He scoffed. "A simple traffic stop."

"Yeah, my father was speeding, but we were running late for my high school graduation. We left the house and on our way to the car, his tire was sitting on a flat. He called Triple A and by the time it was fixed, we had ten minutes to cover twenty miles, so dad floored the Mustang. We were minutes away from the James Brown arena. Just minutes away . . . minutes away from life and death. The blue lights came on and my father pulled over so the officer could run the plates, issue the ticket, and get me to my graduation. Seems easy enough, but it wasn't.

"My dad and I both were kind of antsy, fidgeting because of how close we were yet being so far away. Something about being stopped by the cops made us both nervous.

'He's calling for another unit, son," my dad said, looking in the rearview mirror.

'For what!' I yelled.

'Probably nervous. That's a bad sign. We're going to be here for a while,' Dad said, looking over his shoulder.

'License and registration,' the officer stated, suddenly standing at the window. Dad flipped through his wallet and pulled out his ID and registration card and handed it to him.

'Why were you speeding back there?' the officer asked, hand on his Glock .40, as if the will to shoot surged through him like a circuit board overloading.

'I'm late for my son's graduation, and I'd like to make it there to see him walk across the stage, if you don't mind,' Dad replied, disgusted by the officer's entire vibe; it was so bad it seeped off him and oozed into our space.

'Hey! Slow down, buddy. Just doing my job. I also need to see proof of insurance?' he said, looking over the ID and registration.

"Dad was frustrated and sighed, quickly flipping through his wallet for his insurance card. He went through the wallet twice and realized it wasn't there.

'Move your arm, Scooter,' he said, tapping my arm as it rested on the center console.

"If he had remembered that he'd left his gun in the console, he would have informed the officer first.

'Don't do it!' the officer screamed, backing away from the car and pulling his weapon like a deputy in an old western.

"He sent round after round into the driver's side door, hitting my dad seven times. Luckily I wasn't killed. All I could do was ball up and cover myself as much as possible.

'Get out of the car with your hands up!' the officer finally yelled at me.

"Slowly, with both of my hands raised toward the sky, I exited the car, not knowing if I'd get shot too. My entire body was shaking. My father's blood blotted my white graduation gown like paint splatters. With a huge gun pointing in my face, I lay flat on the ground as instructed, right on top of some of those same shell casings that left the officers weapon after shooting at my father.

"Of course I didn't make it to my graduation, and my dad didn't make it out of that situation alive either. The officer was acquitted. So where's my justice?" A long paused followed before Scooter walked back to his seat and sat down.

Tyrod and Fred looked at each other, shaking their heads. "I guess that's the question everyone keeps asking," Fred said.

"Yeah, and we need to put our heads together to come up with an answer. Preferably one that appeals to our satisfaction," Tyrod added.

* * * * * *

During the next meeting, a young man burst into the room, eyes filled with tears. "They killed my brother!" his voice squeaked out. "They killed my brother." The man fell to his knees, as if all of his breath had been zapped from his lungs. His name was Johnny Parker, known on the streets as JP.

JP was twenty-eight and from the way he told it to the group, he lived a rather good life. His mother married a dedicated family man. He attended a good school and church on the weekend faithfully. Something about him reminded Tyrod of his brother Tyreek, especially when he said, "Christmas and birthdays always made me feel like I'd won the lottery." They were also Tyreek's favorite times of the year once the dough started rolling in. JP told them he had the best clothes, shoes, and games.

But he and his brother started hanging around the wrong people and tried to grow up like true gangstas. JP and his brother forsook their parents' hard work and started gang banging and got involved in a lot of street beef. The crew they ran with was one of the biggest in Augusta and the number one target for law enforcement and rival gangs. Them shooting three-pointers and driving to the lake, soon became them shooting Glock 17s and driving Bonnevilles in the hood.

Luck ran out and JP was convicted of robbery and forced entry and sentenced to ten years. Having already served seven of the ten years, JP was paroled back out onto the streets where his brother had been brutally murdered. The killer was never found. His pain was insurmountable, and he was battling a rage he wasn't sure he could contain much longer.

Trying to do the right thing, he found a job hanging billboards, while he was still working off his last package, making forty dollars an hour. It felt better making honest money than risking his freedom and his family's safety, so at the end of the package, he kept the funds and started working full-time. Six months later, he was laid off with a paycheck that was a little over $400. With no money saved and a car note due, Tyrod saw that JP was on the edge—angry over his brother's murder, yet thirsty for the hustle to get his money up. He also saw a killer. A time bomb just like him and Fred. Waiting to explode. JP would be the perfect candidate for what Tyrod intended to do.

CHAPTER 15

"This is such bullshit!" Christopher Brookes shouted in frustration. Being laid off pending an investigation weighed heavy on the officer's mind. A daytime nap or good-night's sleep had yet to find the once decorated soldier, and when it did, a dream about standing over the guy who was murdered, watching him choke on the last breath of life he'd ever take, took his appetite and his energy. It made him and his wife distant. And to make matters worse, the financial burden was now placed on her. And he was to blame.

The measly dollars he made working security at their neighborhood library was not good enough to keep the family afloat, and the side jobs he did cutting yards and moving furniture, only brought in pennies. His lawyer's latest news did nothing but add to their high stress level. "The way the case is looking right now. The prosecution says it's open and shut. So be prepared to plea out."

Slouching down in his oversize reclining chair listening to the fifth reporter give details of the shooting only increased his ire. "Arrrgh! I fucking hate the news! They're all reporting the same damn thing over and over again!" He clicked the remote to another channel and found the same old story. "Sons-of-bitches!" He slammed the remote down on the table, grabbed the Bud Lite beside it and chugged it down until he was slurping up his own air. Quickly he popped the top on the second can beside it and chugged it down also. The repetitive news report surrounding the shooting made him go from drinking occasionally to drinking every day, sometimes downing a twelve-pack before noon.

"Ooohhh, what's the use? They never tell the full story," he grumbled. "He was a drug-dealing thug! Oh, just screw it!" He picked up the remote and beat the beer cans with it until they flew off the table. His heartbeat increased. Sweat beads dotted his forehead. He grabbed his chest, unable to take in a full breath. "I've gotta get the hell out of here before I friggin' croak! Got-dammit!" Quickly, he stood. Today, he couldn't think of taking another swallow of beer. He had to leave the house before he went insane.

Christopher raced outside and stopped in his tracks. He doubled over, hands on knees and simply focused on taking full breaths. The first few inhales of fresh air calmed his nerves immediately. He hopped in his Chevy Malibu and let the windows down a quarter of the way. He cruised through Gate Five onto Fort Gordon where he drove through the base. Being that this was the first day of hunting season, he wanted to get out early to get the best vantage point and section.

Everything that led up to the shooting ran through his head during the drive. Something felt off, and he had an uncomfortable sensation in his gut. Queasiness seldom found a place inside his body, but this was full-fledged. He only heard "gun," and then the shots that were fired. He remembered the statement he gave to the Office of Internal Affairs. "I was just doing my job," he insisted. "Protecting my fellow officer in the line of duty." It wasn't until the smoke cleared that the realization set in: they'd made a terrible mistake. This was that feeling in his stomach. The end of the road. The end of his career and life.

After unloading his gear, Christopher started on his way, looking forward to putting something else on his mind other than the dog shit he was into.

Perched sixty feet above the ground in a tree stand, he looked through a pair of Nikon binoculars, scanning the fields that surrounded him. Propped next to him was his rifle and 7-millimeter, loaded with eight rounds of ammunition. To line a deer up in his sights and execute the perfect shot was gratifying. It released the anxiety that was pent up inside of him. The bushes moved suddenly. He watched and waited.

Setting his binoculars down, he picked up his rifle, adjusted the lens on the scope, and scanned the area, looking for more movement. The leaves shook on a bush, fifty yards from where he was stationed. Seeing an orange vest, he knew to hold his fire. Hunters were assigned their own part of the field to prevent getting shot. Christopher made a mental note to let the commissioner know and waited until the idiot was out of sight. Minutes later, he lined his rifle up perfectly with a buck that wandered into his peripheral, bigger than most in size.

With controlled breathing, he eased his finger on the trigger. The deer raised his head, turning to face him. He stared at him through the scope.

Boom!

The shot cracked, bringing birds out of their resting places and other animals scrambling for their lives. The deer ran erratically, then fell face forward into the dirt. In a split second, Christopher chambered another round and scanned the area for remaining bucks. He caught a glimpse of one and took the shot. The shot went wild and he missed. Then he set the gun down.

Putting his binoculars inside his bag, he grabbed his gun, and climbed down the ladder, leaving his post. A suction sound stopped him in his tracks. His shirt moistened deep red, as blood flowed freely from where the bullet from a high-powered weapon struck him dead center in the heart. His breathing shortened and his vision gave way; the mini-14 killed Christopher Brookes before he fell backward, landing next to his ATV.

* * * * * *

Fish sat inside the Holiday Inn on Belair Road in Columbia County, eating a Wendy's hamburger, awaiting the next call from his master. He'd been helping more than one law-enforcement agency build drug cases against a number of people in Augusta for close to a year. Ten cases prior, he failed to signal, making a turn off London Boulevard in a drug-infested area. After confirming he had no license, the narcotic's officer pulled Fish out of his car and placed him in handcuffs. Fish sat inside of the narc's car sweating while the AC was on full blast. He was not about the jail life and had no intentions of ever stepping foot inside of a cell. Minutes later, the officer found an ounce and a half of weed and twenty Percocet tens. The officer informed Fish of the discovery and told him he would be facing a few years in jail, if and when he was convicted.

"Give me a dealer, maybe a gun, and all of this vanishes," said the cop, holding up the drugs he found inside Fish's car. Fish reared his head back.

"Do I get to keep my shit?"

"Hell no! That'll cost you more. Two dealers and you can keep your shit. How about it?" The cop smirked, knowing he had Fish where he wanted him.

Fish looked at his weed. He still owed $100 on it and saw two options: keep it and pay Tyreek, or fuck Tyreek.

"Cool, I'm game," he said, releasing steam, like he'd just made the hardest decision of his life. Fish thought, *Ain't no way I'm giving you my boy.* He planned to turn over some low-level dealers from the south side projects he knew. Fuck 'em! After the officers made the first two arrests, turning in only a few ounces of weed, they were not happy. Too many resources were used for the little drugs confiscated.

Fish gave up more dealers on a bigger scale, then told the narcs, "I'm done. Can I get my shit now?"

"Only if you want to be charged with drug trafficking and firearm arm violations, unless you can provide us with something bigger," the officer said with a slight grin.

With his back against the wall, he agreed. Now, Tyreek King was dead. He felt like shit. And he was still being used as a pawn in the fight against drugs in Augusta. The bedside phone rang, startling Fish as he downed the last of his food. He dreaded answering and thought about running, but quickly erased this option, knowing he had no money to get him far, and he would have a drug case hanging over his head whenever he was apprehended.

"Hello?" Fish answered, with his head hung low. He had to find a way out; these crackers didn't care if he lived or died.

"Up and at 'em, buttercup! Time to go to work," said the lead narcotic's officer.

"Whatever, man. This is it after this! I'm done!" Fish shouted, standing up, chest heaving with rage. Tyreek was his boy!

"Shut the fuck up before I put a brick in your car and call Columbia County on your bitch ass! You know you're not built for jail, so you're done when I say you're done, bitch! Now, come downstairs and get ready for work!" the cop shouted into the receiver.

Fish got dressed, grabbed the crumbled pack of Newports, and headed for the door. Regretting that he would have to do the unthinkable.

CHAPTER 16

Alexus and Jake, her cameraman in the field, showed their ID badges to the military police officer at the gates and gained entry. This story was covered exclusively by News Channel 12. They arrived at the scene, and a few hunters and officers were seen wandering around the parking lot. Yellow tape had the area secured off deep in the woods. They stopped short of the tape, and Jake set up his camera. Alexus read over her notes and checked herself in her compact mirror.

"Live in thirty seconds," Jake said, referencing the time on his watch. Alexus ironed her wrinkles away with her hand, then stood in front of the camera with her million-dollar smile on. "Three, two, one," Jake counted down, then pointed to Alexus.

"Today at 6:00 p.m., we have breaking news on Fort Gordon. Today, a police officer with the Richmond County Police Department and ties to the Tyreek King murder was killed during a hunting incident. Officer Christopher Brookes was hunting when he was shot by a high-powered weapon. Investigators are still unsure of the person who shot the gun, and they say it's likely the individual does not know that they struck someone.

"Police are asking everyone who was out on the hunting grounds today to come to the police station for questioning. Our hearts go out to the family and the police department for losing one of their own. Alexus Robinson reporting live from news channel 12. Barnes," Alexus stated publicly to the world.

On the inside, she was thinking, "Fuck him." Chris Brookes

was part of the reason she did not feel the love at home, and why she and Tyrod were going through so much. Tyrod was leaning toward obsession with the officers at RSCO. Always busy, always planning something, or always having to help a support group member with something. She couldn't care less about Brookes' family and the department. Her and Rod's relationship was slipping through her hands, and she was running out of ways to save it. She couldn't remember the last time he was at home for more than twenty minutes.

Alexus's checked the messages on her phone. "Hey, baby. Give me call. Sorry I ain't been around like I should, but you know I love you though. So meet me at the crib. I'm headed that way." He ended the call. She knew he was feeling somewhat guilty. It had been weeks since they'd spent time with each other. He was always busy with the streets and the group. And she kept busy with work. Alexus had never been the type to go looking for a man like a lost puppy or asking why things weren't getting any better between them. There was always some hot story that needed to be reported, and she stayed on top of it. Pregnant and all.

* * * * * *

Alexus heard the beeping throughout the ICU floor at Grady Hospital where lives hung in the balance. She was happy knowing that Denise was getting the best care possible after her brain surgery where they'd removed a section of her skull. Her vital signs were good and her condition was considered stable, even though she was in the coma. A woman was standing in Denise's room, head cast down and hands raised as if an officer had yelled "hands up!"

"Heavenly Father, I ask that you watch over the souls who are ill and keep them on this earth to serve you."

"She's praying," Alexus whispered, halting her steps.

"Better to live for you. If that is not your will, then I ask that the souls that are taken, please be forgiven for the sins they've committed and let them be sent on to rest. In your son Jesus' name, I pray. Amen," Nurse Hannah said.

"Uhm, hello there," Alexus said with a wave as she finally entered the room, closing the curtain.

"Good afternoon. I'm Nurse Hannah. And you are . . ."

"Alexus Robinson. I'm Ms. King's future daughter-in-law," she said.

"Oh, that's wonderful. Good to know she has someone visiting her. Her story touched my heart so much after learning the circumstances surrounding her condition. She's my first patient when I begin my rounds. Well, I actually make her my first patient."

"That's so kind of you."

"Knowing what happened to her son made me feel a kinship to her. Just like Denise's son, my son was also a victim of gun violence here in Atlanta. God, I suffered day and night, just missing his presence. He didn't come around as much once he became involved in that street life though. But maybe that was a good thing." She released a loud breath.

Alexus kept quiet, feeling somewhat convicted by Nurse Hannah's story. She wanted Tyrod to step away from the drug game ASAP, but that hadn't happened. She hoped the lawsuits against those dirty cops brought along a big settlement check, and Tyrod would pursue something else, like his own business.

Nurse Hannah's voice broke her thoughts. "I warned him that the drug dealer's lifestyle and being flashy were only going to land him in jail or in a grave. Wouldn't you know my prophecy had come to pass exactly a year later? I received a devastating phone call about the death of my only son while I was at work treating a gunshot victim. Felt like all the life in me just evaporated." The tall, brown-eyed, slender woman stared beyond Alexus, looking into the past. Chill bumps formed all over Alexus' arms. She didn't know what she would do without Tyrod in her life. He was all she had known for the last twelve years.

"Thank you so much for all you do for Ms. King. Her son Tyrod and I appreciate that."

"Nice of you to say, but that's my job." Nurse Hannah checked Denise's vital signs and IV bag. She then turned her onto her side to prevent her from getting bedsores.

"I can tell just by watching you, that you take such good care of her. I'm going to put her hair up today so it doesn't get matted." Alexus pulled out a brush and some coconut oil and began brushing Denise's hair.

"I can tell you're a really sweet young lady," Nurse Hannah said with a soft smile. She began singing while washing Denise's face.

"The battle is not yours . . . it's the Lords," Alexus joined in. After finishing her song and her task at hand, Nurse Hannah told Denise, "I'll be back to check on you." She left the room, still humming the Yolanda Adams song.

Alexus hoped Ms. King would make a full recovery, but she also hoped Tyrod would make a 180 degree turn and change his life while doing so on the right side of the law. If he kept on taking risks with selling drugs, she knew he'd eventually land himself six-feet under just like Ms. Hannah's son.

* * * * * *

Detective Frank Barton walked into Grady Memorial and approached the receptionist for the fifth time in two weeks. He led the violent crimes unit assigned to investigate criminal offenses dealing with weapons, terrorist threats, and domestic violence, which seemed to be the worst. His new case involved a couple involved in a horrific domestic dispute.

Detective Barton exited the elevator onto the ICU floor, headed for Room 628 to check on his victim. He turned the corner and bumped into Nurse Hannah coming out of Denise King's room. Her clipboard went sailing into the air, and her papers were strewn across the tile floor.

"Ma'am, I'm so sorry. Let me get those for you," Frank Barton said, picking up the items that fell, handing them to her.

"Thank you. I wasn't paying any attention. God bless you," she said, retrieving the remnants. He looked at Nurse Hannah for the first time as recognition set in.

"Ms. Hannah Israel? I'm Detective Frank Barton. I'm working on the homicide case involving your patient. We met a few days ago." He extended his hand for a handshake. She shook his in return.

"Of course, I remember you. How's it going?" She glanced at her watch.

"It's going. Same thing every day, different victim. I was trying to get a statement from one of your patients. Do you know the status of . . ." He looked at his paperwork, referring to his notes, and then asked the name of the victim.

"Yes, he's still in a coma, but he's recovering. He went into surgery just yesterday," Nurse Hannah said, shifting her weight to her right leg as she explained the need for the induced-coma.

"Sure thing, Ms. Israel, and thank you. Could you give me a call personally once he's up?" he asked, pulling a card from the breast pocket of his cheap suit. "I'm hoping he'll be able to tell me who tried to execute him."

* * * * * *

Judges, the prosecuting Attorney, and the Assistant District

Attorney (ADA), along with other high-powered officials from the Augusta area, met in an undisclosed location to discuss the events surrounding the murder investigation involving the six officers. The tapes were viewed by everyone in attendance at one time or another. But to make sure, the video was played again on a large 70-inch television screen.

After the video was viewed, private discussions were formed amongst individuals, until Governor Schreiber called the meeting to order. "As we have seen in the video, the victim was unarmed at the time he was shot, and clearly, someone has to answer for this. We're all on the same side here, so here is what I think. We should go after the lieutenant in charge of the raid and the officer who fired the first shot.

"Let's get the charge reduced to involuntary manslaughter and violating his oath to uphold his sworn duties. We go for the lesser charges possible, outlining all the good he has done and see if we can get him about a year or less. The Feds will charge him for violating the victim's civil rights, so he'll be looking at about five years, total. Then, there is still the lawsuit," said the governor of Georgia.

This would not have been the first time they came together to protect one of their own, and it would not be the last. The all-white panel that conspired to make the situation disappear had one thing in common besides being corrupt in law-enforcement: they disliked blacks! They felt blacks were scum and had no place on earth, unless they were in one of the biggest industries: prison.

"We can try to settle out of court for the wrongful death suit. Lieutenant James is in a lot of hot water, and so is the department. Two innocent people were murdered by the hands of law-enforcement days after the raid, along with one of ours. There's no denying the link between the two. The tape helps confirm that much. We can get ourselves caught up in a scandal if we are not careful," said Mayor Stillwell, loosening his tie as he sat perched in a high-back chair.

"That's understandable. We would do all that we can to protect ours. Lieutenant James is done. He went AWOL and never returned to work after those murders. So he can't be helped, because he's showing guilt."

"But, what about the other six?" the governor asked.

"Well, one was killed in a home invasion, as we all know. Then another one"—Julia Roberto paused to refer to her notes—"Chris Brookes—we just learned he was killed in a hunting accident."

"Oh well, we'll move forward and lend all the support we can to those charged in this case. Their jobs will be questionable, but there's always a chance," said the mayor of Augusta.

"Christopher Brookes was found hours after being murdered by a hunter. The military police secured the area and searched for evidence. Shell casings littered the area, along with other items that could have been left by anyone. The ME removed the contents of Christopher's pocket and discovered he was a police officer with the Richmond County sheriff's office. They were contacted and allowed to send in their own team of investigators to analyze the scene.

"They found nothing out of the ordinary and wrapped up their crews' work. The officer's body was sent to the Fort Gordon medical examiner's office until the ME released his body to Richmond County authorities. Let's reach out to the lawyers and get this thing over as quickly and quietly as possible," Governor Schreiber said while standing, signaling the end of the meeting.

"Whether there's evidence or not to support my suspicion, I believe we should look at the brother of Tyreek King a little closer. He made threatening statements following his arrest that can't be overlooked. Keep an eye on him, but do it discreetly," Mayor Stillwell said to his police superintendent.

Governor Schreiber stopped short of picking up his briefcase and looked at the mayor. He thought on the mayor's suggestion and could not disagree. "Let's make it happen," he said, grabbing his briefcase, then exiting the room.

CHAPTER 17

Six months later . . .

For some reason Tyrod felt as if he wanted to get something off his chest about his past. He felt that Fred was trustworthy and the incident was on his mind so heavy, he couldn't hold it in any longer. He pulled out of the Butler Manor subdivision along with Fred, leaving their secret man cave where they held meetings or brought random females.

"It's crazy how I'm even in this situation right now," Tyrod stated.

"Whatchu mean?" Fred asked.

"I mean the reason I started hustling."

"It was out of survival, I know. Just like most people trying to get by, right?"

"Definitely. My brother Tyreek and I got busted for stealing a teacher's cellphone. Our mom lectured us for the longest about going to jail. Us taking that phone was one of the dumbest, if not worse things we could have ever done."

"Why dumbest?"

"It brought a no-good cop sniffing around. He showed up on our doorstep looking for us. Mama cursed us out . . . crying and screaming and shaking us by the shoulders. Then she sent us to our rooms."

"Rod, I wish I *did* have a mother telling me what to do and not do," Fred said, being brutally honest. "I kinda grew up doing whatever. So what happened? Did the cop try to lock y'all up?"

"Not that day. So the cop was like: 'Don't worry, ma'am. I'm gonna try to pull some strings, so they won't get charged. Are you married?'

"Mom looked surprised. 'Uh . . . no. It's just me and my boys,' she said.

"That po-po was running *game*! My slick ass daddy did my mom like that," Fred said.

"Right, right. So the cop said, 'Being that there's no male figure in the house, I understand that makes it hard to survive and hard to discipline the kids. Especially boys.'

"Six days later, thanks to the *good* officer, me and Reek got charged with theft and sent to an alternative school, along with a gift of a one-year probation. That's how helpful he was."

"Get the fuck outta here, bruh! I thought he was gon' take care of it to impress ya moms. He could've pulled some strings, Rod."

"Hell nah! That ain't what he wanted. He wanted us gone. Within a month, Moms was seeing him on a regular. We called him Officer Jim. He took her out on dates and was helping out with bills, food, and clothes. At first we thought he was cool. He even picked us up from school once. But me and Reek was begging to be cuffed and placed in the back," Tyrod explained.

Fred cracked up laughing. "Ahhh, y'all was doing ride-alongs with Officer Jim, huh?"

"Yup. He started stopping by the school to make sure we weren't getting in any trouble. The more he stayed over to the crib, the more things started changing."

"He wanted to be the authority figure. A daddy."

"Probably. If he had earned it honestly, I wouldn't have had a problem wit' him. But he turned out to be a coward and a pussy and one of the many reasons I hate cops till this day."

"Damn, Rod. So what he do?"

"One night I woke up late as hell to take a piss. I heard some strange ass noises coming from the living room, right? I'm a shorty, so I'm like: what the hell is that? I eased down the hall, feeling my way through the dark and shit. Nigga, do you know I saw my mother bent over the fucking old ass floor model TV, moaning like me and Reek weren't even there. The cop was doing my moms, bruh!"

"You mean 'protecting and serving' the community. "Get the fuck outta here! Straight up?"

"On everything, bruh. That spiteful nigga turned and grinned at me while he was still stroking my moms, bruh. He ain't even try to hide the shit. Disrespectful ass bust his nut, then pulled out and nutted all over her back and butt."

"Ugh . . . got-damn, dawg! That's enough, Rod. I think I'm gonna be sick, and it ain't even my old girl. I would've had to blow that nigga's brains out."

"Man, I was pissed at moms for degrading herself. But it wasn't nothing I could do about it. She grown. She's moms, ya dig? She saw him as a means to an end. Of course I get it now. But damn. That shit's traumatizing as hell."

"I feel you, dawg." Fred nodded. "But still . . . I would have had to put a hot one up in 'im."

"Don't think I didn't want to."

Fred and Tyrod had formed a brotherly bond over the several months that passed and found they had more than their pain in common. "Don't trip," Fred said. "Growing up, my shit was unstable too. I went without basic shit for many days and nights. I had to settle for what was handed down to me.

"But the big difference between my mother and yours is that my old girl was on drugs, and my father was a drug dealer who used to slide through and smash mom on the low for a few rocks.

When she finally approached him about being pregnant, he flipped out and stopped coming through. She refused to abort me because she thought she couldn't have kids. So I guess I'm a miracle. She never had any more children after me though." Fred cleared his throat, ridding himself of the pain that tried to rise. "I can't believe I just told you that bullshit. I ain't never told nobody about my momma."

"So anyway, where we headed to now?" Fred asked from the passenger seat of Tyrod's car.

"I need to go check on Keno and see how thangs running around there," Tyrod expressed and signaled to make a turn.

Fred pulled out a half ounce of loud from his pocket. His status had elevated in the game when he started dealing with Tyrod. He had a weed spot that was doing all right when they first started dealing with each other. Now, they had a weed spot and a spot to sell crack and Percocets.

"Sounds good. I'm rolling."

"Cool." Tyrod headed to Keno's spot, who had gone to school with him and Tyreek. Keno also grew up with them in the same hood.

When Tyrod and Tyreek first stumbled across the book bag containing drugs, a gun, and money as teens, Keno was the one to give them the prices for their merchandise. He put them on back then and continued dealing with them as they got older. Keno worked off of Willow Road on the hill. Traffic was steady and anything with a price tag on it was sold.

Tyrod pointed to the apartments on the hill and smiled to himself. Numerous people did hand to hand transactions, as others stood around waiting for the next sale. They took turns serving, so everyone could get in on the money. That's how Keno had it set up. They sold his work, and the work was fronted by Tyrod, who had hooked up with a more solid connect.

"I'll wait in the car," Fred said, setting his Springfield .45 with an extended clip on his lap. "I don't know these niggas like that. These your folks, no disrespect though."

"Man, you good. This my people spot," Tyrod said and opened his car door, putting out the blunt they were smoking. "Plus, you need to meet Keno."

Fred followed suit, standing outside the car and sticking his gun in his waistband for everyone who was looking to see.

"Who?" came a voice from the other side of Apartment 24, after Rod knocked on the door.

"Rod." He adjusted his shirt to conceal his weight, a Taurus PT 111 in his back pocket.

"What's good, bruh?" Keno said, when he opened the door with his cellphone up to his ear. He stepped to the side so they could gain entry.

"Slow motion, big guy. This my folk, Fred. Fred, Keno," Tyrod said. They slapped hands and nodded at each other. "How shit been for you?" he asked. Keno's spot easily ran through ten to twenty pounds and about a brick on a good week. All breakdown, no weight.

Keno finished up a conversation, then hung up. "The same. Good. When will you be able to holla at me again?"

Tyrod and Fred sat on the sectional. "Whenever you ready, I'm ready," he stated.

"Be here in two minutes. He bringing it off Royal Street," Tyrod said, referring to the money for the package he'd given him. Keno had a small operation running behind Toasties and Big Oak Park.

"Can I use your bathroom, fam'?" Fred asked, standing up.

"Go ahead. It's right down the hall." Keno pointed to the back of his apartment. He tossed his cell on the table and took a wad out of his pocket. "I may need to start getting another half a joint from you. It's picking up around here, so I need to be good when they come," Keno replied, thumbing through the bills.

"That won't be a problem. I'll bring it to you as soon as I come back with the usual."

A knock came at the door. Keno walked over to it, putting his money back in his pocket. "Who?" he asked.

"Careful."

He opened the door. The person on the other side brushed past him. "Man, I gotta piss. Here," Dre said, handing Keno a bag.

"Somebody in there. So you gonna have to wait." He headed down the hall and started pacing. "Man, sit your ass down somewhere," Keno said, sitting down beside Tyrod with the bag he brought in containing money. He passed it to Tyrod as Dre walked back into the living room. He and Rod locked eyes.

"Oh yeah!" Dre said loudly, reaching around his back and producing a revolver. Standing over Tyrod, Dre had the jump on him.

Keno stepped in front of Tyrod, shielding him from the bullet he was sure Dre was going to put through him. "What the fuck! Nigga, put that shit up. Fuck wrong wit'chu?"

"Fuck-nigga know what's going on! He the nigga who broke my nose in the county that I told you about." Dre bit his bottom lip, tightening his grip on the gun he aimed at Tyrod through Keno.

Tyrod stood and stepped from behind Keno. "If you gon' kill me, then do it. I won't beg you to let me live. You deserve what happened to you. So, do you." Tyrod stared Dre in the eyes without a blink.

"Nigga, fuck you!" Dre uttered. "I—"

Fred placed his .45 to Dre's head. His eyes grew wide, now being at a disadvantage.

"Oh yeah!" Fred said, mocking Dre. "Gon' drop that befo' I drop you. I won't ask again." Fred pressed the barrel of his gun further into Dre's head.

"Okay, everybody. Listen . . . just chill. Dre's my cousin. Dre, Rod is my people. We on the same team here. The work we move, he supplies to me. Which means he puts the food on your table. Y'all put the guns down for me," Keno said.

Dre looked at Tyrod, his eyes pleading for his understanding. Dre's gun hand shook, facing another lose-lose situation with Tyrod yet again. He slowly lowered his gun, un-cocked it, and placed in it his waistband.

Fred stared at Tyrod, waiting for the okay to rock Dre to sleep. Tyrod shook his head and motioned for him to lower his gun. Reluctantly, Fred lowered his weapon, but never placed it to his hip. He heard the commotion from the bathroom and came out to even the odds. No way could he let anything happen to Tyrod. The bond they formed would have been like losing a family member.

"Usually, I would have you floating in the Savannah River with holes in your head," Tyrod said, stepping closer to Dre, staring him in his eyes. "For the second time, do not cross me, or try me. I fucks with Keno, so consider him your angel."

Full of pride and bravado, Dre continued trying to mean-mug. Tyrod slid his gun out of his pocket, holding it to his side. "We have two options. Either you can continue to get money with Keno and put this shit behind you. Or, you can leave out of here now, broke, and see me again. No Keno this time," he said, inches away from Dre's face with his finger on the trigger.

Dre matched his stare as he clenched his jaws, tears of rage threatening to fall from his eyes. He swallowed his pride, however, and looked past Tyrod and at Keno, who gave him a look that would agree with him.

"I'm down. It's dead," Dre said, his ego bruised.

"Good. Welcome to the team. Is all of my money in that bag?" Tyrod asked, toying with Dre.

"Yeah, it's all there," he responded, nodding toward the bag.

"Good. Get back to work." Tyrod put his gun away, knowing one day he was going to have to kill Dre. Until that time came, he would use him for what he was worth. Dre left without making eye contact with any of them. Fred and Tyrod watched him leave, knowing it wasn't anywhere near over.

"Hey, sorry about—" Keno said, but Tyrod cut him off.

"You good, G. Thank you, man. You the only reason we both walking out of here. But put a bug in his ear though. Leave that shit alone. 'Cause next time, one of us will die," Tyrod said, grabbing the money-filled bag off the couch.

"True shit. I got you," Keno said.

They said their good-byes and headed out the door, guns in hand. Within a minute they were inside the vehicle.

"That shit was crazy! Fuck nigga wanted to kill you," Fred said as they pulled out of the apartment complex.

"Yeah. If it wasn't for you, I'd be dead. Thank you, fam," Tyrod said, extending his hand to dap Fred.

Fred pushed his hand away. "Fool, you ain't got to thank me. You like my brother," he said, laughing. Tyrod smiled and sped through traffic. "Just drop me to my car though. I gotta go by my spot and handle something before I call it a day," Fred said, splitting a Swisher Sweet with his thumbnail.

"Gotcha, fool," Tyrod said, turning up his music. Future's "Mask Off" quickly filled the car. "I know that fuck-boy gon' try some shit," he said, nodding to the beat.

* * * * * *

After dropping Fred off to his car, Tyrod got a call from his lawyer who needed to meet him ASAP. He drove to the Hibachi Grill off Wrightsboro Road. Hank sat at a table finishing his fried rice, chicken wings, crab meat, and a dish Tyrod wasn't too sure about.

"How are you doing, Mr. Cushman?" he asked, shaking his hand, and taking a seat in front of him.

"Everything is fine, considering I received a call from the DA today," he said, using a napkin to wipe his mouth after sipping his Coca Cola.

Tyrod leaned forward on his elbows. "What they have to say?"

Cushman stood up, throwing a twenty dollar bill on the table and his napkin on the plate. "Not in here. Outside," he said, walking toward the exit.

He unlocked the door to his Benz and got inside. Tyrod got in, lighting a Newport. Cushman started the car and cracked the window. He asked Tyrod twice before not to smoke in his car, and he hated it. "They want us to settle outside of court, and they want that amount to be kept undisclosed to the public."

"Okay?" Tyrod took a drag off his cigarette.

"We are to negotiate privately, meaning through them. You and I cannot let anyone know of the deal." Cushman opened his laptop. "Now, in similar cases that were held in court for the public, these are some of the amounts that were agreed on."

Tyrod looked at the screen and his eyes got big seeing the largest amount was forty million dollars! But they could keep every dime. Tyrod would give them everything he had to have his twin back. Yet, he couldn't change what happened in the past; he could only try to lay out his future. If they were willing to pay for killing Tyreek, then cool. But it would come at a steep price.

"So, what are we asking for?" Tyrod asked, turning the screen back around to him.

"As I have said, these were handled in court. I figure if they want it kept a secret, we must be worth more than these cases. I will shoot extremely high, and they will aim low. We'll debate on what we think it's worth, reminding them that any amount of money for a loved one is not enough. We'll agree on a price, then I will spring out with all of your attorney fees paid and include your mother's doctor bills," Cushman said, placing the laptop inside its case and facing Tyrod.

"That's cool. When does all this take place, and how long before the payout?" Tyrod asked, dumping the ashes out the window.

"It'll start as soon as I set up the date and they agree to be there. Depending on the amount paid, will determine how long before payment comes in."

"I want to be paid in full. One lump sum, or else we can go to court with it. I want you to pay off all my mom's bills, and I want to be reimbursed for the bills already paid. I'll get you the proof of payment on that," Tyrod said, refusing to be dealing with the folks forever on this.

"I'll let it be known, if that's what you desire. Another thing, only two people are being charged in the killing."

Heat rose within. "What do you mean only two people?"

"The officer who fired the first shot, and the supervising officer in charge of the squad. But he's on the run facing charges related to this case. When he's found, he'll be tried and convicted, then sent away for life."

Tyrod tossed his cigarette out the window. Cushman turned up the air conditioner, trying to clear the air, hating the thought of the smoke lingering in his Benz. He needed to drop a bombshell, but he wasn't sure how Tyrod would react. "The officer who shot Tyreek will plea out to manslaughter, and a federal offense that will get him five years, if he's lucky. Or, he will at least serve maybe one or two years max." Cushman purposely gave Tyrod the news on the money first, to brace him for the bullshit.

"Five years? What kind of shit is that? He murdered my brother on camera. Am I the only one who's seen the tape?" he asked, livid. Five years was unheard of for a black man killing someone. But for a cracker, anything was possible. It's not that Tyrod was big on sending niggas to prison, but what happened to the "Justice System," as it was so called?

"Evidently some higher up stepped in on this and is pulling strings. Normally, in a case like this one with a video, they would prosecute and be done with it. But they are standing behind these guys for some reason," Cushman explained.

"When you say higher ups and they, who are you referring to?" Tyrod asked curiously.

"Mayors, judges, and the governor are the people over Georgia. I can try to find out."

"No, don't try to find out. Do find out! That's your job, and that's why you get paid big bucks!" Tyrod stated.

"Sure thing. Give me a few days, and I will let you know what I dug up and when the negotiation is set to take place," Cushman said, shifting in his seat. They were too close to getting the biggest payout of his life for him not to do everything Tyrod asked him to do.

"Yeah, do that." Tyrod got out of the Benz, slamming the door. "No matter what, these folks always find a way to fuck over a nigga," he argued on his way to his Hellcat. He thought about the amount of money Cushman suggested he could get, and how it would be more than enough for him to leave the game alone. Still, the game was what made him into the man he was today, and he knew it wasn't going to be easy to just walk away from it. *Maybe*

I'll pass it down to Keno on a day to day aspect and just play the background.

For the life of him, he couldn't understand the way the system was set up. They placed blacks in a low-income environment by giving them minimal pay, leaving them no other choice but to sell drugs and commit crimes. They set up programs like WIC, food stamps, Medicaid, and housing for women to no longer have to depend on the man of the household. And not to mention, if they find out a woman has a man living in the house, she would no longer be eligible for these benefits. But when shit really gets real, they will kill black males and get away with it with no kind of trial or prosecution.

Tyrod burned rubber out of the parking lot. "Something has to change. Or we're gonna continue to be killed by the people who are supposed to protect and serve with no justice." He shook his head as he grabbed his cell. "First, one has to know where to start to eliminate the problem."

CHAPTER 18

When Alexus came home from the hospital, Tyrod had his mom's crib laid out. Balloons, flowers, and gifts were everywhere around the living room. She gave birth to their healthy baby boy, head covered with hair, weighing eight pounds and seven ounces. To Tyrod, looks could not be determined, but some said Tyreek Major King looked like Tyrod. Some said he looked like Alexus, and people in passing said he favored them both. Tyrod was just happy to have a son named in honor of his twin.

He stuck around the house more than usual, making sure all of his and Alexus's needs were met, leaving Fred to lead the meetings in his absence and report to him what was going on with the brothers. Tyrod could tell Alexus loved seeing him bond with their son much more than how he pampered her. For her to see him put everything aside to be there for her and the baby said a lot and it made her heart happy. But as soon as the weather broke, Tyrod began taking the baby out riding, dressing him in similar outfits.

"So, where are you and my son headed now, Rod? Y'all have been gone practically all day. He's a baby and needs to be at home with his mother."

"Aww, stop hating, Lex. We'll be home soon."

"I'm not hating. I just miss my guys."

"I love you, girl. Chill out and enjoy the quiet time."

"Bye Rod!" Alexus said.

"A'ight. See you in minute."

"Your minutes aren't really minutes. They're more like hours."

121

"Bye, Lex. Peace!" She heard him put down the phone, but he hadn't disconnected the call.

"Your baby is so adorable," Lex overheard some random lady telling Tyrod. "He looks just like you."

"So, I'm adorable too then, huh?" Tyrod replied.

"Nah, you're fine!"

"See how lucky you are, Lil Reek" Tyrod told their son. "To have the ladies checking you out at an early age." Alexus knew an indescribable pride always filled Tyrod's soul whenever he looked at their son. While Tyrod seemed to always be on the move with their baby, Alexus sat at home filled with mixed emotions. She loved seeing Tyrod spending time with their son, and being home was also a plus. But she knew if it wasn't for the baby, he would be doing whatever it was that he was doing out in the streets. She didn't want him to want her because of their son. She wanted him to want her because he genuinely loved her. Plus, every woman knew a baby couldn't keep a man.

"I'm outta this joint. Forget quiet time," Alexus said to the silent room. She headed to Planet Fitness off Peach Orchard Road and utilized their exercise machines to get her body in tiptop shape. She snapped back to her normal size quickly, but wanted to tone up the thickness she gained in her butt and thighs. After running for an hour in two, thirty-minute sessions, she'd do squats to tone up her ass.

Following her workout, she would hit the shower and head to the spa, spending up to two hours getting pampered. Her mind would be at ease while in the pricey spa environment, getting a deep tissue massage and reading. After the spa came the nail salon and last, the hair dresser. Then for her nightcap, she would stop by The Doctor's Office, before heading home. He always knew how to mend the injuries her heart suffered daily.

* * * * * *

"... as the reports are coming in from Augusta, Georgia, if I am hearing correctly, charges have been dropped against two of the officers involved in the killing of Mr. Tyreek King. Our sources tell us that Mr. King was shot by police officers while he was unarmed during a raid. A security camera captured the shooting. Officer Craig Burns is the officer who was said to have been the one who fired the first shot. His charges have been reduced to manslaughter. What does this mean for the two officers? Do they return to duty?" asked Kelly Oxford, a popular news reporter for CNN.

"I'm afraid so, Kelly. They will have to go through an investigation to confirm they are fit, but to answer your question, yes, which I think is crazy," Laura stated, reporting out of Washington, DC.

"To me, this is another way for police—white police, to kill another black man and get away scott-free. There has to be an example made out of these cops. It's happening all over New York, Florida, South and North Carolina, Louisiana and now it's made its way to Augusta, Georgia," Michael Dixon said, also joining in on the reporting news. He worked with the NAACP and covered stories involving black people wrongfully being killed and being targeted because of the color of their skin.

"I'm afraid I am going to have to agree with you on that one because as we've seen all over the United States, these killings are increasing. A former lieutenant, Butler James, is being charged in this killing also. He's on the run from law enforcement at the time, but I am told U.S. Marshalls are doing all they can do to track him down," Laura said to the viewers and the ones in attendance.

Ex-lieutenant Butler James turned off his television and continued to wipe off each round of ammunition with an alcohol wipe. Paranoia set in on him weeks ago, when one of his contacts told him that they turned up the heat on looking for him, and he had additional murder charges pending, the woman and boy he and Holmes took out. He quickly began to revert back to his army days. Butler James slept cushy and moved lighter, moving outside of his comfort zone only under the cover of darkness, and when he had no choice but to go out.

Times when he left, he would drive outside of Columbia, South Carolina, so he wouldn't be seen around his living area, although he'd shaved his head and grew a beard. He'd also lost a substantial amount of weight, making him lighter and quicker on his feet.

Butler James's predicament was a peculiar one. From his experience as an officer, he knew sitting still in one location would eventually catch up to him. Sooner or later, law enforcement always got that tip from too-good citizens doing their job for them. He also knew that after a period, the heat would die down in the immediate area, and the search net would expand. And that's when he would make his move back to the area. The hunted usually got killed first and not the hunter.

Chris Brookes' killing had not gone unnoticed in his eyes. He'd seen that style of killing before, and only by professionals. Either officials were trying to keep the people out of the loop, or maybe it was just an accident. But he would move as if it wasn't accidental. Funds were also getting low for Butler James. He paid his bills up for some time, but kicking out money with nothing coming in was draining him. With only a few hundred dollars left, he had to come up with something. Crazy how one day you could be on one side of the law, then have to fuck the scale of injustice the next.

Butler James grabbed his Norinco MAK-90 and headed outside his home with the exterior lights off. His cellphone vibrated in his pocket. Only two people had his new number and neither knew his location. He stopped in his tracks and back pedaled over to the scrambler and flipped it on. Seeing the name put a smile on his face. Once he heard from his eyes, things would start to shift in a better direction for him. He answered the phone, sitting down in front of the Glock .45 lying on his glass table. If anybody wanted war, he was more than ready.

CHAPTER 19

During a thunderstorm, the Federal Bureau of Prisons (FBOP) bus traveled at forty-five miles per hour on I-20 with forty occupants. Inmates looked out of the windows at traffic, some in awe of having not seen the outside in ten years. Being behind a forty-foot wall in a federal penitentiary, the outside world was only a thought and a distant memory.

The bus pushed through traffic and pouring rain and thunder and lightning, as some inmates gave the driver a hard time when she started to speed up the bus. "You need to slow this motherfucker down! Ya dig," an old head from Washington, DC stated to the Puerto Rican female driver. He had been down for some time and had one hell of a sense of humor.

"You need to find the closest police station and pull this bitch over! We won't do the system no good dead, ya dig!" he continued, as everyone shared a laugh at his expense.

The majority of the inmates on the bus came from Edgefield Federal Correctional Institution (FCI) located in South Carolina. They had served a significant amount of time and were thankful to be away from the medium-security prison. The interruption was welcoming to most, who were going to the United States Penitentiary (USP) in Atlanta where they would be placed on lockdown for up to twenty hours a day, but not for Burns. He dreaded entering the place he sent hundreds to.

The bus made a stop off at McDuffie County jail, which housed federal inmates. Burns was one of the three people to be picked up by the FBOP, sentenced to 40 months for his part in the crime against Tyreek. He feared for his safety every bump of the ride and would request to be placed in protective custody as soon as he arrived at his destination, after Atlanta. His family was torn to pieces when he was sentenced and could not see him going to prison and being okay. There was no doubt he could defend himself, but being a former cop and having killed a black man, Burns knew he was in for a rude awakening.

The bus pulled into a garage attached to the side of Atlanta USP. The gate closed behind them, and the officers on board disengaged themselves, then removed their side-arms. Placing their firearms inside a locked case, they locked it under the bus in the luggage compartment, and led the prisoners through a series of doors and up two flights of stairs.

Burns, being fresh in the system, had to get his picture taken and fill out different paperwork from the others. Officers passed out paper sacks containing four slices of bread, one piece of meat and cheese, and one apple. No drinks! Inmates hurriedly stuffed their mouths, welcoming the meal. They were then led to a hallway, where they stood in line to see medical staff to receive a TB skin test and to be checked for any medical conditions.

Afterward, they were led back to the holding tank in Receiving and Discharge (R&D), where they spent the next hour. Being called out by their name and having to state their prison number, they each received a blanket, sheets, and hygiene products. Once this was completed, they were packed on an elevator and sent to DCU 2, a housing unit for inmates headed to medium and penitentiary compounds.

Close to 300 people shared the DCU 2 floor. Five phones were mounted on the wall and four computers were available for them to email their loved ones on *CorrLinks,* if they had an account set up. Seventy-five inmates roamed the dorm at a fast pace, trying to use the phone in the ridiculous phone line, or take showers and email family. Burns moved unpunctually throughout the dorm. He had no email set up and could not use the phone because he had just got in the system. Standing in front of the sports TV, really paying it little attention, he pondered on ways to get out of his current predicament.

Without a doubt, he let his hatred for blacks get the best of him that fateful night. The day before, a male suspect cursed him and physically assaulted him, and he wanted retribution. When he locked eyes with Tyreek, even more hatred manifested in his heart and a wicked smile graced his face hidden beneath the mask he wore. He'd never seen that much fear in a suspect's eyes before in his life.

"Drop your weapon!" Burns had screamed. He hadn't seen a weapon, just an opportunity to release anger at the idea that a nigger thought he could put his hands on him. He sent the first few rounds into Tyreek with a single pull of his modified AR-15's bump trigger. The rest was history.

"Say Joe, what you in for?" Burns' celly asked, sitting on the end of his bed and stirring his coffee. Burns recoiled at the question, not expecting to be asked about his charges. He turned and faced the massive black figure sitting in front of him with muscles protruding from under his shirt. Tattoos adorned his neck and arms and a look of unclearness that lay across his face.

"Where are you from?" Burns replied, fending off the question.

"Chi-town. Been down for over twenty years."

"Is that right?"

"It is. And I can smell when a man is hiding something, or he's fearful. I've seen plenty of inmates with something to hide for more than one reason. And you're no different. Now, what are you in for?" he asked again.

"Fraudulent checks and tax evasion," Burns said quickly, swallowing hard. He tried to push down the lump in his throat.

"Ah shit, me too, Joe! What code did they charge you with?" he asked.

"Code . . . what do you mean code?" Burns asked, squinting his eyes, as if his celly didn't know what he was talking about.

"Like, for a felon with a gun charge, the code is A 922(g). What they charge you with?" he asked, knowing he was being lied to.

"I can't remember," Burns said, jumping up on his bunk.

"Hm, that's funny. You know, I spend a lot of time in the law library doing work; I just so happened to memorize all the codes."

"Oh okay. But like I said I don't remember."

"You don't remember, huh?" He nodded. "Right. Sure. . . ." He scoffed. "It's been a while since I've been free, but I can still pick a cop out of a lineup of a thousand people. Luckily for you, Burns, I'm headed home in a few months. By now, I would have beat yo ass and greased you up. You're a very lucky man. Very lucky." Burns' face grimaced as tears fell from his eyes. He placed his hand up to his mouth and backed up against the wall. The window caught his attention.

His cell window overlooked the yard on the main compound and the prison commissary. In the distance, he could see train tracks and cargo containers stacked up. A big two-story house was surrounded by trees, almost submerging the house. The Atlanta airport sat in the distance but out of sight. Every minute of the day, it seemed airplanes were coming and going. From his bunk, Burns watched the inmates down below play softball and the planes come and go. God, how he wished he could instantly do the latter.

* * * * * *

"Nine-one-one, what's the location of your emergency?" the dispatcher on duty asked.

"Yes, I am at 2339 Overlook Drive," the caller quickly replied.

"What's your emergency, sir?" she asked, pecking at the keys on the keyboard.

"Well, it's not a real emergency, but someone busted the windows out of my car, and I need to make a police report for the insurance company," said the caller, sitting on the green box between the apartments.

"No problem. A deputy is en route and should be there shortly. Anything else I can do for you?" asked the dispatcher, ready to end the call and answer something more urgent.

"No, ma'am. God bless you all and have a good day," he said, ending the call.

* * * * * *

"Dispatch to 204," came the call over the walkie-talkie.

Eric Wilson was on the night shift and responded to the call. "Two-oh-four, go ahead, dispatch," he said into his walkie-talkie. Eric joined the force six months prior and had high hopes of becoming the sheriff of Augusta one day. His entire family was part of some type of law enforcement agency at one point in time. He wanted to follow in his dad's footsteps and run the department.

"We have a car that's been vandalized at 2339 Overlook apartments." He used a high beam to find the address that was posted on a wooden plaque beside the front door. Finding it, he reported to dispatch.

"I'm at the location." Eric surveyed the scene, seeing the vandalized vehicle. The windows were shattered and the tires were flattened. Profanity was scratched on the body of the car, naming the owner a "pussy, fuck-nigga." He headed to the door and knocked.

"Who is it?" a female voice said from the other side of the door.

"Richmond County Sheriff's Office, ma'am," he stated, shifting his weight from one leg to the other. He rested his hand on his hip, not because his arm needed a break, but because it was close to his Glock 23.

"Richmond County?" he heard the woman saying, right before the door opened. "Well, what's the problem?" she asked through the screen door.

"We received a call about a car being vandalized. Your address was given to the dispatcher," the officer said, grabbing his flashlight and shining it on the door to get a better look.

"No one here called. I am here with my kids, and my car is fine," she said, pointing to a Dodge Charger beside the trash can.

"Then, whose vehicle is that, ma'am? Do you know?" he asked, shining his light on a new model Camry.

"I am not sure, but no one here called you." She closed the door in his face.

He headed to his car and called in the plates to dispatch. Minutes later, he found out. "Dispatch 204, that car is registered to a Kinisha Walker and was reported stolen yesterday," she said, reading from the computer.

"Ten-four. Send another unit please," Eric said, before stepping out of the car to further investigate. He approached the car cautiously, flashlight in one hand, the other resting on his sidearm. He did a quick walk around the car to make sure no one was inside the vehicle, possibly hurt. Satisfied, he opened the door, after knocking on the glass from the shattered window with his flashlight. The inside of the car didn't reveal much. On the floor board, he saw a pair of women's shoes and one earring. He opened the center console and found a bunch of paperwork, mostly bills and the vehicle registration and insurance card.

Opening the glove box, he saw only a cellphone. It was an old flip phone, commonly known as a throw away. He picked it up and went to the contacts list. No contacts were in the phone. The call history revealed nothing. It was as if the phone had either been wiped out or brand new. He placed it down on the seat, when it rang.

Eric held the phone, contemplating answering it. It could belong to the owner, as well as the suspect or suspects. "Hello?" he said, placing the phone to his ear. He got no response. "Hello?" he said once again.

"As we live our lives, we realize certain things we have no control over. We have to accept the fact that someone else, a complete stranger, could cause us great harm mentally and physically," the caller said, even-toned. His words well chosen.

"Sir, I'm sorry, but I'm with the Richmond County Sheriff's Office, and this isn't my phone. Whom were you trying to reach?" Eric asked, standing outside the car.

"I know that isn't your phone. It's mine. And I know you are the police. I called you," the caller said, chuckling.

"Then, I need you to come to the scene so we can do this paperwork." Eric looked around, seeing nothing that caught his eye.

"I am at the scene. I am watching you," the caller said.

"Listen, I am done with the games. Either you come out and let's do this paperwork, or I'll call a tow truck and call it quits," he said, ready to end the conversation, and twice as ready for backup to arrive. Something about the caller gave him the creeps. "And what's your name?" he asked, remembering he never got it.

"Rod . . . Tyrod. Tyrod King! Ring a bell?" Tyrod asked, staring at the officer from his position in a tinted-out Denali truck.

"No, why should it?" Eric asked, clicking the button of his holster off.

"Because your police department killed my brother and a dear friend of mine's family. And tonight, you're gonna pay for it with your life," he said.

The officer had heard about the killing, but it occurred before he was on the force. He told Tyrod as much. "You took an oath to serve and protect, so you're guilty by association, as y'all would put it." Tyrod hung up the phone and turned on the light inside his truck, signaling to Fred it was time.

* * * * * *

Earlier that morning, Fred awoke drenched in sweat. He saw images of his son gurgling blood as he rested in his arms. "Daddy, save me!" Marquise cried. Fred's eyes popped wide open. "Catch the bad guys who did this to me and mommy," his little voice said, echoing in Fred's ears. Images of Tiffany with a hole in her head came into his view. Her jeans and wife-beater were covered in blood. She reached out, trying to pull him into a dark world. He promised himself he'd avenge their deaths, but that wouldn't bring them back. That hurt the most. And somebody had to pay.

Yes, Fred went about his days normally, but the thought of his family was a constant. Now he was kneeling beside Apartment 2335 across the street from the unsuspecting cop. He pulled his .308 from under the branch, setting up the tri-pod. He tied it there when he placed the stolen car there earlier that day. Fred exhaled, resting his body against the earth with the stock of his weapon against his shoulder. Squinting his eye, he peered through the scope. He and Tyrod had been training with one of the brothers from the group on shooting high-powered weapons. He was a retired Navy Seal, rumored to have been part of Seal Team 6.

* * * * * *

Officer Eric Wilson hit the ground, removed his firearm, and pointed it recklessly when the first shot cracked the night silence. "Ahh!" he screamed, scrambling toward his car, firing two shots in the general direction of where the shot came from.

"Officer down! Shots fired! I've been hit!" he screamed into his radio, clutching his leg where the bullet struck. Dispatch requested all units to his location. Grabbing his gun, he peeped over the hood of the car. A bullet ricocheted off the hood and grazed the side of his head. He saw the muzzle flash of the shooter's weapon and returned fire.

* * * * * *

His bullet whizzed by Fred, who quickly changed locations, opting for the cover of the green box. Waiting for Eric's head to pop into view. Tyrod approached the officer from his blindside, brandishing a .44 Charters Arm Bulldog in his hand. He loomed quickly, hearing the sirens in the distance getting closer. The officer was kneeling beside the car, blood leaking from the gash in his head.

"Today, you sacrifice yourself for your country." Tyrod placed the gun at the base of the cop's skull and pulled the trigger.

CHAPTER 20

Local and federal investigators scrutinized the horrendous scene before their eyes. Officer Eric Wilson had been ambushed by two shooters, after responding to a call. The stolen vehicle used to lure the officer was sent to the GBI lab for further inspection for prints and clues. A nickel-sized bullet hole was neatly placed at the base of his skull with gun powder burns around the entrance, indicating the shot was placed at close range. The other two shots came from a high-powered rifle. Shell casings were found yards away from the deceased officer.

Janice Cook, the woman whose address was given to dispatchers, was questioned by authorities. She insisted that no one from her residence had called about the car, but when asked what she saw, she replied, "I saw everything." Janice gave detectives her account of what she saw transpire from the time that Officer Eric Wilson knocked on her door until the dark figure approached him from behind.

"Then he ran to a Denali. It was a newer one," she said, patting her head to cure the itch under her braids.

"What color was it?" the detective asked, taking notes.

"Black," she said. A baby whined in the background. She glanced over her shoulder. "Excuse me, but I have to tend to my kids. I'll be glad to come to the station some other time," she said.

"Sure thing, ma'am. We'll be in touch and thank you," Investigator Charles Reid said. Janice Cook stepped back inside her apartment and closed the door.

Reid approached a lieutenant with the RCSO Division, tearing off a piece of paper from his notes. "Place an APB on this truck and check your records to see when these cars were stolen," he said as he chewed on his dip. The APB was placed on the Denali and was given an armed and dangerous title to go along with it. "And can somebody tell me where the fuck is Tyrod King!" he screamed, looking around at the detectives assigned to the case.

"We're on it," one of the officers responded.

* * * * * *

The Richmond County sheriff officers speed reached over 100 miles per hour racing to the scene. The owner of the Denali truck was visiting a relative in Woodlake and spotted his truck parked in the driveway of an abandoned house. He confirmed that it had been stolen a week prior. A small army of officers quietly assembled outside of the house with a negotiator, prepared to try coaxing the suspects out of the house. SWAT took up position around the house using four sharp shooters to do whatever it took to apprehend the cop killers. Once the signal was given from the lead SWAT member, they made their presence known.

"This is the RCSO! We have the house surrounded. Come outside with your hands up!" said the negotiator, standing behind a bulletproof shield.

Inside the house, Kedrick and his man Tado sat on makeshift chairs created out of stolen milk crates, smoking weed and laughing at the stupid driver of the Denali. They were walking home when he exited the truck, leaving it running. When he disappeared between two houses, Kedrick, the leader of the two, sent Tado to steal the car.

Inside the SUV was a gun, some fire-ass weed, and a few dollars. They took it back to the hood and searched it. Satisfied that they had found everything of value, they went inside to smoke the weed.

"Oh shit! You heard that?" Tado asked, dropping the blunt on the carpet while in the process of passing it.

"Hell yeah, I heard it! What I'm gon' do with this gun?" Kedrick stated, pulling it from his waist. He was also the one who kept the money. He peeped out the window. They were surrounded. Racing into the kitchen, he tossed the gun in the bottom drawer of the stove.

"We gotta get out of here," Tado said, sweat beads forming on his forehead.

"How the hell are we gon' do that? We hit! We better do what they said," Kedrick stated, thinking for the two like he always did.

Hours later, they sat inside the Criminal Investigation Division (CID) on Walton Way. The gun was found and the car was confirmed to be the car in question. It was sprayed with luminol, a chemical that would glow in the dark when blood was present. It would be weeks before results would come back confirming it belonged to Officer Eric Wilson. The .44 was sent to the GBI lab for further examination, along with all the prints recovered from the inside and outside of the car.

Kedrick and Tado were being held on stolen car charges and gun charges. Learning the owner was at the Richmond Hill Market when his truck was stolen, the tapes from the parking lot were secured and looked over until the officers found what they were looking for. A stolen Camry came into view. A male figure hopped out of it and jumped in the driver's seat of the Denali. He was a tall man dressed in dark clothing and a hoodie.

Both Kedrick and Tado were short. The witness also told them a tall man shot the officer. They were still grilled about the murder, just in case they knew something, but officers believed their story.

* * * * * *

"Hey orderly! Four-two-nine needs some ice!" Burns screamed through the crack of his door, trying to catch the inmate before he was sent to his cell for the rest of the night. He still hadn't made the transition from officer to inmate in his few days in the system, but he was figuring some things out. He spent his days reading and standing at the door, watching a piece of the television he saw. For his two hours out, he used that to shower and collect more books for lockdown. He tried using the phone a few times, to no avail.

Getting online was even more complicated. He jumped in front of an inmate from DC who was waiting in the computer line. "Say, slim, the fuck wrong with you? Betta get in the back, slim!" Burns never attempted it again.

"Thank you," Burns said, accepting the coffee bag filled with ice under the door from the orderly. He grabbed his cup and placed a few ice cubes inside. He poured the punch pouch he was given for lunch inside, then hopped up on his bed.

"Don't have the light on all night, Joe. I got to get on that flight to OKC tomorrow. I need some sleep," his celly said from under his blanket.

"Sure," was all Burns said from the top bunk. He shot his celly a bird and mouthed the word "*nigger*," wishing he had the power to kill off all black people. They were useless in his eyes and a wasted creation. Taking his usual place, he sat in the window and watched the planes come and go as he read his book. He sipped his drink, thinking about taking a flight once he was released from captivity. Once he finished serving his time, to him, it was one less nigger, well-killed.

* * * * * *

For three days, JP had sat perched in a secure vantage point. Under the blanket of darkness and the cover of trees, a white pickup truck circled the area and a freight train screeched past. Lights shined through some of the windows, others were darkened throughout the night. Bright lights lit the compound and the area around it like a football stadium. JP did a lot of research on the internet to track down one of his enemies and had gone from jail to jail until he landed in the Federal BOP system.

Tonight the light mist of rain and the ruffle of leaves brought with it a cool chill. His body executed a light shudder, as JP blew in his hands to keep them warm. His 30-06 rested on a tripod on top of a container. His target sat on his bunk reading a book. If JP looked through his scope, he was sure he could read the words on his carton of juice. His enemy adjusted his glasses when looking in the distance, and he stared out of his window. Every night for the past three nights, his light was on until midnight.

It was 10:28 p.m. and time for him to execute and extract. The target was looking out toward the approaching planes. JP flashed a pen light. The mark leaned forward, staring at the train tracks as a light caught his eye. He saw a brighter flash, then dropped from the top bunk.

CHAPTER 21

Another story had developed about one of the cops who killed Tyreek, and Alexus was determined to be on top of it. She emerged out of the front door of the television station. Although she felt exhausted, she hopped in her car and pulled off because duty called. She wanted to be the first to report a cop killer was loose in the city. But at this point, she couldn't be quite sure if it was Tyrod. Either way, she was glad she was interviewing a top dignitary when the story first came in, and she couldn't just leave right away. She didn't know what she would've done if Tyrod or Tyreek's name was mentioned. "Damn, Tyrod," she said, after sighing loudly and dramatically. These were the scenarios that brought Alexus much grief. "Baby." Alexus spoke her heart to him although she was alone. She needed to speak her truth, even if she couldn't bring herself to speak it directly to him. "We're growing older, but nothing about you is changing, or has changed. Neither of us are happy either. So we're definitely not better off. I feel . . . sadder." She imagined Tyrod making promises of better days to come, and she gasped when the thought came to her. *He'd lie to me and tell me everything will be all right but it won't be. It never will be.* That's the moment a few tears fell from her dark brown eyes and slid down her chocolate smooth skin. The risks he took from hustling in the streets were too great, but so were the benefits, ergo the stronghold it had on Tyrod. Alexus was in search of a normal relationship she'd never have as long as she remained with the father of her son. Sure, the fast money had its perks, but she'd settle for a regular working man whom she didn't have to worry about coming home in a body bag any day.

Because of his occupation, she couldn't bring Tyrod to her office Christmas party, or invite him to family dinners or out with her friends. At first, she didn't mind his gangsta lifestyle, because she worked long, odd hours and so did he. But now it was taking a toll on her and the beliefs she brushed aside for what she originally thought would be just a fling. A family needed structure, especially when raising a child. Baby Tyreek had been extra fussy and whined mostly through the night. It would be nice to have some help every now and then. She still had business to take care of with the high demands from her job, but also that empty feeling kept nagging at her, prompting her to demand much better from her fiancé. He was capable of doing more, much more.

Tyrod rarely acknowledged her anymore whenever he was around and was so distant that she didn't know what to say to him. Loneliness kept her company. She knew that he'd lost a lot due to the raids, but if he lived the right way, or even invested the money he made from his dealings, he would not be worried about the money that had been taken. But it was costing them their relationship, on top of the other shit.

They no longer went out on dates or spent time together. Some days he would come home high and drunk, wanting to fuck. She would oblige him because that was her duty as his future wife— not because she was feeling the need to make love. The connection was gone from their interactions. All she felt was a penis inside her core, but not the pleasure that should've come from having her husband. It just felt like touching, let alone putting in work. She was faking orgasms to hurry and bring him to his climax, and she no longer shared the shower afterward. She would go first, or wait until he was finished, settling for a wash-off at times.

Often when Tyrod thought she was at work, she would go out to eat alone and have a drink. She didn't do the clubs—he knew a lot of people around Augusta, and she couldn't have her cover blown, especially when she was supposed to be working. Some days she would get a hotel room and relax, just to be away from Tyrod, or she'd chill with one of the men she met while out and about. She dealt with older dudes, men who were not involved in the streets. It reduced the risk of encountering someone who knew Tyrod. She hated cheating on him, but she had not just physical needs but emotional needs as well. Alexus wanted to feel needed, and needed to feel wanted. She wanted someone who wanted her just as much as she wanted him. Alexus wanted to be number one, but the streets kept winning each and every time Tyrod left the house.

We need a vacation so we can be alone. It's imperative that we talk and I have to lay all of my cards on the table. We've gotta spend some quality time together because if we don't, Tyrod and I are over. Quickly, she picked up the phone and dialed his number. Alexus was sent directly to voicemail, which made her bawl like a baby.

* * * * * *

Fred and Tyrod met with Ernest Vaya, the former Navy Seal to practice on their shooting quality. Ernest had received an honorable discharge after being wounded during a training exercise two years prior, one month after being discharged. He had a run-in with law enforcement that injured him further, causing his rehabilitation last longer and his rage to build.

Inside, the trio returned their hardware to the counter, then said their good-byes. Once they exited the building, Tyrod and Fred went one way having rode together and Ernest went in the opposite direction.

"Yo, Rod. You never did finish telling me the story about your moms and that cop you said you hated. What was his name? Officer Jim, right?"

Tyrod smirked. "Yeah. That's that punk's name."

"Well, go on and finish. What happened that you and your brother dived right into the drug game?"

"After that night I told you I saw him having sex with my mother, he got more possessive and demanding. He cursed my mom out a lot and Reek and I weren't having it. One day he came out of the bathroom and his face instantly twisted up because Reek and I were already eating dinner.

"'If I'm the only one who's providing in this dump, then isn't it only right that I always eat first, Denise!' Officer Jim shouted.

"I was shaking my head because I found it pitiful yet funny. 'We were doing so much better stealing what we needed before he showed his five-O ass up in here,' I told Reek and swiped my plate onto the floor.

"'Get that damn food up from the floor, Tyrod. Let me see you in the room, Denise,' he said, gripping my mom's shoulder. She followed him into her bedroom and the door slammed. Screams and thumps against the wall and bumps against the door followed. Hearing Mom cries sent us right into action. Me and Reek were trying to break down that door. My mom's face had been swollen for days before and her eyes blackened, yet she'd still be all in his pig face for our sakes. But no more.

"'Ma!' I shouted. 'Open the door!' I kept pulling on the knob, but it wasn't moving. Tyreek threw his body against the bedroom door as hard as he could. But it didn't give.

"'Together on three,' I said, joining Tyreek. 'One, two, three!' We ran into the door at full speed. The door gave way, hanging on the lower hinge, and we charged into the room. His five-o ass was standing over our mother, throwing power punches to her gut and face like she was a nigga."

"Oh, I would've murked that nigga. For real," Fred commented.

"We started throwing blows on his left and right, but them punches wasn't hitting on shit for his hulk-looking ass. He hit us both with punches that sent our lil asses flying through the air and landing on our ass.

'Stop it!' my mom screamed as she stood. 'Stop it, Jim!'

'Hit me again, punk!' I said, backing away from him by the seat of my pants. 'We already got yo ass on video for hitting Ma the last two times.'

'Yeah. Don't make us send that shit to the lieutenant or the superintendent at RSCO, and if that doesn't work, then we'll post it to Instagram, Facebook, and YouTube,' Tyreek said, standing and taking Mom out of the room.

"Momma went in the bathroom to clean herself up. Tyreek stood at the door, his chest rose and fell fast as hell as he mean mugged the officer.

'Get the fuck outta here and don't bring ya bitch ass back. Coward ass—hittin' on my mama.'

"Officer Jim's eyes bulged and his chest heaved fast too. We didn't have a tape, but we sure made him believe that we did. He stormed toward the dresser drawer cursing and yelling.

'Fuck all this shit and this fucked up ass house! Your broke ass mother wouldn't have shit if it wasn't for me. Send a tape if you want to. We'll all die. Go on and send a tape and watch what fucking happens,' he threatened, then left the room and returned with three trash bags.

'Know what? None of you are worth me losing my job. I'm leaving, so I won't have to fuck all of y'all up!'

"He packed his shit and never came back."

"I know y'all were glad as hell. His ass was scared y'all were gon' post that shit on social media. That would've been his ass up shit's creek," Fred commented.

"We were glad as hell. Another man like him would never get the opportunity to lay up in the crib. Not ever again. Tyreek and I were going to make sure of it. So we returned to what we knew best—stealing a lot of shit. We made enough to buy a new lawnmower, a weed eater, and some car washing materials. Once we established ourselves around the hood, we washed cars, cut grass, and took out the trash. We made $2,800 in one summer."

"So y'all did have a little hustle going on," Fred said with a brief nod and a smile.

"Yeah, but we found a book bag with some drugs and a gun in it. And it was on from there. I just wish Reek was still here and that mom was okay. She sacrificed a lot for us."

"Yeah, she did."

Traffic was unusually heavy, and Tyrod laid on the horn as a Camaro narrowly missed his car.

HONK!

"Watch where the hell you going, dumbass!" Tyrod shouted, upset that the traffic jam was keeping the beast beneath the hood of his car entrapped.

"Damn, I hate driving up here. These bitches be driving like they ain't got nowhere to go," Tyrod said, sitting back in his bucket seat.

"Ah nigga, you got road rage," Fred replied, laughing at the wrinkles in Tyrod's forehead and his angry expression.

Traffic inched along, and they were approaching I-20. "Yo, Rod. We got the po-po behind us, man. It's an unmarked car." Fred pulled his seatbelt across his chest, then removed his

Springfield from his side, handing it to Tyrod without missing a beat. Tyrod placed both guns inside the compartment when the cop hit the lights.

"Shit!" Fred cursed, shaking his head.

"Just chill. We good. Glad we don't have no dope on us," Tyrod said, noticing the Camaro in front of him also had a light flashing. Tyrod followed the car and pulled into the Starbuck's parking lot followed by the unmarked car.

Two officers hopped out of the car, guns in hand, aimed at the Hellcat. "Driver! Step out of your vehicle with your hands up!" one of the cops ordered, moving sideways, away from his vehicle.

Tyrod did as he was told, placing his hands on the hood of his car. Fred was ordered to get out of the vehicle and joined Tyrod.

"What's this all about?" Tyrod asked as he and Fred were both cuffed.

"Shut the fuck up, you useless sonofabitch! You don't ask the questions, I do," Detective Reid said, turning Tyrod around. He had trailed Tyrod from his mother's home and had been sitting outside of Shooters on Washington Road. He and other investigators couldn't be sure of what role Tyrod King had played in the officers killings, but visiting a gun store/shooting range led Reid to believe that he was on his man.

"And I don't answer questions, my attorney does," Tyrod said, mad that he was handcuffed without explanation.

"Well, fuck your attorney and you too. Who the hell—" Detective Reid stopped short of asking, once locking his eyes onto Fred Sander's face. "Oh shit! What are you two doing together? I should've known," Reid said, stepping back and shaking his head for not making the connection sooner.

"It's a free country. That's what we're doing together," Fred said, meeting Reid's gaze.

"You know, it's strange how some of my cops are turning up dead, and now I have two men who are connected to the fallen, riding together from a shooting range. Any weapons in the car?" he asked, stepping around the nose of the car, helping himself to an unwarranted search.

"Go ahead, knock yourself out," Tyrod said, not worried about them finding anything in his car.

Five minutes later, the two officers were done going through the car.

"Where were the two of you on . . ." Reid paused, flipping through a pad he pulled from his pocket, fetching the date.

"We ain't got nothing to say to you and honestly, I don't care about your fallen cops. If you don't mind, we have shit we need to do," Tyrod said, turning around, motioning with his head for the officer to approach and uncuff them.

"Funny. Let me tell you something. If I find out you two are responsible for these killings of my officers, jail will be the last thing on your mind," Detective Reid said, grabbing Tyrod's arm roughly and uncuffing him. His partner uncuffed Fred.

"Good boy," Fred said to the other officer.

"Get the fuck out of here before I decide to kill a black." Reid smirked, walking toward his car.

"That's a good idea. I wouldn't want to harm an officer of the law," Fred replied as he walked off mean-mugging the officers.

* * * * * *

Detective Reid sat back inside his car and phoned his supervisor in charge of the murder investigation.

"Yeah, what you got?" Lieutenant Forrest asked.

"I followed up on that subject, and guess who he was accompanied by?" Reid asked, pulling into traffic and killing his grill lights.

"Reid, I don't have time to be guessing. I am leading a multiple officers' homicide investigation, not Family Feud."

"Right. Tyrod King and Fred Sanders were riding together to and from a shooting range."

"Fred Sanders, as in the one whose family was murdered by Jones?"

"Yes, one and the same."

"Good job! I am going to lend you more resources to keep tabs on the both of them. I need to know when they take a drink of water," Scott said, before they ended the call.

CHAPTER 22

Governor Schreiber and his comrades came together once again. This time, people were saddened and teary eyed. "Ladies and gentlemen, as we've all heard, Frank Burns was killed today," the governor said, sitting down at the conference table.

"How did he die? Was he stabbed?" asked Mayor Stillwell. The Governor shook his head and pinched the bridge of his nose.

"No . . . not at all. He was shot!" he said. The governor was shocked by the news when he first got it and understood the look on everyone's face.

"What?" everyone said in unison.

"According to federal officials, a sharp shooter took him out in the confined quarters of his cell. That's three officers from Augusta in just a few months, dead."

"One by accident but still dead," said the deputy general.

"I don't think it was an accident anymore. I think it was murder, and all four of these deaths are connected," the governor replied.

"Why would you say that? One died hunting, one was shot in prison, and one while committing a crime, and another ambushed. Where do you draw the connection?" asked Mayor Stillwell, leaning forward on his elbows.

"I believe they are all connected to the case that Burns was convicted on. I don't want to hear anything about a coincidence. People don't get shot in jail by accident," said the governor, and he did have a point.

"So, who do you think is committing these murders?" the prosecutor asked.

"Someone connected to the victim. We need to go back through the files and see who was involved with him. Get your department on it ASAP," he said to the sheriff, sitting quietly throughout the meeting. He nodded once, scribbling down notes.

"Let's not fuck this up. We have someone on the loose killing officers, and they are highly skilled. We need to bring this person to justice, one way or the other," said Governor Schreiber, before sipping his steaming hot coffee.

"Where does Eric fit into all this? You said you think they are all connected to the Burns case. Well, Eric wasn't around then," pointed out the sheriff of Augusta. The governor thought about the question before answering. *Where did Eric fit in? How was he drawn into the equation?*

"I'm not sure, but you know when a murder is committed, especially on an officer, it causes mayhem within law enforcement."

"So, you think we have a serial cop killer on the loose? Jesus!" Sheriff Dickerson said, frightened by the thought.

Governor Schreiber looked the sheriff in the eyes. "Yes, I do, and you need to catch him before you're next."

* * * * * *

Butler James entered Richmond County city limits at night fall, driving the speed limit all the way to his destination. His "ears and eyes" had a place set up for him, until he figured out what he wanted to do. Burns' death confirmed what he already knew. Chris Brookes' death was no accident either.

He shifted through the paperwork he had his "eyes" gather, pertaining to the case when Tyreek King was killed, looking for the brother's information. He remembered the brother's statement when he was brought out of the house. "You bitches killed my brother! Every last one of you bitches will die for this!" he had ranted and put up a helluva fight, breaking one officer's nose and another officer's jaw.

His threat wasn't taken seriously at the time. They assumed it was said out of anger. Now, over a year later, it was all too real. The killer went to great lengths to shoot Officer Burns inside a federal prison. Either he had prior training, or he was that focused on getting retribution.

James found out only a little about Tyrod. But the little information he did find peaked his interests. He and his girl had recently given birth to a son, which he already knew. He had sold his home and a few cars after the case against him was dropped, so his residence was unknown. James flipped through the rest of the paperwork he received. He needed to build a character profile on Tyrod King.

* * * * * *

One week later, Alexus and Rod returned home from a much needed vacation, but Tyrod wasn't sure that it did them much good. During their stay in Miami, they hit the King of Diamonds and did some shopping down Collins Avenue. In his efforts to do better, he bought Alexus a tennis bracelet and diamond earrings. After they spent hours riding jet skis, scuba diving, and swimming with the dolphins, Tyrod was feeling as if it put Alexus and him in a better mood. He smiled at the thought, deciding that he needed to do better by her. But no sooner than they made it to their room to shower and then got dressed for dinner, Alexus cornered him.

"I'm really not happy with the attention you've been showing me, Tyrod King." She only called him by his full name when she was upset.

"I know, baby. I'm sorry."

"And I know I deserve better than this. I've been good to you." He opened his mouth to speak, but she threw up her hand. "I feel . . . neglected and unwanted. And like you—"

He stood before her, took her in his arms and kissed her tears. "You're right, Lex. And I'm sorry that I've been a little evasive lately. And haven't been taking out the time to be with you."

"You say that all the time, Tyrod King." She pouted. "And it's not that you've been a *little evasive*. You just haven't been around at all. Period! It's like . . . I don't even matter." Alexus shrugged.

He grabbed both of her hands and looked her in the eyes. "Trust me on this, Lex. I promise I'll change."

"You'll have to show me, Tyrod King. Because nothing in me believes you anymore." Tyrod held her gaze; he couldn't say anything. "And what's been going on with your group?"

"We just talk, baby. About how our lives have been changed after losing somebody we love."

"And that's all the group does, Tyrod King?" Alexis asked, folding her arms and glancing at him skeptically.

"Yeah. We talk about this hypocritical ass unjust justice system. How do they swear to uphold the law but constantly break it by harassing or killing innocent citizens because they are either afraid of black people or are straight-up racists? If there's hate in their heart, why do they even bother to become a cop to begin with?"

"Good point. Great questions."

"The even better question is: when will all this killing stop? Why do I feel as if the only solution to help them see there's an imbalance is to do something over the top?"

"Know what's funny? I've been sent to investigate a cop shooting."

"Oh yeah?" Tyrod asked, with mild curiosity.

"Mm hmm. The interesting part is that the murdered cop is allegedly connected to Tyreek's shooting."

"Wow, baby. Really!" Tyrod knew she was trying to ascertain his body language and his gaze. He kept everything as normal as possible. Inside, however, he wanted to ask her a million questions. It was imperative that he always stayed ten steps ahead of law enforcement. He needed to contact Cushman to find out if he knew anything about this new investigation.

* * * * * *

Tyrod rode down Gordon Highway, headed to meet Keno. He had been spending time with his son and Alexus ever since they returned home from Miami. They watched movies, cooked dinner, and interacted with their son together. They had an appointment for family pictures the next day and were looking forward to it. He turned on Highland Avenue and noticed two tinted Ford Taurus' behind him. When he made the next left on Damascus Road, both cars did the same. There was no doubt that both cars belonged to the police department.

Approaching Wrightsboro Road, Tyrod sped up just a tad and made the right, headed back toward Highland. Both cars made the turn as he had. He stood on the gas and quickly accelerated forward, as the 707-horsepower pinned him to the seat. He weaved in and out of traffic for about half a mile, and then hopped out at the Circle K. Both cars quickly approached the gas station, pulling beside his car.

"The fuck is wrong with you driving like that?" asked the investigator, hopping out of the car. His face was balled up and he glared at Tyrod and his car with a look of disgust.

"It's not every day that I am being followed. I feared for my safety, so I pulled into a public location." Tyrod leaned against his car, hands clasped in front of him.

"Well good! Put your hands behind your back," said the second officer, pulling out a pair of handcuffs.

"For what?" Tyrod exclaimed, standing face to face with the cops, demanding answers.

"Questioning, big shot. You ever heard of that?" The officer walked behind Tyrod.

"Then, maybe you should call my lawyer. Because I don't have nothing to say about nothing," Tyrod replied, now cuffed and being led to the backseat of the unmarked vehicle.

For nearly two hours, Tyrod sat inside an interrogation room waiting on Cushman to arrive. The detectives took it upon themselves to inform Tyrod that this was about the officer being killed that was involved in Tyreek's case. "So what do you have to say?" the ginger headed, green-eyed detective asked.

He wrote Cushman's number down on a piece of paper and slid it to them. His attorney advised him to sit through the interview and answer the questions, unless he thought it was to entrap him or lead him in an incriminating manner. Once he explained why he thought that was logical in his case, Tyrod agreed. Cushman's only directive was to wait until he got to the station.

The pot belly investigator with four-day-old stubble entered the room with legal pads, coffee, and a tape recorder. He sat across from Tyrod and his lawyer. They sat quietly, flipped through notes, sharing glances with each other occasionally.

"We have other things to do, so if you guys could hurry," Cushman said, agitated and offended by the detective's tactics. He sat on the opposite side of the table long enough to know when he was being strung along.

"Yes, sorry, just getting all my notes in order. Mr. King, how are you doing? I'm—"

"Not important. Let's get to the questions and skip the formalities," Tyrod said, his face contorting into a look of displeasure.

"Right, Mr. King, where were you on . . ." He paused, referring to his notes, "on May 16, 2018?"

Tyrod stared at him with a dead-pan expression. "With friends."

"What about December 7, 2018?" he asked, referring to the date Officer Eric Wilson was gunned down.

"I was with my lawyer having a late dinner," Tyrod stated, lying through his teeth.

"Can you verify that, Mr. Cushman?" he asked, looking him in the eyes.

"Yes, I can," Cushman said, not showing any indication he too was lying. Tyrod knew he had to have been caught off guard by him implicating him in his alibi, but Cushman told him to sit through it, so he had to help Tyrod out.

"On December 7, 2018, we had an officer ambushed and killed in Overlook Apartments. A witness saw you walk up to the officer and shoot him at point blank range and flee the scene in a Denali truck. Then, we find two gentlemen inside a house with the car parked out front, and we confiscated a firearm we believe to have been used in the murder. Again, we have someone matching your description seen walking away from a Denali truck. Can you explain it?" asked the investigator.

"It's a lot of people that match my description, but it wasn't me," Tyrod said, keeping his composure in check and his answers short.

"Then, why were your prints found on the truck, Mr. King?" he asked. It was a long shot, not having any of the results from the lab back. He watched Tyrod closely for any signs of deception.

"For one, my prints ain't inside no damn truck, and if my prints were inside that truck, I would not be down here for questioning. I'd be in here for murder. So cut the bullshit," Tyrod said, ready to go.

"I find it strange that officers involved in your brother's case are dying. How do you feel about these officers involved in his case?" the detective asked, leaning up on the table.

"Don't answer that question. How would you feel if someone killed your brother?" Cushman said. He picked up his pen, wrote on his notepad, and placed the pad in front of Tyrod's face. It read: two more minutes.

"Were you in any contact with these officers? Ever thought about hurting one of them?" Pot Belly asked.

"Gentlemen, this meeting is over. If you have any more questions for my client, contact me, please. I would hate to file harassment charges against the department. Mr. King is done here," Cushman said, grabbing his briefcase and pushing in his chair.

"Sure thing, ah Tyrod . . . just so you know, we will be watching you, so behave yourself," the redheaded detective who had been silent the entire time said, rising and adjusting his tie.

"Watch all you want," Tyrod said, before walking out of the office with Cushman.

"What the hell was that back there, man?" Cushman grumbled as he quickened his pace toward his Benz. "Using me for an alibi? Do you know if I am found lying that I could be charged and prosecuted? What were you thinking?" he asked, once they were a safe distance away from CID. His face was red and worry lines stretched across his forehead.

"Listen, man, you told me to have the interview, so I did. He asked me a question and I didn't have an answer. So I used the first thing that popped in my head. Chill the fuck out!" Tyrod said, walking to the passenger side of Cushman's Benz.

"All I am saying is, we could get in a lot of trouble. Were you involved with these crimes?" Cushman started the car and plugged up his cellphone.

"All I am saying is: I pay you, so do what it takes to protect me, plain and simple. And it should not matter if I was there or not. Do your damn job and shut up!" Tyrod said, sparking a Newport and shaking his head in contempt. If his law firm was not the best, Tyrod would fire his ass.

"My car is at Circle K on Wrightsboro and Highland. Can you drop me by there?" he asked, dumping ashes out the window. Cushman shook his head yeah and proceeded to drive down Walton Way into traffic.

* * * * * *

Butler James was staked out across the street, looking for one of the lead investigators to arrive when Tyrod exited the building with the Mighty Cushman, as he was known to the justice department. Putting his car in gear, he picked up on the tail and followed Tyrod and Cushman in his Benz at a safe distance.

CHAPTER 23

Fred and Tyrod sat outside their meeting place on the back porch, awaiting the arrival of the group. He informed Fred of the events that occurred the day before, adding, "Man, they're just going through the motions. Backtracking through those bitches' history, leading up to their deaths."

As he thought of the situation at hand, Fred sipped on his Budweiser slowly. "I think we should still change some tactics," he stated. "We also need to have strong ass alibis. We can't miss a beat, Rod."

"You're right! But we can't be in two places at the same time," Tyrod said, staring in the distance on the privacy fence, his mind working in overdrive.

"But they questioned you, not me. I can handle the other two until we can find the nigga James. We gon' handle his ass together."

Tyrod nodded in agreement. "I feel the same, fam', but we in this together. You got the info on the other two already?"

"I checked out a few of the leads, and they ain't check out," Fred stated, referring to the day he rode by James's house and found out he no longer resided there.

"What if we bring it to the group?"

Fred let out a deep breath and gave a light chuckle. He wiped his mouth after taking another sip of his beer. "What we're doing is some serious shit, Rod. If the cops find out about the group and put pressure on them, they may just crack," he retorted.

"I don't know about you, but all I can look forward to is seeing these bitches dead. If they could put us closer to them, then so be it. I'm ready to breed mayhem," Tyrod said. "As far as I'm concerned, even if I lost my life in the process, it would all be worth it."

"I feel you, bruh. I'm ready to put it all on the line," Fred said, as rage manifested all over again. He never escaped a day without the images of his family, slaughtered like cattle, creeping into his mind. Hearing his son's voice caused him the most anguish.

"Then, we bring it to the group." Tyrod dapped up Fred.

* * * * * *

Members in the spacious room were conversing about various topics. Usually, the meeting would be conducted like an AA meeting. People would vent to get the stress off their chests, as everyone sat around and listened. Everyone in attendance had gone through something similar and would listen intensely, using methods others used to cope with the pain they endured. Tonight, things were different. Members ended their conversations after seeing Tyrod and Fred enter the room.

"How is everyone feeling today?" Tyrod asked.

"Good, my brother," the members replied. They referred to one another as "brothers" after coming together and realizing the strong connection the men had with one another in the group.

"There's something Fred and I have been talking about lately, and we want to bring something to the table. To be all the way up front with you, everyone must be on a need to know basis. When we start conducting these matters, you are asked to keep what you know to yourself and not speak about any of this outside of these walls, not even to each other," Tyrod said. Everyone listened closely. No smiles were seen. Fred took a stance beside Tyrod next to the bar against the kitchen wall.

"We're going to take this group to the next level. If anyone doesn't wish to go to that level, which I assure you will be dangerous, then we ask that you leave within the next sixty seconds," Fred said, looking at his watch. Members glanced around to see who would make their exit. No one made the move, but suddenly the father of a twenty-three-year-old son who had been shot and killed by a rookie cop.

"Brother, what is it exactly that we will be doing that you say will be so dangerous?" he asked from his seat on the curved sectional.

"Again, all I am going to be able to tell you guys right this second is that the change may consist of danger. I can't and will not disclose the meaning of these words with everyone. We all in this room are playing a different role in life. Some of us, the same role. But you will only know what you need to know so that you can be successful," Fred stated.

"Uhhhm, I'm going to have bail out, brothers. I have a wife and kids at home who depend on me. I can't chance my boys growing up without their father. Most of us have seen the results of that as well as have become the stereotype of a fatherless child. I understand the pain we all feel and that strong desire for justice, but I'll leave my thirst for justice and vengeance in the hands of God."

"Who said anything about vengeance?"

"I did. That's why I joined. But today, I realize that's not what I really want. I want my son back. And it's not going to happen. No matter who goes to jail, or how many people I kill. He's not coming back. Not in this lifetime." The guy stared at each man as his sad, brown eyes swept around the room. "My family will fall apart without me, and I can't do that with a clear conscience," the guy named Samuel said. "The streets are hungry for my sons, cops and the prison system wanna eat 'em up too, but I'm hungrier. Hungry enough to see them beat the shit out of this dog ass world by becoming successful—morally, spiritually, and career-wise. I gotta raise them as best as I can so they won't repeat my mistakes and the mistakes of their deceased older brother."

Something pricked Tyrod's heart as he thought of his own son. But he let anger, hatred, and payback take over. "I understand you, yet I don't."

"Same here, bruh," Samuel replied.

"I thought we were in this all together, but only you know what's best for you, Sam. Take care, brother. I ain't mad at ya." Deep down inside Tyrod wished that his father had loved him and Tyreek like Samuel loved his children. Maybe he wouldn't be in the predicament he was currently in.

"You too, brother," Samuel said, "And you too." He shook both Tyrod and Fred's hand. Samuel dapped up the rest of the brothers and made his way toward the exit.

"Hold up, Sam! I'm out too, brothers," another young guy said. Three more men made their exit.

Once they made their departure, Fred looked at his watch again. "The time to leave is up. So I take it the rest of us are all in, right?" he asked with his arms outstretched. Everyone nodded, including Tyrod.

By the end of the night, the rest of the men spoke to Tyrod and Fred in private and vowed that what was discussed was just between them. When going up against a force, you had to be a force. Strength lied in numbers and experience!

* * * * * *

"How do you feel about everyone after letting them know their roles?" Tyrod asked Fred. They sat in a Burger King drive-thru.

"Let's see if they start sharing stories with one another first before we proceed. In a week or two, we will know. We will also see who will obtain the info first!" Fred said from the passenger seat. Everyone was valuable to them in one way or another.

"True shit! Until then, we just sit back and chill. What you got planned?" Tyrod asked Fred, retrieving the food from the window.

"I may kick it with shorty that I been telling you about. She cool as shit, fam', and a nigga really starting to catch feelings." Fred pulled his large fry from the bag.

"You tender-dick nigga! Pussy got you whooped already, fool," Tyrod joked.

"It ain't even all about the sex. She down to earth and she got plans and goals. I believe she got some other shit going on too. She really reminds me of my wife a lot," Fred said, getting choked up thinking about his girl.

"Then, maybe you should go after her a little harder, fam'. She could be heaven sent," Tyrod said, steering and eating at the same time.

Fred unwrapped his whopper and took a huge bite. "In a way, that's how I feel too, but I also feel like it's too early, so I keep my distance from her sometimes, even though it be killing me."

"You know what's best. I think you should see her more and get a better feel for her and see if she is the one for you. Ain't no sense in wasting your time," said Tyrod. "Don't let the opportunity pass you by." They rode quietly, listening to Foxie Lo as they headed to Tyreek's house.

Tyrod pulled into the double garage and parked next to Tyreek's motorcycle; it was too difficult for him to part with or ride the bike. The first time he tried to take it for a ride, he damn near sideswiped a car, blinded by his tears. And no matter how he tried, the pain just wouldn't go away. Keeping the house was his way of holding on to Tyreek. So was keeping everything just the way his brother left it. The only thing that changed was the food and drinks in the refrigerator.

"So, you think fam' gon' be able to come through with every toy?"

"For some reason, yeah. I don't normally trust niggas to do the shit they say they gon' do, but he gives me a different vibe. He also asked to be brought in hands on with our project. So he seems willing and ready to put in work," Fred said, gathering his belongings out of the backseat of Tyrod's car. They decided since the police didn't know anything about him, he wouldn't drive any vehicle he owned near Tyrod. They always met in different locations. And the only address he had for him was at Tyreek's house.

"I hope you right. I was thinking about catching both of those niggas at the same time. How does that sound?" Tyrod asked.

"How we gon' do that?" Fred asked, with a puzzled frown. Tyrod smiled. Fred smiled back. He knew exactly how it was going to be planned.

CHAPTER 24

Dre sat inside the trap on Royal Street, bagging up everything from grams to ounces. The two spots he and Keno operated did numbers daily and rarely saw a day where big dollars weren't made. When Dre and Tyrod bumped heads a few weeks back, all he could see was blood. And he wanted to put a bullet through Tyrod's head. *Badly*. Keno, however, stressed the importance of Tyrod's life to their daily dealings and how the relationship they had with him was valuable.

"Man, you want your dumb, black ass to rot in prison for the rest of your life? Or you want to be out here making more and more money? Nigga, you ain't never had this many bills in yo' pocket before in yo' life!"

Unfazed by what Keno thought, Dre's mind was set on revenge. Keno wasn't forced to wear a face mask because his nose was severely dislocated and his face severely fractured. No matter how much money Tyrod put on his plate, Dre was going to see that he met his fate one way or another.

Now that he had the knowledge that Tyrod was responsible for the drugs and not Keno, Dre cooked up the drugs and kept a portion without Keno noticing. New customers, he would charge more and keep the extras. But all of it was on a smaller scale. And he followed Tyrod after he picked up his money, just to see where he deposited it. Tyrod would enter numerous locations and stay for extended periods of time. Sometimes for hours. Then, he tracked Tyrod home. Dre was going to use the people he held influence over outside of Keno to help him get at Tyrod. But he needed loyal people, people he could trust not to cross him or run their mouths in the process. He kept doing his normal drops, but Keno was paying much more attention to his every move.

Dre knew Keno was counting the money twice that he dropped off to make sure everything was right. Dre had never given Keno any problems before, but since the incident between him and Tyrod, he knew Keno wasn't sure that he wouldn't pull a shitty move. He and Dre grew up in the same household, and he knew Dre better than anyone. "I can tell you still got ill intentions toward my man Tyrod, but what can I do about it, besides make sure you don't act it out and jeopardize our business relationship, and more importantly, my friendship with him. All I'm asking is that you keep a cool head and let's get this money," Keno advised.

"Easy for you to say. It wasn't you who got played like a bitch. That nigga humiliated me. I got beat in front of niggas. But yeah, just keep getting this money, right? That's more important." He scoffed.

Unable to find a solid way to get at Tyrod without screwing up the whole move, or plotting a foolproof way of dealing with Tyrod, Dre came up with the next best plan. Late nights into the wee hours of the morning, the traffic to the apartments would die down. Little to no people remained outside at that house, and that would be the perfect time to strike.

He placed numerous calls to Keno and got no answer. Riding around the corner, he spotted Keno's car and knew he was inside asleep. Dre knew that Keno had a freak on the regular always at the spot that fucked him crazy. Sucked the life out of him, then fucked him to death again. Leaving the trap spot vulnerable.

* * * * * *

Once she was sure that Keno was out, she rolled out of bed and got the black LV bag he dropped between the sofa and the wall in the living room. Her eyes grew to the size of basketballs, seeing all the bills in one bag. She had fucked her share of dope boys and clipped a lot of them, but damn! None of them had bags lying around like Keno. After removing the wads of cash from the bag, she went back to the other bedroom where she left her "ho bag,' as she liked to call it. She wrapped the money inside a shirt, and then stuffed the shirt down the leg of a pair of pants, then zipped the bag.

Tiptoeing back to the bedroom where Keno slept, someone kicked in the back door with so much force, it came off the hinges, and she pissed herself. Keno woke up after hearing the sound. A little disoriented, he looked next to him and did not see Trina. He got up to investigate.

"Fuck nigga, lay down!" the first man said, as he entered the room brandishing a 20-gauge coast-to-coast pump. A ski mask covered his face, and he was dressed in all black. "Now!" he ordered, seeing that Keno was not responding to his order quickly enough.

Two more men entered the room. The last of the two held Trina by her hair. Blood trickled down her face from a gash that had been opened, due to the force of the Beretta meeting her forehead.

"Where the money and dope? We don't have all day! Where it's at, fuck nigga?" said the first guy, pointing the gun in Keno's face.

"Man, look. I don—" He struck Keno in the face with the stock of the gun repeatedly. Keno's face swelled instantly and blood squirted from the gash across his cheek. He felt like he was going to lose consciousness.

"Where it's at, boy?" Last time I'm asking." He racked the slide of his shotgun, ejecting a live round to the floor.

Keno spat out a glob of blood with a few teeth, disregarding the hole the slug left behind. "Nigga, I ain't giving your broke ass shit! Kill me, nigga!" he spat with venom, meaning every word.

"What?" the second dude exclaimed. Throughout the entire ordeal, he remained silent. He was out of pocket and had no business being there, but his hand was forced in the matter. "Give the money up! This ain't no reason to die," he said, stepping up with a .45 in his grasp.

"It's behind the sofa," Trina said, speaking up, unable to see Keno take another blow. Nor could she take a chance of them searching the house and finding the money she stole.

"You dumb ass bitch! You better bounce when they do 'cause I'm fucking you—"

Keno was met with vicious blows to the head, rendering him unconscious. After getting the money and dope they came for, the three men left. Trina dialed 911 and exited the house with her "'ho bag" right behind them.

CHAPTER 25

"Mmmhh, yes baby! Yess!" Alexus purred, as Tyrod spread her ass cheeks and entered her softly from behind. He guided himself inside her slowly, savoring the feeling. It had been some time since Tyrod made love to her.

"You like that?" he asked her, going deeper but steady with his pace. With each stroke, he felt her spot up against his length and it drove her insane.

"Yes, baby! I love it. Give me more! Fuck me!" she said while throwing her ass back, causing his pace to quicken and deliver harder thrusts. Giving up on the loving, he matched her pace, smashing into her juices. "Ahhh boy, fuck me! Fuck me! Yes, yess, yess!" Alexus screamed over the volume of Rod's ringing cellphone. He stood up, bringing Alexus to her feet, and then swooped her up in his arms. She straddled him as he guided his dick inside of her walls.

"Shit!" Tyrod grunted as his mood heightened. Blood rushed to his dick. The sound of her ass smacking against his skin and her titties bouncing always got the best of him. Alexus' eyes rolled up in her head as she screamed out in ecstasy, loving each stroke.

"Ooh, Rod! Beat this pussy, nigga. Beat it!" And that's all it took. Hearing her talk crazy to him while he did his thing always put him in a trance he couldn't come out of. He released his seed deep into her and continued to stroke her slowly, while still releasing. Alexus was a cold freak, so Tyrod knew she wanted more. He put her down on the bed and placed his dick inside her mouth, so she could get him back right. His cellphone sat beside him, ringing again for the fourth time. At this time of morning, it had to be important.

His eyes narrowed at seeing an unrecognizable number on the display. He declined the call, believing it could be someone calling the wrong number. They called right back as soon as he set the phone down. Alexus continued doing her thing, but the phone was throwing her off.

"What? What?" Tyrod said, answering the phone. He grabbed the back of Alexus' head, encouraging her to continue.

"Yo, Rod, this Dre," he said.

"What's up? It's early as fuck, fool. What you need? And I thought we agreed Keno was our point guard," Tyrod said, not digging the call from Dre. His dick went soft, and Alexus snatched her head back so quick, his dick scraped her teeth on the way out.

"Ouch!" Tyrod screamed, looking at her as she stormed out of the room.

"We did, but Keno's in the hospital! I think he got robbed," Dre said.

"What? What you mean you think? How come you don't know? Is he okay?" Tyrod asked, reaching for his boxers and pants.

"He good, but he fucked up. And like I said, I don't really know if he was robbed. I haven't spoken to him yet," Dre said.

"What hospital he at?" Tyrod asked, throwing his shirt over his head.

"University," Dre told him.

Tyrod hung up without saying good-bye or thank you.

* * * * * *

Dre paced the ER waiting room, fuming. Not only had he been disrespected by Tyrod once again, but the money was short and his goons did not follow his instructions. He specifically told them not to harm Keno, just rough him up little and get the money, but make it look real. Everyone claimed to not know where the $10,000 went that he knew was in the bag. But Dre vowed not to let the move slide.

The doctors said Keno was beaten badly with a weapon, more than likely a firearm. When he came in, he wasn't responding to the doctors, but his vitals were stable. He was given a mild sedative and was filled with pain killers. When the sedative wore off, Keno woke up in a heap of pain but was happy to be alive. His right eye was completely closed and the left wasn't far behind it. His two front teeth were broken off in the gums and both lips were swollen and busted.

* * * * * *

Tyrod rushed into University Hospital ER and approached the desk. A few people were in front of him, being checked in for minor problems. Tyrod kept his cool, wanting to barge up to the receptionist, pass up everyone and demand to know which room Keno was in. Luckily, he spotted Dre, who stood talking to the nurse. As Tyrod approached, he and Dre locked eyes for a split second, and Tyrod saw something about him that he could not place. He walked up on the end of the conversation they were having. ". . . will be fine. He just needs some rest and to wait on the swelling to go down," said the nurse.

"When can I see him?" Tyrod asked, after she finished speaking. Dre gave him a look that went unnoticed by the nurse but not Tyrod.

"In about twenty minutes. He is being cleaned and bandaged up," she said, smiling at Tyrod.

"Cool, thank you," he said, returning the smile and going back outside through the double doors. Dre followed him. Tyrod pulled out a cigarette and turned on his heels as he fired it up.

"What the fuck happened?" Tyrod asked, feeling better about talking about it outside, but still not feeling the idea of holding the conversation with Dre.

"Back door was kicked in. Cleaned him out, I'm assuming, since he hasn't been turned over to the police," Dre said, pulling out a cigarette of his own. He sat down on the bench, while Tyrod opted to stand.

"Cleaned him out of what? What all did he have?" Tyrod asked, in between pulls of the Newport.

"I took him the money for you earlier, and I know he still had a lil green and pills left. So, unless you got the money, they got that," Dre said, looking at Tyrod as he dumped his ashes. He hoped he put just enough into his answer to ward off any more questions. Tyrod shook his head, knowing he should have gone and got the money when Keno told him. He wasn't tripping about the money as much as he was that his partner was laid up in the hospital swollen up. But he still had his mother's doctor's bills he was footing as well. So Tyrod felt crossed in three ways.

"Keno didn't say shit about no nigga on some other side?" he asked Dre, while thumping his cigarette down on the ground.

"Nah, he ain't say shit to me," Dre replied, shaking his head.

They entered the room and both of their stomachs twisted in knots. Lumps, knots, and bruises were all over Keno's face. His lips were three times their normal size, and his eyes were swollen.

"Look what the wind done blew in," Keno said through his clenched jaws. He looked through the slit of his left eye and sat up slowly in pain, as they closed the door behind them.

"You good, cuzzo?" Dre asked Keno. Keno and Tyrod both gave him a look that said, "hell no, asshole!" Dre took the facial expressions to the chin, knowing that it was a dumb question.

"I'm good, Dre. When I catch that bitch Trina, man I'm

fucking her up, on God!" Keno said, meaning every word he spoke.

"What she do? Who the hell is Trina?" Tyrod asked, moving the table with the wheels on it to the side. Keno gave them the entire night's events, leading up to being knocked out cold. Dre listened to every detail, feeling like a traitor. His cousin was laid up in the hospital fucked up because of him.

"Don't worry, cuz. I'ma get the niggas that did this as soon as I find out who responsible," Dre promised Keno, as if he was innocent.

Hours later, at daybreak, Keno was released from the hospital. Tyrod drove him home, telling him to get rest and stay away from the trap until he could move around. Keno suggested letting Dre run the spot while he was out of commission. Tyrod didn't like the thought of it at all, but he needed to get back what was taken.

"I'll straighten you on that change when I get back moving. But Dre can handle both the spots. He got Steve 'round there with him at his spot, so he can just come run mine," Keno said, sitting down on the sofa.

"Just get right. You don't owe me shit. It's all part of the game, Keno. I'll set it up with Dre 'round there, so don't worry," he said, not wanting to let Dre run shit of his, but Keno felt he could handle it, so he agreed. He hoped he didn't come to regret his decision.

CHAPTER 26

Cop cars could be seen for what looked like miles. Cars from different counties in Georgia, some further way, drove slowly with lights flashing and sirens off. The grieving family traveled behind the police cars in a variety of cars. Every eye was wet, as they mourned the loss of Officer Eric Wilson. News stations were amongst the cars and the crowd leading toward the burial site. The officers and family packed the church to the max, so no public figures were allowed inside. They were left to stand outside, but had the privilege of going to the burial.

Tyrod trailed the sea of cars, dressed in a black suit with white pinstripes and black Jimmy Choo shoes. A blood-red Donald Trump tie was knotted perfectly around his neck. The gold frames he wore gave him a business appeal. Tyrod exited his car, however, in search of Lieutenant Eddy. He had Tyrod down at the station for questioning about recent homicides, so he wanted to show him that he supported law enforcement.

Finding him standing alone, Tyrod approached him, removed his frames, and nodded. "Hello."

"What are you doing here, asshole?" Lieutenant Eddy hawked up a loogie and spat it at Tyrod's feet.

"I came here to support the law enforcement officers with my fellow citizens. Sorry for your loss." Tyrod stared at the silver casket bearing a flag and roses, carried by fellow uniformed officers wearing white gloves. Each man took calculated steps as they approached the canopy over the open grave.

"You should be somewhere selling drugs. Not here amongst us positive folks of Augusta," the detective hissed, trying to shoo Tyrod off like he was a dog.

"It's crazy how the city will bury you cops amongst us when y'all die. But place y'all above us while y'all are alive," he said, shaking his head. "You see that tombstone over there?" Tyrod pointed at Tyreek's grave.

"Yes, I see it, and I don't actually care about it. All I care about is burying the officer I feel you killed," he said, grilling Tyrod.

"See. That's y'all problem. Y'all only care about yourselves. But I care about that grave. That's my brother's grave. I remember standing over there just a feet away, feeling empty, lost, and hurt! Wishing I could trade places with him. Wishing we could share one more conversation. Anything!

"But, I was robbed of that by the men in your department, you know? Do you know what it feels like to see your brother stretched out in front of you, shot to pieces, and you can't do shit to help him?" Tyrod focused on the preacher giving his prayers and reading from the good book. Not the casket being lowered, or the news stations getting an aerial view using drones. Four news stations were in attendance and six drones occupied the air space around the cemetery.

"Yes, I actually do. I was there when he was found." Lieutenant Eddy pointed at Officer Eric Wilson's casket. "I saw the medical examiner load him onto that gurney and place a white sheet over his body. So, yes, I do know what it feels like," he said, ready to bust Tyrod in his shit.

"I kind of understand where you're coming from. But I mean *hearing* the gunshots. Seeing your twin brother dead on the ground. While being led out in handcuffs," Tyrod stated.

"Then I guess I don't. We live two different lifestyles. Yours require you to go to jail, and mine requires me to lock you up. Big deal! But what I do know is that you do not deserve to be here, and I would like it if you left," the detective said over the loud cry that came from relatives, as the casket started to descend into the cold earth.

"No problem, Detective. I just wanted to show my gratitude and support to you guys during this troubled time. Have a nice day!" Tyrod turned to leave.

"Don't mention it, asshole. I will get you one day, you prick," the detective spat.

With a smile plastered on his face, Tyrod stopped. "Now, that is no way to talk to anyone, officer. Show a little respect for the dead."

"Fuck you, black bitch! Go to hell!" Eddy said through clenched jaws, turning red. His chest heaved as his eyes bulged out of his head.

With a smirk, Rod stared into his eyes, and then put on his glasses. "Nah, fuck y'all!" he stated and walked away.

Tyrod walked up to the partially lowered casket, picked up three white roses lying on top, and took them over to Tyreek's grave. He kneeled at his brother's grave and kissed the tombstone. "I love you, Reek. This one is for you, so open those eyes," he said, touching Tyreek's name that was engraved in the stone. Afterward, he walked over to Fred's son and wife's graves, leaving them a rose as well. "Fred sends his love, and he wants you to know, this one is also for you."

* * * * * *

Yards away, Butler James looked through the scope from the top of the Old Regency Mall across the street from the cemetery. He focused his sights on his Beast Master 308 and Tyrod and the officer having their conversation. He chewed on a piece of gum, as he calmly shifted his position to be in the best spot to take the best shot.

* * * * * *

Alexus was reporting live from the field. Jake flew their company drone over the funeral procession. Well over two thousand people were present, half being law enforcement personnel. She promised to keep the viewers posted on updates as they came.

Once the final prayer was said and the crowd began to disperse, the news stations packed up their equipment and prepared to leave. Alexus and Jake still had their drone up, in anticipation of anything else they could uncover. Watching the other three news stations leave, she wondered why three drones still hovered above. Just as she was about to mention it to Jake, She spotted Tyrod and frowned. *What the hell is he doing here?*

On their way back to the news van, the three drones moved in closer to the ground. Seeing them, an officer walked over to Alexus and Jake. "They're too close. You're gonna have to move them back."

"Those are not ours," Alexus said, wrapping up her favorite microphone. Nobody wanted to make any statements at a time like this anyway. The drones whizzed past them at full speed.

Boom! Boom!

Both hit at the same time, sending officers and body parts flying. The smell of burning flesh wafted in the air as everyone took cover, screaming and running to cars and hiding behind tombstones.

* * * * * *

Stunned by the homemade explosives, Tyrod took cover like everybody else behind a headstone. A piece of it chipped off almost quicker than he could duck.

"Shots fired!" officers shouted, scrambling about, uncertain where the bullets came from. Side arms were drawn from the safety of cover as the sniper open fired, hitting whatever he could. The shooting lasted only seconds, then ceased. Lieutenant Eddy gaped at the carnage, holding his head in his hands as surviving officers jumped into action assisting the fallen, and dispatching all units and EMTs for the bodies piled on top of each other.

Tyrod stood and replaced the three roses which had fallen off of Tyreek, Tiffany, and Marquise's headstones. As he scanned the area, admiring a job well done, he locked eyes with Detective Eddy, gave a shrug of his shoulders, and smiled deviously enough to get a reaction.

"You bitch!" He rushed Tyrod.

Once he was close enough, he cocked back and hit Tyrod flush in the nose, knocking him to the ground. Jumping on top of him, Eddy landed punches to his face before he was snatched off of him by his fellow officers. Remembering the third drone in the sky, Tyrod counted his losses, pulled out a handkerchief, and wiped his bloody nose.

"You hit like a bitch! I hope y'all ready to add this to the lawsuit," he said.

Lieutenant Eddy was restrained as he spat venom from his mouth, promising to be the death of Tyrod one way or the other.

* * * * * *

Taking advantage of his tantrum, Butler James packed his gun into the carrying case, shimmied down the ladder, and hopped in his car, leaving the small area through the back of the apartment complex of Regency Village. He didn't kill Tyrod, but his day would soon come. So far, the few police he injured would have to be good enough.

* * * * * *

Jake brought the drone down and pulled out the cameras as Alexus grabbed the mic, ready to cover the next big event happening in Augusta, Georgia. "Give me one second, Jake," she said, speed walking to catch up to the drama unfolding in front of her. Alexus couldn't believe she'd witnessed the pandemonium caused at the burial, or that the police officer attacked Tyrod. She was glad to have caught it all on camera.

As Alexus approach, she noticed Tyrod's demeanor changed. He looked confused, as if he'd failed to notice her amongst the reporters.

"Rod, are you, okay?" she asked, cutting her eyes to the detective, then back at Tyrod's bloody nose.

"Yeah, I'm good, baby. Finish up your job. I'll be fine." He placed his hand on the small of her back, guiding her in the direction from which she had come. The sooner she was headed back to work the better.

"I want you to know, *Detective*. I have your unprofessional actions on camera," she snapped, being led away by Tyrod. "It's cops like you that give the department a bad name," Alexus spat over her shoulder.

"Just know that you also have the actions of your thug boyfriend on camera as well. He's a cop killer, and he gives the community a bad name. And I will bring him down."

She eyed him harder. He eyed her back, disgust on his face. "Tread lightly, young lady, or you may get caught up in the mix of things," he said, ice-grilling Alexus and meaning every word. For all he knew, she could have been flying the drones.

Alexus stormed ahead of Tyrod. He had to walk fast to catch up to her. Away from the cops and Jake, Alexus stopped short and stared at Tyrod. She searched his face beyond the blood for answers. She wondered if the detective's words held any truth.

She came up with no answers in Tyrod's blank expression, the same expression he wore for over the past year.

"Are you?" she asked, staring in his eyes. No longer sure who the man was standing in front of her. Since losing Tyreek, she tried to look past the change because of the pain he was enduring, but he'd become someone she didn't like.

"Am I what?" Tyrod threw the handkerchief to the ground beside a plot.

"Don't fucking play with me, Rod! Are you a cop killer? Have you been killing cops?" Tears built in Alexus's eyes. When the first officer that was involved in Tyreek's case died, she thought, *See how fast life comes back to haunt you!* But when the second officer died, she began to wonder what was really going on.

He was never home, and on the nights when he did come home, Tyrod spent those nights pacing, after their son Tyreek went to sleep. He wasn't the same anymore, and she wanted the old Tyrod back so badly.

Tyrod spat blood on the ground, then looked at Alexus. His gaze was cold and held no answer to her question. "Alexus, if I was or wasn't responsible, shouldn't make a difference to you. So finish up your work and meet me at the crib." His dancing around the question let her know he was guilty. A lump formed in her throat as tears rolled down her face.

"No, I won't meet you at home. Our son Tyreek and I will be leaving until you can end this chaos and cold-blooded murders that you have caused. I will not have my son anywhere near you when they kick down the front door, guns blazing. None of this will bring him back, Tyrod King, and I'm sorry. But we need you too. You can't be here for us if you're in jail or dead, and Tyreek would want you to be here for your family."

Tyrod almost snapped. "You don't know what Reek would

want!" But he held his anger inside. He was doing exactly what Tyreek would want: causing widespread havoc. Shutting shit down around the city.

Staring in her eyes, he wished he could feel something for Alexus and their relationship, but he couldn't at the moment. His mental stability had a block that had to be removed. Alexus's words about his son did ring true, though. Baby Tyreek didn't need to be around, in case shit got out of hand.

"No, don't go. I'll leave. I don't need y'all bouncing from place to place like y'all homeless. Give me some time to get my shit in order, then we can move back in together." She cried harder. "Alexus, I love you and I do want us to work. But I'm hurting in a way you could never know. Just give me some time," he said, pulling her into his embrace and squeezing tight. Openly she sobbed, hating to see Tyrod in his current state. She held on to him, not wanting to let go. She felt a tap on her shoulder.

"Sorry to intrude," Jake said, breaking up the moment. "But we have like ten seconds, then we are live." He pointed to the area in his camera that was set up behind the yellow tape. Throughout the commotion, Alexus forgot she had a job that she was in the middle of. She pulled away from Tyrod's grasp. A hint of tears threatened to fall from his eyes. She placed a hand on his cheek, brushing it away.

"Be careful. Your son and I need you with us. I love you," she said, walking off with Jake and his camera. Taking a stance in front of him, Alexus dabbed at her eyes as to not mess up her makeup, while Jake counted down.

"Hello, I'm Alexus Robinson reporting live from a scene I can only describe as"—She paused, blinking away a tear—"Murder and mayhem." Little did the viewers know how close it hit home for their favorite reporter. All except one was blinded by the fact.

CHAPTER 27

Nurse Hannah started her shift the same as any other day. She prayed for those inside and outside of the hospital, asking God to be there for everyone. After entering the ICU floor where her patients were, she held brief conversations to uplift the other nurses at the nurses' station. Eventually, she sanitized her hands and began checking her patients' charts. She headed to Denise's room first, oil in hand. Once she approached her bedside, she opened the bottle, dabbed some oil on her fingertip, and gently placed them on Denise's forehead and said a prayer.

Once she finished giving her a bath and cleaning the room, she went on to her next patient. Down the hall in the rehabilitation ward, Quan Bryant gripped the bed rail, forcing himself to sit up. He had been in a coma for a long period and doctors wanted to give up on him, but his family and friends were deep into church and believed in God. They knew He held the final say so, so if He wanted to take Quan away from them, it would have to happen while he was on the machine.

Nurse Hannah entered the rehab ward and spotted Quan doing what little he could for himself. The gunshot he suffered caused significant brain damage, so certain things would take time for him to learn again, if ever. She smiled, seeing a determined Quan doing the simple things that were such a big accomplishment for him. Now he could feed himself and say some words without stuttering. He pushed himself to do hard things for a person in his position, and when he failed, he would try again.

"Hi, Quan. How's it going?" she asked, rubbing the back of the hand that he cradled the remote in. He turned his head facing her and forced a smile that was weak and painful.

"Hey, Ms. Hannah. It's going . . . going good." Quan let out a deep breath after his reply. His lungs were strained, so he was left with breathing tubes in his nose.

She pulled out her oil and placed some on his forehead, as she had done for the past several months, then bowed her head in prayer. He did the same. "Heavenly Father, I want to thank you for watching over this child, Lord. Father, you know best and you spared this child's life for a reason, Father, and we thank you. I ask that you help him find his purpose on this earth and live for you, Lord.

"We are living witness that prayer works," she added. "So we continue to ask for your guidance and strength. Thank you, Lord. Forgive him for all his sins and cleanse his soul. In your son, Jesus Christ's name, we pray, Amen!" Nurse Hannah ended her prayer with a light tap to his hand.

Quan smiled. "Yo-yo . . . your pr-prayers al-always do, do, do something for me. Although . . . I . . . I can't recall the events after being shot. I ca-can . . . tell from my condition that I am blessed."

"Amen, Quan. Most people who get shot in the head don't live to see the next fraction of a second. Here you are months later, watching television in a hospital bed." Nurse Hannah gave a proud smile.

"Thanks, Ms. Hannah. I rea . . . really need the pr-prayers you give me. Can I ba . . . bathe today?" he asked, wishing he could get up and walk again before he could accomplish that task.

"I'll get your RN to help—"

A call came over the system. Doctors were being summoned to a room by a call button.

"Quan, I'll be back to check on you, and I'll let your nurse know you need a bath. I have an emergency," she said, rushing from the room.

* * * * * *

Denise King came to with a banging-ass headache and blurred vision. She did not know where she was at first, but the beeping sounds were all too familiar. She didn't remember how she got there. She racked her brain trying to come up with an explanation, but kept coming up empty-handed on all of her thoughts. Seeing the device lying next to her, she grabbed it and pushed the button. Pain shot through her head with this small achievement. A voice came back to her, asking what they could do for her.

"I . . . I need . . ." she said as her head spun, not sure of what she needed, or what to ask for. Spittle rolled from the corners of her mouth, dripping down her chin, and onto her gown. Her face was numb, but the pain in her head was equivalent to a head-on collision. Medical personnel stormed into the room, along with Nurse Hannah, happy to see her revived.

"Thank you, Lord, for watching over your child," Ms. Hannah silently prayed, also knowing Denise King had another battle to fight. She still didn't know she had suffered the loss of her son.

* * * * * *

In record time Tyrod arrived at Grady Memorial Hospital along with Alexus and the baby. He carried his son in his arms, and he nearly sprinted through the hospital with Alexus on his heels. They hadn't seen each other for a few days, but talked daily. Her job kept her busy, and his group meetings started increasing after going to the next level. Some meetings were conducted one on one, outside of the normal meeting area. Some were in places one could not start to imagine.

Nurse Hannah stood just outside Denise's room, writing on

the chart hanging on the wall. This wasn't his and Nurse Hannah's first time meeting. "I could tell you were her child from miles away," she said the first time they met.

She rubbed the baby's cheek. He smiled his baby smile at her and immediately stretched out his arms for her, an effect she had on most children. "God bless your soul. How are you guys doing?" she asked.

"We are good, Nurse Hannah. Even better, now that she's out of this coma. How is she doing?" Tyrod asked, handing baby Tyreek to her once she hung the chart back in its place.

"I'll let her doctor know you are here so he can come in and explain everything to you. But right now she is in a great deal of pain, which is expected." Nurse Hannah handed the baby back to Alexus, who stood next to Tyrod.

Tyrod's mind went to 7,000 RPMs after hearing his mother's status. He had already struggled with Denise being in a coma. Now that she had come out of it, he prayed he didn't lose her, or couldn't cover her costs. Over the year she spent in the hospital, her medical bills consumed most of the money he made in the streets. He was what one would consider well-off, however, that was in the past, like the hit he took when Keno was robbed. They still had no clue who had been that bold, but there would be hell to pay when he found out.

Tyrod entered his mother's room, trying to maintain some enthusiasm. But seeing her laid up in the hospital bed helpless and in pain did something to him. It sent chills through his body. That's why his visits were rare and quick. His mother had been stripped of her beauty. The once attractive, round face was now slim and crackly. Her weight had been replaced by bones pressing firmly against her skin. And she looked as if she had aged fifteen years.

"Hey, Ma," Tyrod said, approaching her bedside with Alexus and their son beside him. She moved her head slowly toward the sound of his voice and focused on the three of them, with a curious expression, like they smelled. Her right eye would not blink when she attempted to do so, only her left. Drool ran freely from the corners of her mouth.

"Hey, did you bring my medicine?" she asked Tyrod, confusing him with her doctor.

"No, Mom. This is your son, Tyrod, and I brought your grandson to see you, along with Alexus." Tyrod leaned closer so she could see his face.

"Oh. Hi, boy. How you doing?" she said, her voice sounding different when she spoke. "And what's all this about a grandson? I don't have no grandkids."

"Yes, you do have grandson now, Ms. King," Alexus said, smiling. She turned the baby to face her, so she could get a good look. Alexus wanted to hand him to her, but seeing her weakened state, she thought better of it.

She looked at their bundle of joy wrapped inside Alexus's arms and gave off what appeared to be smile. Her lips barely moved, as saliva continued to roll down her face. Alexus handed little Tyreek to Tyrod and wiped it away. Disregarding her current state, they sat with Denise for over an hour, talking and uplifting her spirits as much as they could. She seemed to enjoy the conversation, but Tyrod could tell she was embarrassed by her current state and would probably never be the same.

For minutes at a time she would turn her head away when speaking and zone out, as if in deep thought. Then she'd suddenly turned toward them with her eyes wide. "Now, where the hell is that brother of yours?" she asked out of the blue. "I guess he was too busy to come and check on his mom, huh?" Denise shook her head, hair braided prison style, and scalp recently greased. Tyrod made a mental note to thank Nurse Hannah again before they left. She promised him that she'd personally see to it that Denise was taken care of properly, and she had yet to let him down.

For a moment, Tyrod looked at Alexus, then back to his mom. It hadn't dawned on him that Denise did not remember Tyreek's death. Although he wanted to believe she put it all in the back of her brain, dealing with it how he'd learned how to deal with it. He racked his brain looking for the best way to explain that her son, his twin brother, was dead.

"So where is he?" she asked, as Alexus wiped away her drool again. He and Alexus exchanged glances. Tyrod was afraid that she may not survive the news of her son's death all over again. But how do you ease the news of the death of a son on a mother?

"Mom, it's hard to explain," he said, hugging his son close, trying not to tear up. "But the day you—"

Knock, knock, knock.

Nurse Hannah peeked her head into the room during the second hardest time in Tyrod's life. A man dressed in bright blue scrubs stood beside her. Not only was Tyrod about to relive the entire situation over again, he wasn't ready to drop the bombshell on his mom. He wiped his forehead with the back of his hand, trying to play it off. God must have known she would not have taken the news well.

"I'm sorry to interrupt, but we have to get some tests run on Ms. King that will take a few hours, so I need to borrow her if you guys don't mind," the man said, smiling.

"Before you go," Tyrod replied, "can we talk for a minute?"

They stood in the hallway while the man got Denise ready for transport. "Ms. Hannah, my mom doesn't remember my brother being killed. I would like to keep it that way until I find the best way to deliver the news to her," he said, remembering he told her about his brother's death on his first visit.

"Sure thing, Mr. King, that's fine by me. But what about her having cancer? We are supposed to notify the patient, but given the situation, we could have you do so?"

He shook his head at the thought and sadly agreed. "I'll tell her.

They left the hospital after saying their good-byes and headed back toward I-20 east. The ride seemed longer now than it ever did. Alexus and Rod spoke on and off, trying to keep his mind off the problems at hand while Tyreek played and talked his baby talk in the backseat. He reminded Tyrod of his brother every day and clung to Tyrod just like Tyreek did. Once back in Augusta, he dropped his family off at home, then went to Fred's spot, wondering how he was going to break the bad news to his mother.

CHAPTER 28

Dre stood in the middle of his living room on Royal Street in front of the three people responsible for beating Keno and stealing from him. His 23 model Glock was secured by his jeans and belt and murder filled his eyes. "So, which one of you disloyal sons-of-bitches took the money?" Dre asked, looking from each of his flunkies standing in front of him.

Everybody said, "not me" with terror etched on their faces, shaking their heads.

"Yo, Dre. You trippin'! Nobody stole nothin'. All three of us was in sight of the money at all times," Jaylon said, gesturing toward the bag of money lying on the ground.

"That's real, Dre. Nobody touched anything. Maybe Keno did something with it," Josh said, speaking up on their behalf. Dre thought about the last statement and quickly dismissed the notion. Dre felt he was being played by all three of them.

"Nigga, save that shit! Keno never came short with his money, and that's a known fact. So one of y'all niggas gone pay for this shit. I ain't about to have a youngin' trying to bullshit me. So, who's it gon' be?" Dre removed his firearm from his side. "And I told you niggas no matter what, don't fuck my family up. Now, he at home, face on swoll." Dre pointed the Glock at the trio.

A tennis ball size lump formed in Fish's throat that he couldn't swallow, as he eyed Dre and his gun, regretting ever meeting up with this clown ass nigga again. What started out as Fish buying small quantities of drugs from Dre and fucking some of the same 'hos and their friends, evolved into him becoming one of his do-boys. He started holding drugs for Dre without being paid, and Dre would wake him up out his sleep at odd hours of the night demanding, "Bring me what the fuck I need, nigga. Or else!"

When Fish got popped, he overlooked Dre because he feared him. Now, he wished he would have been the *first* person he set up because he would not have been in his current situation. "Dre, we all on the same side here," he managed to say. "I'm sorry about what happened to Keno, but he wouldn't give up the money. And we couldn't afford to come back empty-handed, so we did what we had to do to please you. But we a team, man."

"Keno never been short on Rod's money, so that's out of the question. But you the one responsible for beating my cousin, right?" Dre asked Josh, madder about the $10,000 that was missing than Keno getting his ass whooped.

Josh dropped his head and nodded yes in defeat. Fish's eyes popped out of his head at the mention of Tyrod's name, petrified of the day Tyrod ever laid eyes on him again. How could he ever face a man who lost his brother because he could not bear to go to jail for a few months, if that, for a petty drug offense?

Dre stepped up to Josh with the speed of a cheetah and swung his gun at his head. It landed with a loud crack. Josh fell to the floor balled up like a baby in the womb, as Dre came down with more vicious blows. With each strike, blood squirted out of the gashes in Josh's head.

"Yo, Dre! That's enough!" Jaylon said, grabbing his arm. Dre spun around, gun aimed. "Uugghh!" Jaylon screamed, falling to the floor, holding his bloody knee in agony.

"Y'all niggas got me fucked up! Get y'all bitch asses out of here before I kill one of y'all!" Dre screamed, kicking Jaylon in the head.

Fish hurried to the door, terrified he would be next. Yet, if he got in trouble, he had a plan. He kept the hidden device close. It was given to him by the cops he worked with, just for situations like this. The only thing was, they didn't know he had taken part in a robbery. However, they did know he was supposed to be working close with Dre, trying to bring him and Keno down. Keno had the hill wide open, and it didn't take long for law enforcement to get wind of the traffic.

"Fish!" His heart froze in his chest. "Get these niggas outta my shit! And hurry up!" Dre tucked his gun back inside his waistband and stepped over Josh.

Josh lay on the floor, moaning in pain, resembling Keno, battered and bruised. Fish stood Jaylon up first and carried him out to the car. He came back inside to get Josh and had to sling him over his shoulder because walking was beyond his power. "Ay, Fish," Dre said when he reached the door. Fish turned to face him.

Dre removed the smallest rubber banded knots from the pile of money and passed it to Fish. "Get at me tomorrow. We got shit to do, all right!"

Fish looked at Dre, holding it out to him as though he should have been grateful. *This all I get for my work?* he thought. "Cool," he said on his way out the door, ready to report to his watch dog. "I got ya!"

* * * * * *

Butler James pulled away from the curb after throwing his cigarette out the window and rode inconspicuously in his Turbo 4, 3.6-liter Camaro v-6 SS. The 455-horsepower engine wasn't as fast as the car ahead of him, but it was fast enough for what the fugitive cop needed it for. After watching the residence for what seemed like days, it finally paid off. James cruised by his target when he pulled into the yard and parked. He smiled to himself, seeing where they had arrived.

* * * * * *

GBI Investigator Charles Reid sat outside of Fred's house, snapping pictures. He had his eyes on Tyrod also, but he'd lost track of him for a few days when he moved out of his mother's house. Reid was called to the scene along with federal agents, when the drones delivered the bombs at Officer Eric Wilson's funeral. Besides a lot of police being killed and injured, the two officers that had returned to duty after being acquitted of all charges surrounding Tyreek's death were both blown up. It was concluded they were the primary targets of the attack.

Investigator Reid and other state and federal agents canvassed the scene and did not see anything that stood out. The local detective, Dan Eddy, spoke on the presence of Tyrod King. "It wasn't illegal for him to be there," he stated, spitting out his wad of tobacco. "But after reviewing the footage from the news stations, we discovered the officers were blown up, away from the grave where King set the flowers."

Lieutenant Eddy opened a pack of Red Man chewing tobacco and plopped a plug in his awaiting mouth. "At first it looked like he was dropping the flowers off on top of a loved one's grave. But after reviewing it over sixteen times, you can tell he was clearly marking off the no-strike zone, away from his loved ones. The grave sites were that of Tyreek King and the family of Frederick Carl Sanders, whose family was killed by Butler James. So, Fred Sanders could more than likely be one of the drone operators. We just need to find out who assisted him."

CHAPTER 29

Tyrod puffed on his blunt after stressing to Fred about his mom's health. Fred listened attentively to his friend, as he did during meetings. Now, most conversations were about revenge and murder. Still everyone was handled on a need to know basis and was given information relevant only to their roles. Fred gave Tyrod the best advice that he could on the situation, which wasn't much at all. He knew Tyrod needed someone to vent to, so he was there. After a few blunts and conversation with his homie, Tyrod felt good.

"Bruh, I love you to death, and I ain't about to kick your ass out, but I got a lil something lined up for tonight. So, you're welcome to stay, but I'm 'bout to bounce," Fred said, grabbing his trusted Beretta with an extended magazine off the sofa.

"So, you and shawty getting serious?" Tyrod asked Fred, standing to his feet.

"Nigga, who said it was her? I got other women," Fred said, picking up his keys from the coffee table. Knowing for certain, she was all he wanted.

* * * * * *

Investigator Reid was reading over paperwork when he spotted the silver Camaro that rode past him, and he could have sworn it was Butler James driving, even as it pulled into a yard a few houses down and parked out of sight from his rearview mirror.

* * * * * *

Butler James had been parked down the street from Fred's house when he noticed Reid's Charger also staking out the house his target had pulled up to. Seeing a family leave their home, he pulled into their driveway once they were out of sight and parked on the side of the house. Thanking God nobody had dogs, because they would have been going crazy, he hopped over the chain link fence with a ski mask, hiding his face, and removed his Glock from his waist, waiting on his target.

* * * * * *

"All right, fool. Hit me in the a.m. and make sure you get that info for tomorrow," Tyrod said, dapping up Fred. He opened his car door and got inside his Hellcat, as Fred trekked to his truck, anxious to see his new woman. Movement behind his house caught Fred's eyes as he backed out of the driveway.

The shots came back to back in quick succession.

Doom! Doom! Doom!

Backing out of the driveway recklessly once the shots were fired, Tyrod hit Fred's truck before his car went into the ditch, rendering the Hellcat useless. Fred jumped out of the truck and returned gunfire at the figure now standing in his driveway. After grabbing his .45 out of his glove compartment, Tyrod exited his car and joined the fight once Fred put down strong cover fire.

* * * * * *

"Shots fired! Shots fired!" Reid frantically called out on his walkie-talkie right after he'd let off six rounds.

* * * * * *

Taking cover behind the house, James let off another round on his way back to his getaway car. One round found Fred's bulletproof vest. In an instant, he backed his Camaro out of the driveway, damn near on two wheels, pulling off from the scene in a blur.

Reid sent the eleven shots he had left inside his clip at the car, then ran and jumped into his government-issued vehicle, giving chase to the fleeing subject. Having put two and two together.

* * * * * *

With his gun still in his hand, Tyrod raced to his car that was stuck inside the ditch and removed his personal sack of weed and any other evidence that could get him in jail while Fred waited anxiously to disappear. Tyrod hopped in his truck.

"What the fuck's going on and who could that have been? You making enemies? Posted outside your shit while the police staking out? Who you done pissed off?" he asked, making light of the situation.

"I don't know what the hell's going on. I don't have no enemies," Fred admitted, racing down Bobby Jones Expressway.

"You know the dude in the Charger was a cop, right?"

"Yeah, I'm not sure what he got going on. But I'm gonna keep my eyes open though. Shit, the spots I got probably shut down, even though I'm never there," Fred said, shaking his head at the thought of losing money for the next few days.

"That's smart and you don't need to go back there. Find a different spot. Her man might come back," Tyrod said, punching Fred on the arm as he died laughing at Fred shaking his head and smiling.

"That pussy so good, he got to shoot me then. 'Cause I ain't cutting her off for nobody," Fred said, seriously. "Man, I think I love her."

CHAPTER 30

Cushman went back and forth on the phone for hours with the government before stating, "If my client and I do not have our demands met, we first will expose this closed meeting to the public and sue the department for everything you own. So, it's either our way or OUR WAY! The ball is in your court. I expect a call back in the next ten minutes, so my client can be done with this bull. Good-bye!" He hung up the phone, propped his feet on his desk, and loosened his cufflinks.

Nine minutes later, the phone was ringing. "Yes, how may I help you?" Cushman answered, knowing who it was. When you had the government by the balls just as he had, they always responded rather quickly.

"Okay, Mr. Cushman, my colleagues and I agree with the terms and fees that are requested by you and your client." He demanded funds for Tyrod's lawyer fees, his mother's doctor's bills to the date, and Tyrod's pain and suffering.

"However," the governor added, "it's going to take a few weeks before we can clear that type of cash without it going unnoticed. We'll get with you as soon as we've gotten clearance." He had to go through high officials at the White House and explain their situation and demand from the lawyer and client. They were not happy about the situation at all, but what could they do?

"I'll let my client know, sir, but just so you know, I'll be filing the same suit in a matter of hours for another client. I'm sure you remember the deaths of the mother and son, killed by law enforcement officials. Or, we could close that matter out of court, just as soon as this one is taken care of. But I'll be asking for double this amount," Cushman said, clicking the top of his pen.

"What! It'll take the rest of my life to get that type of money from officials without it being know to the public," Governor Schreiber stated, clenching his hand around the receiver of the phone tightly.

"Well, you don't have the rest of your life, Mr. Governor. You have . . ." Cushman looked at his Rolex. "One hour and twenty minutes before I file." Cushman hung up the phone, not waiting for a reply. He promised Fred and Tyrod that he would suck every penny from the system humanly possible for the great loss that they both suffered. And he was going to honor his word.

* * * * * *

After the scene was processed and Investigator Reid was interviewed, they were sure Butler James was the perpetrator in the shooting, although shell casings confirmed nothing but caliber and location of the shooter when the shots were fired. Tyrod's car was taken to the police station to be searched for projectiles to be removed, to see if they yielded any clues. Attempts to contact Tyrod and Fred went unanswered. They went by his mother's address, only to be told by Alexus that he no longer lived there.

They staked out both locations in hopes of spotting the two, but neither of them surfaced. There were no cases pending against the two; however, they did not have Fred in their system as owning a firearm legally. James' presence was kept under wraps from the public and officials that didn't need to know. They feared him returning into hiding if the info was known to the citizens of Augusta. Little light was shed on the situation that transpired, but law enforcement had its bases covered. They needed to get the right players in the right spot to build the perfect case.

* * * * * *

Tyrod left his hotel room in a Chevy Tahoe after he received a call from his lawyer and was informed they should meet. They agreed on Buffalo Wild Wings for the meeting where Cushman explained the payout would come in a lump sum in the next few weeks. "And I got a call from the police about the shooting that you guys were involved in the other day," Cushman stated.

Tyrod wiped his hands on his napkin. "*Involved in?* This fool started shooting at us from out of nowhere." And he still didn't have a clue who it was or why?

"Well, they want to talk to you and return your car. I think we should do a sit down, which they are prepared to do at my request. I can assure you no charges will be brought against you," Cushman stated.

"There you go suggesting meetings and shit. The only reason I'm going to agree with this shit is because I need my car back. I hate riding in this big ass truck."

"Then, I will have them meet with us here." Cushman pulled out his phone.

Thirty minutes later, two detectives walked into the restaurant and took a seat at the booth with them. Eddy held a sour expression on his face, and Reid looked the same. Reid sat in front of Cushman and Eddy sat across from Tyrod. They exchanged stares, before Cushman and Reid caught the exchange.

"You two got some sort of problem?" Reid asked, glancing between Tyrod and Eddy.

Tyrod sniffed, rubbed his thumb across his nose, and continued to glare at Eddy, who didn't break his stare, as he envisioned leaning across the table and landing a swift jab to Rod's jaw. "I'm cool. I don't have a problem with the little idiot," Eddy said, grabbing Tyrod's drink and taking a sip.

Appearing unfazed by displaying a smile, Tyrod stood up, and then hit Eddy in the jaw, sending him sailing onto the floor. Eddy leaped to his feet, swinging wildly. Cushman and Reid jumped up to separate the two. Reaching around Cushman, Tyrod gave Eddy one final blow to the head before they pulled them apart while patrons looked on in disbelief. Even though alcohol was served in the establishment, it was uncommon for a fight to break out.

The manager raced up to the men. "I'm going to need for all of you to leave, or I will be calling the cops."

Reid flashed his badge. "Sorry about that. But everything is now under control." The man nodded nervously and walked away, assuring the patrons it was a police matter, and they were safe. Reid turned to Tyrod in haste, wanting to slap the smirk off his face. "What the hell is your problem?"

"He assaulted me the other day at the funeral. Just a little payback!" Tyrod said, sitting back down.

"Fuck you, bitch!" Eddy hissed, trying to contain his desire to pull out his gun and splatter Tyrod's brains all over the place. He pointed his angry finger at Rod. "And I'm gonna get you for this and for those cops. You fucking nigger!"

Tyrod laughed harder. "I've been called worse."

"Cut the bullshit, Tyrod. And Cushman, you need to inform your client that he can't go around assaulting law enforcement officers."

Cushman cut his eyes at Tyrod, ready to be done with him and his case. He had enough enemies, and he was getting tired of riding around in last year's Benz.

"He's correct, Tyrod," he said, hoping to keep him from being locked up long enough to get paid. Although the money he made dealing with thugs was good, he hated the babysitting and having to remedy their spontaneous bullshit. But this was one of the biggest settlements of his career. So he had no other choice. After this was over, he couldn't care less what happened to him or Fred Sanders.

"You could be arrested for that," he added.

Reid cut him a nasty glance for his sarcastic remark, and then turned his attention on Eddy. "Dan, control yourself! Here and now is not the time." Eddy seemed to swell even more. He patted his shoulder. "Head outside to the car to cool down. I'll handle this!" Reid said.

"I'm good," Eddy responded, about to sit back down.

"It was not a suggestion; it was an order, sir," Reid said, being the lead on the case.

Dan stormed out of the restaurant heatedly. "I hope he kills his black ass!"

"Sorry about that, but he had it coming," Tyrod said, watching him exit.

Reid held his peace, letting it be known that he was the officer in charge on the scene. But it was not his reason for being there. "Mr. King, do you know the person that was shooting at you? And why?" he asked Tyrod.

"No. He was wearing a mask, and who said he was gunning for me?"

"Well, he was shooting at the both of you," Reid said. Tyrod's forehead wrinkled slightly. Seeing the expression on Tyrod's face, he continued, knowing he sparked something.

"And who exactly is he?" Tyrod asked, suspecting he knew more than he was letting on.

"Mr. King. I'm afraid you might be in grave danger." Even though Tyrod was considered a cop killer, until that could be proven in a court of law, he would have to ensure the safety of Tyrod and Fred as any other citizen. But he didn't have to necessarily tell him from who. Yes, James was a rogue cop on the loose, but he would never be forgiven if he sold him out. "So I'm going to need for you to come clean about who you might've crossed. And what you might know about the attempt on your life."

"Nobody I can think of," Tyrod retorted. "Unless, one of you plan on doing to me what you did to my brother." Reid cut his eyes at Tyrod, never wanting to punch a man so strongly before in his life. Done with the back and forth, Tyrod sat back. He and Fred had now become the hunted.

"My client has nothing to do with those officers being killed. How close are officials to finding this guy anyway?" Cushman asked.

"We aren't close at all," he said. "But that's not why we are here. I think your client knows more than he is letting on." If it came down to him or James, as bad as James made all law enforcement officers look, he still preferred he take Tyrod out.

"Well, whoever he is, let him find me. I won't hide from nobody. Especially a—" He smiled. "When can I get my car?" Tyrod asked, remembering they had taken out every cop involved but one. And whoever came for them was no amateur. Not the way he was firing rounds off, void of cover. Only somebody with protection would've been so bold, and somebody trained to shoot.

"You can pick it up from impound." He handed Tyrod a card. Tyrod passed it to Cushman.

"Take care of that for me and send it to Kendrick's Paint and Body, location five." Tyrod stood, thanked the officer, and turned to leave.

"Mr. King!" Reid called out.

"Yeah?" Tyrod turned around.

"We know you're responsible for these killings. As soon as we get a pinch of evidence, you're going to the death chamber. You understand me?" he asked, staring hard at him.

"We're all in the death chamber, officer. Wear your gas mask," Tyrod said with a smile.

* * * * * *

Armed with pertinent information that Tyrod received from a support group member, he knew the game had changed big time. The cop he desired to kill was now trying to kill him, and a slew of officers were trying to bring him down. His future didn't look so promising, so he had to go hardcore in his search and turn up the heat. He picked Fred up later that night, explaining their dilemma and relaying what he'd learned.

"So if we want to catch this fool, we're gonna have to smoke him out. So he has a son and a daughter. I couldn't confirm the son's identity, but the daughter wasn't so hard to find. She lives on Lumpkin Road. She's married and has two kids. So roughing them up or threatening their lives should get him."

* * * * * *

JP and Fred rode silently, as Tyrod turned onto the street with various tools to get these people talking. If they refused, then they couldn't know anything about his whereabouts for sure, or they had a death wish they were ready to fulfill. At 1:00 a.m., the streets were dark and deserted. They exited the car and went around the house to check for anything out of the normal. Satisfied, JP approached the back door with his lock-picking tools. After five minutes of trying, they gained entry into the house and took in the environment: the light was on above the stove, big screen TV in the living room was also on.

Seeing that the house was much too quiet, they crept past pictures of the family hanging along the walls leading down the narrow hallway. Inside the first bedroom they approached, two kids lay on separate beds, fast asleep. A SpongeBob rerun watched over the brother and sister. Without waking them, JP and Tyrod bound them with a nylon rope and duct tape while Fred stayed in the hallway, gun in hand. Once they were done, they carried them into their parents' room.

Rita and Scott had, had a long day with the kids. They took them to Adventure Crossing and to Airstrike. After leaving Airstrike, they went to eat and returned home to catch a movie. Within minutes, everyone became sleepy and turned in for the night. Rita and Scott enjoyed a brief sexual encounter before falling asleep. They dozed off in each other's arms, both spent.

Tyrod placed the barrel of his gun against Scott's head before nudging him awake. Scott's eyes popped open to a masked intruder standing over him with a large caliber weapon pressed against his skull. Two other mask figures stood next to their bed, behind their son and daughter.

"What—" Scott said before he was silenced with a hand to his lips.

"Shhh." Tyrod pointed at the kids to show him they meant business. JP woke Rita. Seeing the masked men, she let out an ear-piercing scream until she was knocked out with a blow to her chin.

"Shit!" JP said, shaking his hand from the pain.

Once the trio rushed the family into the living room, they ordered them to sit on the floor. Scott cursed himself for not arming the alarm system before going to bed. Guns were aimed at them as Rita began to come to.

"Rita, how nice of you to join us. I'm going to remove your tape now, and if you scream, my friend will kill one of your kids. Understood?" Rita nodded as tears freely streamed down her face. The tape was snatched off her face.

"Ouch!" she said, softly rubbing her face with her hands tied together in front of her.

Tyrod pulled a chair in front of Rita and sat directly in front of her. She could not see his face, but his eyes showed no mercy. "I have some questions for you, and I need honest answers. If you are not truthful, someone or maybe all of you will suffer gravely. Understood?" he asked, looking into her soul.

"Y . . . yes, I understand," she said, sobbing.

"When was the last time you seen or heard from your father?" He had no time for small talk.

Rita racked her brain for the correct answer. She and her dad spoke frequently before he was wanted. Now, he only called every now and then. When he did call, it was always from a different number. "It's been about a month since he called me," she said, getting her tears under control.

"How do you get in touch with him?" he asked.

"I don't. He always calls me," she answered. She wasn't sure what these goons wanted with her dad, but it could not have been good.

"I need for you to get the numbers he calls you from, and I also need to know locations. I want to know where he goes and the names of people he deals with. You know, the ones he is close with," Tyrod said.

"I erase all the numbers he calls from, and I'm not sure who he deals with, or where he goes," she lied, blinking quickly and fidgeting with her tied hands.

Tyrod motioned JP, and he came over with the little boy. With a slight nod of Tyrod's head, JP pulled the box cutter out and severed one of the little boy's fingers. He screamed and shook violently, as if he were having a seizure. His screams were muffled by the duct tape but could still be heard.

"Noo! You bastards!" she screamed and was met with a blow to the head.

Scott jumped up from his spot and didn't make it one inch before he was shot with Fred's silenced .45. The shot ripped through his thigh, sending him crashing through the coffee table.

"Don't lie to me again. Names, addresses, and numbers! You have one minute to get all the info, or the girl dies first," Tyrod said, pointing to the sobbing baby girl. Fred turned his gun on the girl at the mention of her death. He'd lost his son to the shady game, so he was officially cold-hearted.

"Okay, I need my phone," she said. "It's in my room on the nightstand."

JP went and got it. She quickly rambled off each of his close contacts while Tyrod wrote everything down because growing up, he knew what taking one's cell phone could do to you.

"When we leave, I need you to contact your dad and tell him he will be seeing us soon. I also need you to give him a message for me!" Fred said, speaking for the first time.

"Okay. Whatever it is, I'll tell him," she said while shaking, seeing her son and husband bleeding badly. To her dismay, Fred pointed the gun at Scott's head and pulled the trigger. Then he turned and shot the little boy in the chest, followed by two holes in the little girl's head.

"Nooooo!" she shrieked. "Oh God! Why . . . Jesus, why?" she repeatedly screamed. Falling out of her chair, she wailed with her head on the floor, wanting to die as well.

"Tell him payback is a bitch!" Fred said.

CHAPTER 31

"Three family members were murdered in the wee hours of the morning on a quiet residential street. According to police, it's been confirmed that two of the victims are children: a boy, age seven, and his sister, age five, along with their father, Scott Conner, were shot several times at close range. Investigators are still on the scene, but as far as we know, no suspects have been named at this time. We will keep you updated as we get the information. This is Alexus Robinson reporting Live from News Channel 12."

Alexus got the call at 4:00 a.m., waking her up out of her sleep. She was told to make sure she made this story her priority and to get on the scene as soon as possible. "All of these killings going on in Augusta need to stop," her boss Angela expressed more than once. And she agreed. Kids were killing kids and somebody was killing cops. And Alexus was convinced it was Tyrod King.

It had been days since Alexus and their son Tyreek had heard from or seen him and to her it was for the better. The less she saw of him, the easier it was for her to walk away, needing more than what he could give her. It was time she focused on herself and her happiness. Tyrod presented too much danger.

* * * * * *

Butler James caught the ass end of the news report from the sexy anchorwoman who was almost in tears upon reporting that a family was murdered, but he didn't catch the names. Murders were all too common in Augusta, so it didn't surprise him in the least. Attentive to the task at hand, he attached the shell catcher to the side of his Bushmaster, after modifying the trigger and placing a suppressor on the front.

As 7:00 a.m. rolled around, James stood inside the kitchen sipping coffee. He did 500 pushups when he woke up, causing him to miss the news. He walked into the living room and flipped through the channels to get an accurate update. His cup crashed to the floor, spilling its contents everywhere. With his head low, James pulled his hair as the pain intensified in his soul. His only grandkids were both murdered by the hands of a ruthless killer. He could not think of a reason why someone would want to kill two kids. His family. Then he thought of Tyrod and Fred. Snatching up his bulletproof vest and his AR-15, he rushed out of the house. He had to contact his daughter.

* * * * * *

Keno's wounds healed up quickly, for the most part. He had seen Dre a few times since he'd been staying at the house recouping. When he went out the house, he went strapped times two. He was not taking any chances with the streets after what happened to him. He was checking for Trina, but he could not find her. He would have never given up the money, threatened with death or not; he wasn't with the shits.

On a whim, Keno decided to pop up on Dre and see how he was doing in the spot. From the outside, everything seemed normal: traffic was in and out of the apartments as usual, and everyone seemed to be on point. Inside the trap was a different story. Going inside the house, Keno saw two naked women having sex with each other on his couch. Dre sat off to the side, sniffing coke from a glass mirror. Stacks of money lay on the coffee table with a few ounces of dope. A dude Keno had never seen before sat in the recliner smoking a blunt while naked, stroking his dick.

"What the fuck you got going on in here, folk?" Keno said, as everyone finally noticed him standing inside the house. Everyone was so zoned out on their drug of choice and the bitches that no one heard him enter with his key.

"Oh shit! What's good, dawg? You like that shit, huh?" Dre asked, gesturing toward the two females who didn't seem to care that Keno had entered the house tripping.

"Fuck no, nigga! This where we grind, nigga. Not no fucking 'ho house. Nigga, put your fucking clothes on, fool! And you bitches get dressed!" Keno snapped, disgusted with Dre and his childish actions.

"Bruh, you trippin'! We just enjoying the fruits of our labor. Loosen up!" Dre put the mirror down.

"Nah, nigga. You got shit twisted. You enjoying the fruits of *my* labor! You need to tighten up and leave that shit alone. I would've never put you on if I knew you were fucking with that shit!"

Everyone was dressed now and all standing around looking crazy. Dre went to the stacks of money and counted off $500. He went to hand it to the girls, but met resistance from Keno. "Fuck no! You got me fucked up! All y'all get the fuck out! Y'all 'hos ain't getting paid shit!" he shouted, slapping the money to the floor. Some of it flew across the room and landed on a bag in the corner. He picked it up and turned to Dre. "Where this come from?"

Eyebrows raised in confusion. Dre waved Keno off. "I bought it, that's where. You ain't the only one who can buy one of those you know." Dre gathered the remainder of his things.

Keno unzipped the bag. The same threads that were dangling in his bag were also in the same position. Keno shook his head and tossed the bag to Dre. "You right, G. I thought that was mine. Y'all kick it though. The spot closed." Everyone filed out of the apartment. He closed the door behind them. Peering out the blinds, he saw Dre screaming at the dude that had been naked. Keno closed the blinds and sat down, trying to process what he just learned from his pop-up visit.

CHAPTER 32

Tyrod made the unscheduled visit to his mom a few days after coming into contact with the James family. He knew it was only a matter of time before he would either be killed, or put in jail, so he needed to visit his mom and be the bearer of bad news. He watched her as she sat in the room filled with recovering patients. A hospital counselor spoke to the people going through their recovery, knowing they would need a push not to give up.

"Hey, Mom! I see you moving around a little better. I missed you!" Tyrod said, giving her a hug and placing a kiss on her forehead.

"Yes, I am. I can't wait to get home. This place makes me feel so old, son. How is that grandbaby of mine?" she asked, adjusting her body in her seat.

"He's good, Ma. Getting bigger." He took a seat across from her.

"So why didn't your brother come this time? What's the excuse?" She stared at Tyrod, waiting for an answer.

He sighed deeply and scooted his chair closer to his mother, their knees touching. Taking her hands inside his, he stared her in the eyes. He didn't want to tell her about Tyreek while she was in her current state, but he had no choice. Tomorrow was not promised to him, and at the rate he was going, he was not sure about his future. This wasn't quite how he wanted this to turn out, but he wasn't all that upset about it either. Alexus was a great mom and eventually she'd find somebody who'd do right in helping her to raise their son. That was his only hope. He'd gone too far to turn back. The pain and heartache over the loss of his twin brother deadened all of his sensibilities. His mother did not deserve to hear about Tyreek from anyone else but her son.

"Ma, it's obvious you do not remember what happened that got you here. Tyreek was killed by the police during a raid. They came to the house to inform you of what happened, and you passed out and hit your head. You were in a coma for over a year." Pain surged through his hands and into his mom's hands. Her face showed a look of confusion.

"So, those visions I was having were true? In my dreams two detectives were knocking on my door," she said.

No tears fell from her eyes. "Oh no, baby. I don't . . . My God, Tyrod. You must be in so much pain, son. I know how close of a bond you had with your brother—it was strong and unbreakable." She tried to stand on her own, but her knees were a little weaker. Tyrod helped her to her feet, then she placed her arms around his neck and hugged him tightly.

"It's gon' be okay, baby. Let God deal with it. He knows what's best for us all," she said, feeling the pain in her gut.

"Yeah, I feel you, Ma. God also uses his kids to carry out things. We'll make it through this together though. But there is one more thing I got to tell you," he said, pulling away from her embrace.

"What?" she asked, numb to everything.

"They found out you have cancer. It's treatable, but—"

"Boy, I already knew that. I overheard the doctors talking when they thought I was asleep," she said, trying to smile.

Tyrod felt better about not having to drop two bombshells, and went on to tell her about the lawsuit that was about to be paid out and assured her the funds needed for the surgery would be available. They talked for a few more hours, then he left, promising to return. He passed a guy in a walker on his way out the door.

"Excuse me," Tyrod said, standing aside as the dude entered the rehabilitation room. They stood there, staring at each other for several seconds.

"You all right, bruh?" Tyrod asked.

"Yeah, man . . . It's just . . . never mind." The guy pushed his walker forward, looking back over his shoulder at Tyrod for a final time.

* * * * * *

Quan Bryant looked over his shoulder at the man walking down the hall. He looked so familiar that he racked his brain trying to place where he knew the person from. Sitting down, he folded his walker and rested it at his side. He closed his eyes to think of where he knew the dude from.

"Keyshawn!" Quan shouted, and recalled being dragged into Keyshawn's bullshit about robbing a dude from Augusta. Quan was reluctant to partake in the robbery, but needed the money. Doing so yielded him no money and a bullet to the head. But, was he wrong? Was he just seeing things?

"Hey, Quan. How you doing, baby?" Ms. King asked, taking a seat back in her chair. Over the course of time, she was gaining more and more strength. Still, she could not blink her eyes or smile completely, but she pushed forward, encouraged strongly by Nurse Hannah.

"I'm okay, Ms. King. How about yourself?" he asked her, looking at the Atlanta news.

"I'm good, baby. Can't complain. I see you moving around better." She could now use her strength to lift the two-pound medicine ball high above her head. She tried to smile. The rehab was going well for both of them as patients of Nurse Hannah. Denise was coming along a little slower because of the severe nerve damage, but Quan Bryant was doing very well. He could now sit up without struggling and straining too hard and he was learning how to walk with a walker.

"Yes, I try," he said.

From talking with Ms. King, he remembered she too was from Augusta. He looked closely at her and saw the resemblance now. She spoke highly of her kids, so he knew Tyrod was indeed her son. "Was that your son that just left out?" he asked.

"Yes, that's my baby. He told me my other son was killed. I didn't know until today!"

"Oh my God. Sorry to hear that. I don't know how it feels to lose a child, but I know how it feels to lose a brother. Terrible feeling," Quan said, thinking of his boys, Keyshawn and Stu.

"Sorry to hear that, baby. But we'll be okay. Just keep trusting in the Lord, and don't lose faith!" She stood to her feet, a bit winded from the bad news about Tyreek.

"Okay, Ms. King. See you later, and sorry to hear about your son," Quan replied.

"Thanks baby." She finally walked off.

Quan watched her leave and thought, *"Bitch, fuck both of your sons! You gon' lose one more as soon as I'm able.* He headed back to his room to make a phone call.

CHAPTER 33

Dre kicked himself in the ass for keeping the stupid ass Louis Vuitton bag he was supposed to get rid of after the robbery, but left it inside of his car, needing to transport things. He also had Fish in the apartment and was glad Keno did not recognize him. Keno's actions, however, after dropping by the house, left a sour taste in Dre's mouth. He understood he was going against the rules by using drugs and having bitches in the trap. But Keno could have talked to him using a different tone. He felt Keno was throwing around his muscle to make him look small in front of his guests.

He had already gone against the grain once, and after what happened on the hill, he was willing to do it again. Was it the drugs making him think like this? Or maybe it was him not being able to hold on to any money, when he had all the tools he needed right in front of him! Tyrod did not have a big operation at all, but it was enough to keep them happy.

* * * * * *

Tyrod and Fred decided to do something they hadn't done in a long time: enjoy themselves! They both were dressed like grown ass men and could have any woman they wanted. Their boss status, along with the killer demeanor they carried, made them stand out to the women in Club 706. Stepping inside the door, the odor of kush, musk, and cigarettes invaded their nostrils. The base from the speakers rattled their bodies, as Tee Grizzly's "First Day Out" played loudly throughout the club. And the bar was crowded. Tyrod stopped a waitress, handed her 4 one-hundred-dollar bills, and told her to bring two Coronas and a bottle of Ace of Spades.

Drink in hand, they made their way toward the dance floor. Women danced half naked, not caring about the roaming hands or eyes. Two sexy friends standing by the VIP section, immediately spotted Fred and Tyrod. They made their way over to the ropes, standing next to the security guard. "How much, big guy?" Fred asked the guard.

"Four hundred . . . and you get a bottle of top shelf. Your pick!" He accepted the money from Fred, who requested another bottle of Ace, and they were granted entry inside the VIP section.

Tyrod held his hand out in front of him while smiling and said to the beautiful women, "After y'all." They smiled, then went inside leading the way. The light-skinned girl was taller and thicker, while the brown skinned chick was shorter and toned perfectly. Her ass rested on her backside perfectly, and as the two females walked, Fred and Tyrod were satisfied.

"What you ladies doing in here looking all lonely? Y'all men should kick y'all ass!" Fred said, as they sat down.

"What men?" the brown-skinned girl said.

"What's y'all names?" Tyrod asked, looking at the taller of the two.

"I'm Christy and that's Erica," she said as she pointed to her brown-skinned home girl. They sat around talking and sipping on their drinks until they ran through two bottles. Everyone was feeling themselves and ready for the real. Seeing the money being spent, there was no way the girls were going to let them two get away without a sample. Christy rubbed Tyrod's dick under the table, bringing it to attention. She unbuckled and unzipped his pants, pulling his dick out of its confined space. Knocking back the rest of her liquor, she went under the table. Peeping the move, Fred followed suit and pulled his dick out.

Christy and Erica sucked away like their lives depended on it. Moans could not be heard over the music, but onlookers could tell by the look on Tyrod and Fred's faces that they were getting served. The girls were also well known for picking out ballers and had no shame in their game. Pussy paid the bills, and they both slurped and moaned, bringing their new customers to their climax. Satisfied with their performance, Fred insisted they leave the club and take it to the next level. Tyrod, on the other hand, let the liquor get the best of him and let the girl suck him up.

Christy looked at Fred and rubbed her fingers together. "No disrespect. Y'all cute as shit, but we got bills to pay, baby!"

Not wanting to be caught dead in Augusta fucking around, Tyrod drove to Colombia County where the chances of seeing someone who knew him and Alexus were slim. Inside the room, Fred set his phone up against the mirror facing the bed. If he was going to have to pay for the pussy, he was getting a video out of it. Showing no mercy, Tyrod and Fred dicked the friends down, then paid the women on their way to the parking lot.

* * * * * *

Tyrod was pulling out of the parking lot when he suddenly stopped.

"What's up, fool? You need me to drive?" Fred asked, thinking he was too intoxicated to handle the 2017 Impala they rented while their cars were in the shop.

"Nah." Tyrod backed the car up then parked beside a blue Chevy Malibu. He reached under the seat for his pistol. Seeing the move, Fred followed suit. "Oh, hell naw! I think I just saw Fish go into the hotel," he said, straining his eyes and looking at the dude standing at the desk.

"Yo, Rod. Man, are you absolutely sure you saw him? You know it's cameras out here, right?" said Fred, hoping Tyrod understood they would have to proceed with caution.

Tyrod continued to watch through the double doors, as the man talked to the clerk at the desk. He saw the dude digging in his pocket, then turned briefly. "Yeah, that's him! I got to get this nigga tonight. Ain't no question!" Tyrod said, temperature boiling.

"How about we just snatch him up? We might be able to use him."

"Use him for what? Target practice?" Tyrod asked, confused.

"Nah, just think about it. Look at it this way," Fred said, laying down his speech.

* * * * * *

On Royal Street, Fish and Dre had females over at the trap snorting coke and drinking liquor. Fish had never indulged in cocaine, but after being forced to do so by Dre, he gave in. After he got his first drain, he wanted more and more. They fucked the women and snorted lines off their breasts well into the night. Fish was drunk. As he parked his car and headed for the front of the motel, fumbling around with the contents of his pockets, he looked for his room key, pulling out blunt wrappers, condoms, and empty baggies of cocaine, but no key. He removed his wallet from his back pocket, flipped through it, and came up empty-handed. Going inside the motel, he went to the front desk.

Fish looked over his shoulder and saw the gentleman enter through the sliding glass doors. He was well-dressed and walked light, approaching the desk. The lady scanned a card, then passed it to Fish as the dude stood right behind him. Fish turned to leave. "Big homie, you think you can give me a jump? Me and my homie's car won't start?" Fred said, looking frustrated.

Fish was in no mood to go back outside after going back and forth with the desk clerk. He could not find his ID, so she had to contact the person who rented the room for him. He was drunk, high, broke, and ready to get some rest. "I would, bruh, but I'm dumb tired and drunk." He gave a phony, weak smile. He didn't care how they got home, or if they got home.

Fred dug in his pocket and pulled out $200 in twenties. He pushed his hand forward, shoving the bills at Fish. "This should do it for the inconvenience, playa."

The sight of the bills instantly made him think of buying more coke from Dre. Accepting the bills, he put a real smile on his face. "I got ya!" he said, leading the way outside.

"Y'all got cables?" he asked. A man stood in front of the car with his head stuck under the hood, looking over the engine with the light on his cellphone. Fred walked up to him while talking to Fish. "That's me right there." Fish pointed to the car next to the broken down Impala. After he started his ride, he popped the hood, happy to be of assistance.

Fred stood beside the man looking under the hood. "Yeah, man. Can you grab them off the floor of the backseat?" he asked.

"Oh sure." Fish walked to the back door and opened it. He didn't see any cables, so he felt around under the seat. Unable to find them, he stood to get out of the backseat. "I don't s—" He turned around to the barrel of a gun in his face. Fish's breath got caught in his throat and his insides died, as he trembled noticeably on the outside.

"Nice to see you, Fish. Get in the car!" Tyrod pushed the gun into Fish's eye, forcing him to get in the car and got in behind him.

CHAPTER 34

Although the two best detectives in Augusta interviewed Rita about the men who murdered her family, Reid was positive that it was Tyrod and Fred. He wasn't sure about the third party, but one thing he did know was they were getting worse with their crimes. Killing cops was bad enough, but executing kids was sickening and on a whole different level. Rita told him everything the intruders said to her. Her father's background wasn't clean, however, nothing happened that warranted the death of James's family.

Five days later, Rita and her brother stood in the Charlie Reid Funeral Home on Laney Walker Boulevard, picking out caskets and making funeral arrangements for her husband and children. Her life had been flipped upside down in one night, and she doubted if she would ever recover from the agony. Her night was spent crying her eyes out and wishing death upon the guilty parties responsible for making her have to bury her kids at a young age. A mother's worst fear.

The inside of her son's pearl casket was light blue and a soft pink lined the inside of her daughter's pearl casket. A cherry woodgrain casket with gold handles and a white interior held the cold, lifeless body of her husband Scott, who wore a Brook's Brother double-breasted navy suit. The insurance policies would leave her depressed, suicidal, and filthy rich. Rita already dreaded seeing one cent of that money. She would trade places with them all in a heartbeat.

Crying and screaming disrupted her grieving. A funeral was taking place inside the chapel, and the grief was almost unbearable as the people were ushered in. She could not only relate to their pain, but her hot tears burned with grief and righteous indignation.

After the funeral and repast ended, Rita was alone in the room. She was on her knees praying beside the caskets of her deceased husband Scott and the kids. She rocked back and forth with her hands clasped tensely in front of her. As quietly as possible, James slid inside the room waiting on her to finish praying, fighting bitter tears. When she was done, Rita went to each casket and placed a kiss on all of their foreheads, told each corpse how much she loved them, and how much she would miss them.

"I promise I'm going to try to—"

A sniffle made her spin around. Emotions raged through her body. She saw blood, felt hate, love, and comfort all in the same moment. Rita didn't know if she was supposed to run up to him and slap him, hug him, or simply call the police to haul him off to jail. Tears built up all over again, seeing the cause of her family's death standing in front of her.

While looking up from her position, she glanced at the Stetson hanging low on his head, but was able to glimpse the pained expression on his face that matched hers. Obviously, he was feeling remorseful. He was not there to protect them when they needed him the most. He failed his grandkids and his daughter. Miserably stepping forward, he held his arms outstretched, with tears flowing down his face. The little girl inside Rita ran into her father's arms, crying freely. He rubbed his hands through her hair as he did when she was little. He held her tight as the tears flowed freely.

"Baby, I'm so sorry I wasn't around to protect them. Please forgive me," he said, sniffling.

"It's nothing you could've done. They would've just killed all of us if you were there. They wanted you, Dad." She broke away from his embrace. "What have you done?"

"What do you mean they wanted me?"

"I mean they asked about your whereabouts, about when we spoke, and who you deal with."

"What did they say exactly?"

She ran down the encounter from the beginning when they woke up, to the guy asking her to deliver his message for him. As she described the shots, her father shuddered as if he could hear and feel them as if they had entered his own body. "I have no doubt who the assailants are; I just need to find them and put an end to the madness once and for all, even if that means dying."

"Do what you gotta do," Rita said, looking him square in the eyes.

"Dad?" His son walked inside the room. He also hadn't heard from him in a while and was equally shocked to see him here, with all the coverage he had about the case hanging above his head. Pulling the curtains back, what was left of the James family talked for hours. Their dad's presence did nothing to cure the pain or fill the void, but they were happy to see him. They cherished the time because at any second, he could be walking inside a cell, never to return, or laid in a casket, never to see the light of day again.

* * * * * *

Being restrained for hours on end had fucked Fish's mind up completely. The beating and the bullets he expected to receive never came. Although, if looks could kill, he would have been dead in the parking lot. He was left alone while Tyrod and Fred talked quietly in a different room. He couldn't hear what they were saying, but he just knew it concerned his death. All he could do at the moment was wait and see while in the grips of fear.

Once they returned to the room, Tyrod placed a gun on the nightstand. They both stood next to him, one man on his left, the other to his right. Fish couldn't stop his heart from racing; he couldn't breathe.

"You want to live or die?" Tyrod asked. To Fish, that was the craziest question he had ever heard. Instantly, his breathing returned to normal.

"I wanna live, man," he responded.

Tyrod told him the requirements for living, and he couldn't turn down the offer. He was the cause of his brother being dead and the reason Tyrod started out for revenge, so what the hell? He'd sold his soul once, so once again would not hurt him.

"But man, what I don't understand is why? Man, my brother argued with me that you were cool and shit—"

"Rod, man, it whatn't supposed to go down like that. Reek *was* my boy, no matter how foul shit may seem. And even that shit with Dre—"

"What shit with Dre?"

"Man, he set up the robbery, threatened to kill us if we didn't do it, then took everything. He got some kind of payback shit for you. Real bad."

"I see," Tyrod said, glancing at Fred, whose brows rose in response to the new information.

After contacting his handler, Fish showed up at the narcotics unit, unscathed. When asked about the kidnapping, he told the truth. "He was just seeking closure as to why I set up his brother. And naw, he didn't kidnap me." Fish spread his arms. "See, I'm fine."

CHAPTER 35

Tyrod had only spent a short time with his son after he dropped off a few things for him and Alexus, then headed back out with shit to do. Before he stepped foot out of the door, Tyrod realized the kind of grip the streets and revenge had on him. He placed the bag he brought along with him at the foot of the bed containing a point blank body armor vest. He'd barely even met Alexus' gaze.

"You gotta wear that everywhere you go, Lex," he instructed. Maybe it was all for the best. "I'm out," he said, closing the door quietly. He had to meet up with Fred and JP about the little issue with Dre. Keno had been getting a lot of complaints from his most trusted customers. Dre was shorting them on drugs, and the product had switched grades. The spot on Royal Street also started to bring in less money than usual, which made it easier for Keno to continue slowly pulling the Royal Street operation from under Dre's control and doing most of his work out of the apartment.

After telling Tyrod about finding the bag inside his crib, Tyrod advised, "Man, Dre made a move on you, using you as a pawn. And cousin or not, you can't trust the nigga. Ain't no way you can have two of the same bags with the exact problem."

Tyrod gave Fred and JP the information they would need to find Dre, which wasn't much, but he also kept it away from Keno. Dre was still Keno's family; he wouldn't want to see him dead. But they both would be better off without Dre in the picture. He didn't

231

care about Keno when he got him beat over a couple of dollars. So fuck 'im.

"Give me one second," Tyrod said to them, stepping aside to answer his ringing cellphone. Cushman's name was displayed on the screen. "Hello."

"What's up, Mr. King?" Cushman said, excitedly. Trying to sound cool.

"Oh, nothing much . . . same ol' thing. How about yourself?"

"I'm good. Life is going. I've got good news for you," Cushman replied.

"Good news? Hell, I need some of that. What's up?"

"I just got off the phone with the government's lawyers. They were cleared for the funds to settle this case. Eighty-nine point five million dollars to be exact. They also will cover any fees and your mother's hospital bills," he said, equally excited about his ten percent.

Tyrod gave a light smile, happy to receive the money, but not happy about the blood that was shed to collect.

"So, what they need for me to do?" he asked, leaning against the side of Keno's car.

"Well, they need an active bank account to send the funds to that can be verified as yours. I guess it'll take a few weeks for them to get it all cleared. That should be it," Cushman said.

"A few weeks? I'm really sick of waiting on these folks. I don't even have an active account after the raid."

"Well, we could always have the check made out to my law firm. That'll also speed up the process of payment."

"Cool. Do that shit, man and get back at me," Tyrod said, relieved that he didn't have to go through the motions.

"No problem. I'm going to get these forms typed up. I'll need you to sign, then we'll be cleared to move forward."

"Sounds good, Cushman."

"I'll call you shortly so I can meet you, or you can stop by the office."

"Do that." Tyrod ended the call.

Tyrod told Fred about his phone call with Cushman and the amount he would soon receive. Fred's mouth dropped. The amount was astonishing for the hood figure who only saw thousands of dollars, let alone millions. They wrapped up their conversation, then headed out after promising Keno that they'd be in touch.

* * * * * *

Fish drove down Deans Bridge Road as he headed to meet with Detective Scott. *Finally, I can get out of the snitching business and star over anew.* He'd heard too many promises that, that time would be his last, but this time was etched in stone. Fish turned on Gordon Highway, then pulled into the Budget Inn seconds later. He chose to meet there because mostly junkies and prostitutes frequented there at nighttime. The chances of him being spotted there were slim to none.

He stepped inside of the cheaply furnished room as Scott pulled into the parking lot. He exited his Camaro then walked in behind Fish. They spoke for close to an hour, Scott stating more than once that Fish could stay on as a paid CI.

"Nah. No thanks, man. I'm done with all of this," Fish replied.

"You sure?"

Fish batted down every attempt Scott made, opting for the job he said he had lined up for him at a local phone store since Fish refused to leave the area.

"It's been a pleasure working with you, Fish. Honestly. And I am a man of my word, so here you go," Detective Scott said, pulling the drugs that he had confiscated from him months ago.

The same drugs that started all of Fish's troubles and led him down a treacherous path.

"Get the fuck outta here! I'm good on that. You might have a car waiting to pull me over and bust me for that shit, so you can try to keep me working." Fish walked toward the door, preparing to exit.

Detective Scott shook his head at the thought of Fish getting smart. "You're in the hood *wit' your peeps*, so you're feeling mighty mouthy, huh Fish? Whatever!" He followed Fish outside to his car. Prostitutes, users, and a few low-level dealers could be seen moving about and he wanted no parts of that. Fish got in and sped off.

* * * * * *

Inside his Camaro, Detective Scott watched Fish's taillight disappear around the corner before backing out of his parking spot. He had to find someone soon to help him continue to build cases for him, but his main priority was finding Tyrod and Fred and putting them away for life.

"Fuck!" he cursed, slamming on brakes to avoid hitting a drunken person lying in the middle of the street. He leaned on the horn to no avail, the drunk just lying there, still clutching his bottle of booze. "Get your ass out of the friggin' street, idiot!" Detective Scott shouted. Angrily, he threw open the door and stepped out onto the pavement.

"Hey!" he shouted, nudging the man with his foot. He aimed his flashlight into the man's face, trying to bring him out of his stupor.

"Ummm." The drunk rolled over onto his side, tossing the beer bottle he held in his hand. He then balled up into the fetal position, clutching his stomach.

"Hey, you! Get out of the street, buddy, before I haul your ass in for public intoxication." Scott kicked the man lightly on his back.

In a flash the drunk turned over, not seeming so drunk after all. His eyes were wide and clear yet focused and sent a chill racing down Scott's spine. He clutched a compact Glock .40 in his hand. Scott stumbled backward, trying to pull his own Glock, but the attempt was useless. Ernest's first shot was fired from a sitting position that crashed into the detective's gut, doubling him over. Standing to his feet, Ernest ran up on the officer and placed the barrel of his gun against Scott's head.

"On behalf of my brothers, United Through Pain, I hereby pronounce you deceased." Ernest placed one shot between Scott's eyes, slamming his head against the hood of the car, before falling to the ground to his final resting place.

CHAPTER 36

Ms. King went through her final days inside the rehabilitation ward at Grady Memorial gaining back the much-needed strength to most of her body. Nurse Hannah was there for her every step of way. Ms. King's mental state had slipped a little after hearing about Tyreek's death, which in turn slowed down her recovery process. She would sit in on sessions thinking of Tyreek's life and cry openly. Nurse Hannah would sit and listen to the stories about Tyreek and empathized, knowing the feeling all too well from the loss of her own son. She offered her unwavering support.

Finishing with the medicine ball, Denise headed over to the hot tub to relax her muscles. As she entered the room, she spotted Quan drying off his thin arms outside of the stand-up shower.

"How you doing, Quan, baby?" Denise asked, stepping up the two steps slowly, one at a time, holding the rail.

"I'm good, Ms. King. How are you?" Quan asked, trading the towel for a T-shirt given to him by the hospital. It was hard for him to talk to Denise now, knowing her son was responsible for putting a bullet in his head. Night after night he fought with the devil, contemplating going inside Denise's room and beating her half to death for what her son had caused him and his friends, although it wasn't her fault.

"I'm getting better. I hear we are both on our way home in the next week or so. I can't wait to lay in my own bed. I got to find me a church to join once I get out of here because the Lord has been good to me, and I need to repay him with worship." She sat inside the heated water as the jets spewed pressured water her way.

"I may need to find me a church also. Ms. Hannah gon' make me come back to hers if I don't."

"So you two know each other well, huh?"

"I knew her son really well. We were best friends before he was killed." Quan cut an evil glare at Denise, but she hadn't noticed.

"I am so sorry to hear that, Quan. I hope you are dealing with it the best way possible. Maybe you should meet my son. Being that you both lost someone you were close to. Y'all may be able to relate to each other in a way that no one else can."

"Yeah, thanks but no thanks. I am not trying to get to know anyone new." He gathered all of his things, ready to make his exit. He could no longer take hearing Denise's voice, or hearing about the man who killed his friends and placed a bullet in his head.

"Sure, I can understand that. Well, I hope you get into that church when you go home because God has a higher calling for the both of us, and that's a fact."

"I will, and the same to you," he said, waving good-bye before turning to leave. He hoped he did see Denise and her son one day at church. He also hoped to have them both lying flat on their backs, bleeding out. Quan wouldn't make a move until the timing was right, but when it was . . .

* * * * * *

Tyrod was having a hard time trying to locate Dre along with everyone else. When he ran the lead down across town in River Glenn, they found out Dre was now smoking crack and had no address. They knew users were around there; they hadn't seen him since his latest heist of thirteen grams of crack from one of the local dealers. However, they spread the word that they were indeed looking for him and money would be paid for his whereabouts. "JP, we just want you to know that you're 100% official in our eyes," Tyrod said, speaking for both he and Fred.

"Especially in my eyes after putting in that work for us," Fred added. "You always make loyal decisions when it comes down to it."

"Thanks, man," JP said with a serious expression. "I appreciate that."

"I respect your drive, too. You remind me of myself and my brother when we were growing up."

"No doubt." JP nodded. "Thanks, Rod. That means a lot to me coming from you and Fred," JP responded.

The trio were having a drink inside of Robbies while playing a game of pool when Tyrod received a phone call. Seeing Ms. Hannah's name on the display, he quickly excused himself from the game and went to a quieter spot.

"Hello?"

"Hi Tyrod. I have some great news for you today," Nurse Hannah sang.

"Oh yeah? What is it?" Tyrod smiled.

"Your mom will be discharged later today once her doctor comes on shift. Do you think you can be here around 7:30?"

"Hell yeah! Thank you so much, Nurse Hannah, and I will call you once I leave." He happily ended the call and joined his boys.

"Ay yo, check it. My momma being released from the hospital later today, so I got to swing through and pick her up. That situation can wait until some other time." Tyrod downed his drink and placed the empty glass on the bar once he finished.

"Hell yeah! That's what's up. I'm tryna meet ma dukes though, fool," Fred said, glad to hear Ms. King was finally coming home.

"Me too, fool. That's all of our momma now. We brothers!" JP said, meaning every word.

"Shiiiiid. No problem then. Fred, we got to drive your truck though. I ain't trying to ride her back home in the Hellcat."

"Say no more," Fred replied.

They finished their game and left Robbies, feeling better than they had in a while.

The moment they entered Tyrod's car, he called Alexus.

"Baby, Momma's coming home!"

"Oh my God! That's great, baby. I'm so happy for her and for you!" Alexus responded.

"I can't wait to bring her home."

"Me too. I know our son is going to love bonding with her too. It's been a long time coming."

"Yeah, it sure has."

"Bae, would you mind if I covered your mom's exit from the hospital for the local news?"

"Nah. I don't mind. Not at all. It'll be all good, especially because the public will be reminded that those fuckin' dirty ass cops killed Tyreek. I want them to remember." A long silence followed. "Hello?" he finally said.

"I'm still here, baby. I'm just so thankful to God for the awesome staff at Grady Memorial. I'll be there at the hospital a few hours before her actual discharge." Alexus hated how fast Tyrod had gone from being overjoyed to blazing hot rage. She wondered if his desire for revenge would ever end.

* * * * * * *

Lieutenant James sat in a corner booth at the Waffle House on Gordon Highway talking to his "eyes." He had the only two people in his corner trying to dig up info to put an end to the King Family. His grandkids being murdered made him say "Fuck the consequences" and pull out all stops to get to Tyrod and whomever he was connected too. And he'd hit the jackpot!

"Okay, so I have the address for his mother's home, which is now being occupied by his fiancé, which you already know. He hasn't been staying there, and neither has she on some nights. I have followed her numerous times. I see her with this dude a lot, during the wrong times.

"His mother is still in the hospital in Atlanta. I just got wind that she is being released today at 7:30," his Eyes said as if reading from a script.

"Which hospital in Atlanta?" James asked, with fire in his heart and ice in his voice.

"Grady Memorial Hospital."

"Okay, so I got time to make it there today," James said, looking at the clock on the wall. He took a sip of his hot cup of coffee.

"Listen, I know you lost a lot and you want to strike while the iron is hot, but I think you are going a little too far with this last part. His mother and family had nothing to do with any of this stuff, you know?"

James shook his head in disbelief as he stood inside the booth, placing his Cleveland Cavaliers hat on his head low. He then placed a pair of Ray Ban shades over his eyes. "Neither did mine," he said, leaving the man sitting there to pay the bill.

CHAPTER 37

Fred glided the F-150 on 20 West as Tyrod and JP put fire to the end of one of the blunts they'd just finished rolling. Tyrod blew out a cloud of smoke, and he realized it felt good to have people by his side. Both Fred and JP were eager to meet Ms. King. They were happy for Tyrod, knowing that he would come around to being himself more, having his mother home under his care.

Having phoned Nurse Hannah, Tyrod got his mother's sizes from her to ensure she had a fresh outfit to throw on once he got there. She could do her own shopping when she felt the need to do so. They pulled into the South DeKalb mall parking lot at 5:06 p.m. and rushed the stores. What was supposed to be a quick in and out turned into an hour shopping spree. Tyrod even ended up getting Ms. King six outfits and three pairs of shoes.

They left the mall and grabbed a bite to eat. Fred parked his truck in front of the hospital, refusing to have Ms. King walk too far.

"At least get the guns from under the seats and out of the truck and leave on your hazard lights," JP suggested. Now with the hazard lights on and the guns out of the truck, they walked outside.

* * * * * *

"Father, please continue to watch over your child as he goes home to rest and get well. Please keep his hand from doing any evil, and let his mind be opened to know you and your son Jesus Christ, my lord and savior. He needs a change of heart and mind,

Father. I know that you can do all things, but he has to believe you can do them also. In Jesus' name. Amen," Nurse Hannah said a strong prayer for Quan as he was signing his release paperwork.

"Quan, I know I'll see you in church on Sunday, right?"

"Yes ma'am," he replied.

"You know you could've easily wound up dead just like my son, but God spared your life for a reason. I want you to go out there and live life as straight as an arrow. You hear me? I don't want to see you back up in here or worse, Quan. Downstairs on a cold slab of steel with a Y-incision going down your torso." Nurse Hannah stood from the end of the bed she sat on.

"I understand, Ms. Hannah. But like I told you before, nothing in this world will stop me from killing the man responsible for Keyshawn's death. And I meant that," Quan said, tying his shoes.

Nurse Hannah closed her eyes and shook her head. "Lord knows I believe in him and in his son Jesus Christ. I know they are the Alpha and Omega and all of us will be judged by the Most High. But Quan, if you can put your hands on the man that killed my Keyshawn, let me know what I can do to help," she said, tears streaming from her face. Never in a million years did she ever think she'd possess what it took to murder someone, but if she could have a go at the person responsible for killing her baby, then she was all in.

Quan's eyes bucked and his forehead wrinkled with confusion. "Ms. Hannah, are you being sarcastic?"

"No child, I am not. I mean it. I did not believe in revenge because the Lord says he'll take care of the vengeance part, but my soul—my spirit aches so bad for Keyshawn. I miss my boy so much, and every time I think of him, I hurt all over again. I . . . I don't know Quan. I think I'm losing my faith and letting my flesh do the thinking for me."

"Well, you can help me," Quan said flatly, looking at her wipe away the traces of tears from her ashen face.

"What do you mean? What do I have to do?" she asked. "Baby, I can't do no drive-by."

"Naw, naw, Ms. Hannah. All you have to do is get me inside Ms. King's room today before she leaves, and it will be all over with."

"What? Why Ms. King's room? What are you talking about?" she said, looking both confused and agitated.

"Ms. King's son is the one who killed Keyshawn and Stu and shot me in the head. At first when I saw him, I couldn't be too sure. But then I started to remember bits and pieces before being shot. It's definitely him." Quan explained everything to her about how Keyshawn planned on robbing Tyrod and how it all went wrong.

Ms. Hannah, not being from the streets, felt sorry for Tyrod and the time of the incident. But now that her son was dead, and knowing the guy responsible was within her reach made her lose her compassion. She couldn't care less about Tyrod King. He had made a foolish decision and he didn't deserve to live. She shook her head at her son Keyshawn's lifestyle and choices also, thinking carefully about what she was going to do. She was willing to trade places with her son, but there were no do overs in his life. Both men were guilty. Why should Denise King's son get to continue living his evil life?

With malice in her heart she agreed, "I'll do it."

CHAPTER 38

Everyone, including Alexus and her cameraman Jake sat inside of Denise's room talking and laughing. It seemed her release from the hospital had everyone's spirits uplifted.

"Ms. King, don't forget we'll be filming your departure once you come down to the main entrance of the hospital.

"I remember. It's for Channel 12 News in Augusta. Oh hell! I don't care if it was for the world news. As long as I am leaving, I don't care," she said, bringing everyone to laughter.

"See you when you come down," Jake said as he and Alexus made their exit.

No sooner than they left did Tyrod, Fred, and JP enter the room.

Denise gasped. "Oh my God!" She took the flowers and shopping bag that Tyrod gently pushed toward her.

"These are for you, Ma. Glad you're coming home." She hugged Tyrod so tight.

"Dag, Ma. I know you got all of your strength back now. That was a strong bear hug. I could barely breathe," Tyrod joked.

"Tyrod, did you see Alexus and Jake. They just left a couple minutes ago."

"No. They probably got on the elevator just as we were getting off."

Nurse Hannah entered, stealing everyone's attention. She looked tired. Dark circles were just beneath her eyes. Everyone continued to help get Denise's things together.

"Hello, Nurse Hannah? How are you feeling today?" Denise said with a smile that suddenly turned into worry.

"I'm a little weary today, Denise." Her normal cheerful aura was now gone, replaced with a depressing air. She gave Denise a weak smile.

"You're all ready to go, I see." Nurse Hannah looked at all of the things packed up.

"Yes. Jesus knows I need my own bed. Thank you so much for looking after me. The Lord will bless you a million times over, you hear?" Denise stepped up to Nurse Hannah, wrapping her arms around her, giving her the same hug she'd given Tyrod. Nurse Hannah closed her eyes, almost forgetting the heartache Denise's son caused her.

"No problem. I have your number, so I will be calling to check up on you." Nurse Hannah knew she'd never place a call to Denise. Ever. "The doctor will be in shortly, and Quan wanted to say good-bye before you left."

* * * * * *

Butler James sat across from the entrance talking to a patient, who thought he was a nurse. His blue scrubs and cleaning cart did help him blend in amongst the others. Just as he finished talking with the patient, he spotted Fred and Tyrod and another man he didn't know when they first entered the hospital. James rolled his cart along the hallway, still unnoticed as he headed to the rehabilitation unit.

Pushing his cart along the hallway, James checked for Ms. King's name on the chart but came up empty-handed. He walked around the ward looking for his prey. He saw an unevenly proportioned nurse rounding the corner and headed straight at him.

"Excuse me. Do you know where Ms. Denise King's room is?" he asked with a hand against a dust mop on the cart.

"If you would, sir. I will need a second to check it out for you. I am not sure," she said, walking toward a counter manned by a nurse in full gear.

Glancing around, he saw a nurse pushing a man down the hall in a wheelchair. His head was lightly bandaged and he held a Grady Memorial Hospital bag in his lap.

"Sir, you could just follow that nurse wheeling that man in the wheelchair. That's her nurse heading that way now, she said, remembering Nurse Hannah working with her.

"Thank you," he said, following about twenty yards away. He saw them enter a room, and that's when he pushed the cart to the side, opting for the feel of his Glock .40.

"Hi, Quan, I see you're all ready to go," Denise said, seeing him being wheeled into her room.

"Yeah, I thought we should be wheeled down together since they won't let us walk," he said with his hands in his lap. He never acknowledged the others in the room. He wanted to see if Tyrod could make the connection before his life ended.

"Then I guess we better get going then, because I just signed my papers. Thank the Lord." Tyrod helped her get seated in the wheelchair.

Quan placed his hands inside of the bag and gripped the Smith and Wesson, sending a charge through his body. He glanced around; no one seemed to know who he was, and that sent him into a rage.

If snatching the gun out of the bag so fast didn't shock Tyrod, then the quickness with which JP responded did. "Hold up there, playboy. I don't think that's in your best interest right this second," JP said, standing off to Tyrod and Ms. King's right.

"Quan, put down that damn gun, boy! What's the matter with you?" Ms. King asked, afraid of the situation unfolding.

Quan stood from the wheelchair. Ms. Hannah moved it to the side and crossed her arms across her chest, eyeing Tyrod. "The problem with me is your son. Ain't that right, *Ty*?" he asked, taking a step closer and so did JP.

Tyrod racked his brain as he still had one hand on the back of the wheelchair, as the other found its place next to his leg, inches away from his gun. He only recalled the incident in Atlanta and one didn't even end in violence. Then only one of those people knew him as Ty.

"Whatever you got to handle with me, you need to do just that. My mom's ain't got shit to do with this, so catch me at a later date," Tyrod said, unsure of how this dude would end this situation. He saw murder in the dude's eyes; it even radiated from his body. Not good.

"Man, stop acting like you don't know what's crackin'. Too bad when you killed my man you didn't give him that option. *And* you shot me in the head," he said, pulling the trigger in a rage, hitting Tyrod smack dead in the chest. The force of the bullet knocked the wind out of him and he fell backward.

On cue, JP began blasting away, putting four holes in the shooter's chest, two of them fatal, entering his heart. Fred pulled his gun, kneeling beside Tyrod and trying to pull him up into a sitting position.

"My God! Nurse Hannah, help him!" Denise screamed.

"I'm okay. I'm all right," he assured her, showing his mother a piece of the vest around his shoulder.

"Thank God you are okay. What the hell was he talking about?" she asked.

"It's nothing. Let's get the hell out of here before the cops get here," he said, heading toward the door. Suddenly, he stopped in his tracks.

Nurse Hannah stood there with tears streaming down her face as she pointed Quan's gun at Tyrod's head.

"My son is nothing?" she asked, sobbing as her hands shook uncontrollably

"Your son?" Tyrod replied, appearing confused. Fred and JP had guns trained on the grieving nurse.

"Yes. Keyshawn Harris. You gunned him down at Magic City parking lot like some kind of animal. Now he's nothing." She never received the answer she was looking for.

Lieutenant James opened the door, and fired recklessly into the room, shooting Nurse Hannah in the back of the head. Tyrod quickly pulled Denise to the floor and pulled his own weapon to join in the gun fight.

JP crouched next to the door and sent four blind shots into the hallway. Two return shots followed slamming into the frame of the door, narrowly missing his head.

"We gotta get out of this room! It's our only chance of getting out of here alive. Fred and I will put down the cover fire while you take my mom down the hall out of the back exit," he said to JP.

Ms. King kept her hands covering her head, crying and screaming out her fear and confusion. Tyrod picked her up and put her in the wheelchair.

"I'm sorry, Ma. I'm sorry." Everyone was ready to carry out their part. If Tyrod trusted anyone with his mom's life, then it would be JP without question. "Take good care of her, JP," he said.

"You know it!" JP responded.

On the count of three, Fred and Tyrod burst into the hallway, guns blazing. James was caught off guard and had to seek shelter behind a metal laundry cart. JP rolled Ms. King out of harm's way, pushing her down the hall to the rear exit. Relieved, Tyrod walked up on the cart firing round after round, in hopes of penetrating it to no avail.

James was forced to run out into the open as they approached. He shot over his shoulder as a bullet ripped into his left thigh as he ran. He dragged himself around the corner, sending two shots in Tyrod's direction.

"That's that cracker Lieutenant Butler James, right?" Fred asked, replacing his empty clip with a fresh magazine.

"Looks like him. C'mon!" Tyrod replied, rounding the corner first, seeing a trail of blood.

After turning a second corner, they came face to face with James holding a young, white RN around the neck, using her as a human shield. "Put your gun down, or she won't live to see tomorrow," James shouted, his Glock aimed at the woman's head.

"Fuck her!" Tyrod shouted, stepping closer and trying to get a better shot off. If need be, both he and the girl could die.

"I see you're still a defiant little bastard nigger boy, huh kid? Never did change."

"Bitch, you don't know shit about me. Watch your fucking mouth."

"Oh, I know about you. Remember, I used to fuck your cheap ass mother way back when you and your bad ass brother Tyreek were in school stealing. Remember that, boy?" he challenged with hate in his voice.

As his wrath exploded, Tyrod either forgot or didn't care what happened to the RN. He sent seven shots into both of them, leaving them both wide-eyed and lifeless on the floor.

"Let's go, Rod. Cops will be here in a second," Fred said, snapping him out of his daze.

CHAPTER 39

Tyrod and Fred ran outside and came face to face with Jake holding a Smith and Wesson .380 to Alexus' head. He stood behind her using her as a shield.

"Ay, dude, don't do this," Tyrod said, aiming his gun in Jake's direction. Fred had set his gun down without second guessing it. Tyrod looked at him out the corner of his eyes with a perplexed expression.

"I do have to do this, and I will do this. You killed my niece and nephew, you bastard! And I take it my dad is dead too, isn't he? Isn't he!" Jake screamed, pointing the gun at Tyrod.

"Yeah, he is. That shit is over with. We both caused the other family a great deal of pain. Let's stop it here. Put the gun down and let her go. No hard feelings."

"No hard feelings? Are you crazy!" he said.

"Ay, Rod. Put it down, fam'," Fred said softly, while staring ahead.

Alexus stared back at Fred with her mouth hanging open. Her current situation was bad but had gotten worse upon seeing Fred along with Tyrod, exiting the hospital.

"Hell no, nigga!" Tyrod said softly.

"Jake, please! You're scaring me," Alexus said.

"Scared? You should be. Tell your husband to put the gun down," Jake said, pointing the gun at Tyrod. Tyrod didn't have a clean shot, or he would have taken it already.

"Husband!" Fred said, loudly gaining everyone's attention.

253

"Yeah, husband. That's her husband," Jake said.

Alexus closed her eyes, blinking away tears. Tyrod picked up on the exchange.

"Yeah, that's my wife, Alexus. Alexus meet Fred, my homie. Bad way to meet," Tyrod said, still aiming his gun at what he could see of Jake. "Why does it matter to you?"

Fred looked over to Tyrod and faced him head on. "That's the girl I've been telling you about," he said, holding his breath.

My wife? Tyrod thought. "What? Bitch, you been cheating on me?" he asked, pointing the gun at Alexus now. Fred sensed the sudden change in Tyrod and tried to convince him.

"No! Don't, Rod," he said.

Several cop cars were pulling into the parking lot. Tyrod glared at Fred and released a shot.

"Ahhh!" Fred screamed, dropping to the ground.

Tyrod scowled at Alexus as she slowly shook her head no.

"Tyrod. No! No!" Alexus cried.

Boom! Boom!

He fired two times, hitting her twice in the chest. Alexus fell from Jake's hold and lay flat against the concrete. Surprised by Tyrod's action, Jake fired off two wild shots that missed Tyrod by a few inches, but Tyrod returned fire that landed in Jake's forehead. His limp body body crumbled to the ground. Seeing all three bodies still before him, Tyrod threw the gun to the ground, got down on his knees, and locked his hands behind his head.

The police swarmed the area, cuffing Rod and placing him in the police vehicle. He closed his eyes, finally feeling some sense of peace for the first time since he'd lost Tyreek.

Epilogue

Tyrod was taken to court, where his bond was denied. He had been charged with well over ten murders and drug charges. His mom and JP sat in attendance throughout the proceedings. Ms. King cursed, seeing her son led out in cuffs. He called her after making it back to the county jail. "Yes, I'm here, baby; how you doing?" she asked, after accepting the call.

"I'm holding up. You know you don't have to worry about me. JP been taking you to the appointments?"

"I been going but not back there. I can't walk in there after all that went on," she said.

"Did you get in touch with Cushman?"

"His phone number is disconnected. He told me at first that he had to wait on the money to clear, then he turned his phone off. JP rode by the office, and he no longer works there," she said.

"Don't even trip. I'll holler at him when I get out. You talked to Alexus?"

"She called to check on me, but she hasn't been by. JP says she's with that man." Tyrod had given Alexus a point-blank body armor vest the last time he visited her. He told her the situation had gone from bad to worse, so she needed to wear it always. He didn't want to kill her, but he wanted her to hurt exactly how he was hurt.

"That's what's up. Tell JP I need him to get in touch with Keno for me and the guys in the group. Tell him we were prepared for this, so I need him to handle shit for me since I am down."

"Okay, baby. I love you, and I will be down there to visit you soon."

"Don't bother," Tyrod said when the lady announced that he had one minute remaining.

"Why not?" she asked, thinking Tyrod was giving up.

"Because I'll be coming to visit you soon. I love you, and I'll call you later," Tyrod said, ending the conversation.

The murder and mayhem had stopped in Augusta, for now.

THE END

Author's Bio

Pierce J. Anfield was born in South Augusta, Georgia where he grew up with his parents and siblings.

He began reading to help him get through the devastating loss of his beloved family members. The more books he read, the more he had come to admire the passion, skill, and experience that was poured into creating each story world.

Deeply inspired, Pierce believed he too had the ability to give life to a novel. Always up for a challenge, he grabbed his pen and pad and some time later he completed his first full-length novel, *Murder Breeds Mayhem*.

The author hopes that each reader will receive the lessons ingrained in his book. Pierce is currently working on his next novel. He has two beautiful daughters, Taliyah A. Clifford and Promise Jiovanna Anfield.

IN THIS INTRIGUING TALE OF FAMILY DYSFUNCTION, RELATIONSHIPS ARE TORN, SECRETS EMERGE, AND MANY HEARTS ARE ANNIHILATED

TRACES
of my
Blood
SERENITI HALL

7 FIGURE PUBLICATIONS PRESENTS...

LIFE OF A
Star
BASED ON A TRUE STORY
ASHERDEE DIAMOND

7 FIGURE PUBLICATIONS PRESENTS...

CRIME SCENE DO NOT CROSS

A
TREACHEROUS
Hustle
Hitting a LICK for the love of a PIMP
A FALICIA BLAKELY STORY
SERENITI HALL

THE FALICIA BLAKELY LETTERS
FROM A
PIMP

"Daddy still loves you"

To: Falicia
From: Ike

SERENITI HALL